ADRIFT

ADRIFT

A Folly Beach Mystery

BILL NOEL

Cover photo and design by Bill Noel

Author photo and map by Susan Noel

ISBN: 978-1-958414-99-6

Enigma House Press

Goshen, Kentucky 40026

Enigmahousepress.com

BILL NOEL'S
FOLLY
BEACH
SOUTH CAROLINA

1 Rita's
2 Dude's surf shop *
3 Sand Dollar
4 Haunted House *
5 Loggerhead's
6 Snapper Jacks
7 St. James Gate
8 Surf Bar
9 Cal's *
10 Mr. John's Beach Store
11 Landrum Gallery/Barb's Books *
12 The Crab Shack
13 City Hall/Public Safety
14 Sean Aker, Attorney *

15 Planet Follywood
16 Woody's Pizza
17 The Washout
18 Post Office
19 Pewter Hardware *
20 Lost Dog Cafe
21 Bert's Market
22 The Edge *

* From my imagination to yours.

Other Folly Beach Mysteries by Bill Noel

Folly

The Pier

Washout

The Edge

The Marsh

Ghosts

Missing

Final Cut

First Light

Boneyard Beach

Silent Night

Dead Center

Discord

A Folly Beach Mystery COLLECTION

Dark Horse

Joy

A Folly Beach Mystery COLLECTION II

No Joke

Relic

A Folly Beach Mystery COLLECTION III

Faith

A Folly Beach Christmas Mystery COLLECTION

CHAPTER ONE

I answered the phone to hear Virgil Debonnet, say, "Chris, you'll never guess what I found." My friend was out of breath, sounding like he'd run a marathon.

His call disturbed my early-morning cup of coffee as I sat in my seldom-used kitchen while pondering nothing.

"The fountain of youth." I said, suspecting I was wrong. I had a difficult time being serious when someone starts a conversation asking me to guess something.

"Your guessing sucks."

I smiled then said, "Want me to try again?"

I heard him exhale before saying, "No, you'll never get it."

I met Virgil a year ago and we'd quickly become friends. Like many of my acquaintances on Folly Beach, the small, South Carolina barrier island I call home, God bestowed upon him an abundance of quirks.

"What did you find?"

"A dead body. Can you believe that? It was—"

The fountain of youth would've been higher on my list.

"Where are you?"

"Boat ramp parking lot. Don't you want to know—"

This wasn't a conversation I wanted over the phone. "Meet me at the Dog. I'll be there in fifteen minutes."

"I have an open spot in my calendar." He laughed as his breathing began to approach normal. "See you there."

Virgil had countless open spots in his calendar. He was in his early forties but hadn't worked in years.

I'd avoided exercise most of my sixty-nine years, but since I was a few, okay, more than a few pounds overweight, I was determined to walk whenever possible. The Lost Dog Cafe was fewer than six blocks from my cottage, so hoofing it didn't provide much of a challenge. I stepped out the door and was surprised by the dense fog blanketing the island. Fog wasn't unusual in April, but today's version was fog on steroids. I felt I'd have to part it with my hands, an irrational feeling, but it still popped into my head.

The Lost Dog Cafe was a half-block off Center Street, the center of most retail establishments on my six-mile-long, half-mile-wide slice of heaven. Since I fixed food about as often as kangaroos knock on my front door, the Dog was my go-to spot for breakfast. Unfortunate for me, fortunate for the restaurant, it was also the favorite breakfast spot for countless vacationers plus many locals. I peeked in the door, looked around, but didn't see Virgil. Being early, the restaurant wasn't full, so I selected a table on the front patio. The hostess escorted me to the vacant table and before I had time to settle, Virgil rounded the corner.

He was my height at five-foot-ten but much thinner than I am. He wore a long-sleeve, button-down white dress shirt with frayed cuffs, navy blue chinos, and his prized possession, resoled Gucci loafers. His fashionably long, black hair was slicked back. One of his quirks was he wore sunglasses regardless of time of day or amount of sun. They looked even stranger this morning as he emerged from the fog.

"Sorry it took so long to get here," he said as he took a seat. "The constabulary wouldn't allow me to leave until I answered 3,000 questions. I pled the fifth amendment when that cute Officer Bishop enquired about the size of my Jockey shorts."

"Virgil?"

He raised his right arm and pointed his hand at me, palm out. "Yes, Christopher, I made up that part. Regardless, there was a plethora of questions."

Before he could make anything else up, Temple, one of the servers, appeared to ask what we wanted to drink.

I said coffee, Virgil asked if they had kopi luwak coffee.

Being the professional, Temple said no, without giving any hint if she knew what it was. I knew I didn't.

"Good," Virgil said, "It cost fifty-nine dollars a cup. I can't afford it. How about a cup of normal-people coffee?"

"Coming right up," Temple said. It may have been my imagination, but she left the table quicker than necessary.

Virgil watched her go, then turned to me. "Kopi luwak is the most expensive coffee in the world. I had a cup back when I was rich. Tasted like crap."

I didn't waste time asking why he asked if the Dog had any. Virgil had been a stock market analyst, had inherited a mansion overlooking the Charleston Harbor, all before losing everything through horrible investments, gambling losses, battles with illegal substances, and failed squabbles with the

IRS. He now lived in a tiny apartment in a building that could best be described in need of a total remodel, or demolition.

Temple was quick with our coffee, then asked if we were ready to order.

Virgil said, "Perhaps give Mr. Landrum and me a few minutes, Miss Temple."

She left to ask if the couple at the table behind us needed anything.

I said, "Dead body?"

"I've had more traumatic sunrise experiences than a vampire. Today topped them all. Chris, as you know, I'm unencumbered with a job, so I have countless hours to, well, to do whatever I choose to do. I've learned this enchanting island has a certain optimistic glow early in the morn. Optimism is a rare commodity in this era of mere glimmers of optimism, so I choose to seek it out. Early morning walks meet that need. In fact, I've been taking—"

"Virgil, dead body?"

"I'm setting the stage. You in a hurry to get somewhere?"

"Set on."

Temple returned before Virgil could continue constructing the stage for his drama. This time we were ready for her. I said I'd have French toast, the breakfast I order most every visit to the Dog. Virgil said he'd have to stick with a bagel adding that his current net worth was slightly north of seven dollars. She headed to the kitchen to take a significant bite out of his life savings.

Virgil turned to me. "Most mornings I like to take in the sights of sunrise over the Atlantic. This morning, I decided to saunter the other direction seeing if any action was stirring at the Folly River. In hindsight, I grievously chose the wrong destination. As you can see, the fog has shrouded our island like a cotton blanket over, well, something under the blanket."

I nodded, hoping construction on the stage would be completed before supper.

"I arrived in the parking lot for the boat ramp to find not a creature stirring, or if there had been, the fog made it impossible for me to detect movement. Only half the bridge off the island was visible through the thick low-lying cloud. Additionally, there were three vessels bobbing in the water, only three I saw, that is. Two medium-sized boats and one attractive sailboat drew my attention." He hesitated, sighed, then said. "That is until I walked to the edge of the river where I noticed an aluminum jon boat trapped in the tall grasses at water's edge." Virgil closed his eyes, shook his head, and said, "That, my friend, brings me to the dead body."

Poor timing brought Temple to the table with our food. I thanked her, hoping it didn't knock Virgil off his story. I'd heard enough about the stage.

Virgil spread cream cheese on his bagel, looked toward the small parking area in front of the restaurant, then said, "A gentleman was lying prone in the boat. Two thoughts came to mind. First, why didn't I take my morning walk along the ocean? Second, a call to the local law enforcement officials seemed in order."

"How did you know he was dead?"

"The boat was down the sharp decline in land so I couldn't get to him."

I repeated, "How did you know he was dead?"

"I suppose because he was lying in a puddle of blood that appeared large enough to stock a blood bank. Chris, I doubt any was left in him. Let me tell you, my friend, this was no way for me to begin an optimistic day." He shook his head. "In hindsight, I should add my day was more optimistic than that of the boat man."

"What happened next?"

"I was surrounded by more emergency vehicles than appear in the Christmas parade. I suppose the law enforcement officials who descended on the scene considered me the number one suspect in causing the demise of the boat man. I assured them I was the citizen who called to report the body which, I suppose, made me appear a bit less guilty. When Chief LaMond arrived, she first rolled her eyes when she saw me, then told the other cops she knew me, adding that while I could be a pain in her lovely posterior, I was probably not the person who ended the life of the boat man."

Cindy LaMond, who held the official title of Director of Public Safety but was referred to by everyone as the Folly Beach Police Chief, was a good friend who knew Virgil as a result of a double murder a few months earlier. He, along with a couple of my other friends, had stumbled into solving the crime. That, for some reason, had left a lasting impression on the Chief.

"Virgil, do they know what happened to the man?"

"Possibly, but they didn't choose to impart that information."

"Did you recognize him?"

"Don't know his name, but I've seen him in a couple of local drinking establishments with his butt parked at the bar. As you may know, when there is an uptick in my financial status, I enjoy an adult beverage, or two, or, well, you get the idea."

I did. "Describe him."

"Older than me. Maybe in his fifties, black hair going grey around the temples, I'd guess a couple inches taller although since he was dead he didn't stand for me to compare. Had a distinguished air about him. Not this morning, but when he was in the bars. That's about it. Know him?"

"Doesn't sound familiar."

"No need to. You won't be running into him other than at a funeral home." Virgil took another bite of bagel, rubbed his temple, then said, "Before I called you, I called Charles, you know, because he's a private detective. I got his voicemail so I left a message where I might have mentioned that I found a body. Since you're part of his detective agency, I called you next."

Charles Fowler has been my best friend since I'd arrived on Folly Beach a dozen years ago. He and I had rapidly bonded even though we're as alike as a raisin to a filet mignon. He's also a self-proclaimed private detective, a status he claims to have earned by reading every detective novel written in the last two hundred years, an exaggeration, but only slight. Since I'd known him, he and, truth be told, I have stumbled into assisting the police solve several murders. The how is much too long a story to share.

I was now getting a glimmer of why Virgil made me the third choice of calls this morning.

My thought was confirmed when he said, "I have no idea how we'll do it, but we've got to find out who killed him."

Virgil's ringing phone broke his proclamation. He nearly jumped out of the chair, indicating he wasn't as calm as I'd thought. He stared at it like it was a cobra getting ready to strike, then answered. After listening to whomever was on the other end for a few seconds, Virgil said, "The Dog," then seconds later, added, "Okay," before returning the phone to the table.

I'm no psychic but would bet we'd be getting an addition to our table.

I said, "Charles?"

Virgil nodded.

"On his way?"

Virgil nodded again then repeated, "We've got to find out who killed him."

No, we don't, I thought, but history has taught me thinking and doing are two different things. Here we go again.

CHAPTER TWO

I heard Charles's hand-carved wood cane he's carried ever since I've known him tapping the walkway in front of the patio before I saw him. Despite several attempts over the decade to find out, he'd never explained why the cane was his constant companion. That can also be said about his obsession with wearing long-sleeve college-logoed T-shirts or sweatshirts regardless of the weather. Today it was a green and white Slippery Rock University T-shirt.

"Who turned on the fog machine?" he asked as he lowered his body in the chair. "Thought I was going to have to use the handy-dandy GPS machine in my phone to find my way here."

Charles was a couple of years younger than I, a couple of inches shorter, more than a couple of pounds lighter, and with his three-day old, scruffy whisker growth, could pass as a street person.

"Morning, Charles," Virgil said. "Glad you successfully weaved your way through the zero visibility we're enjoying."

Charles's apartment was four blocks from the restaurant.

"Morning, Charles," I said.

"Morning, Charles," Temple three-peated, as she set a mug of coffee in front of my friend.

"Temple, you're a lifesaver. Think you can round up another order of French toast, or did Chris eat up your supply?"

"Think I can find one," Temple said, then pivoted before heading to find another order for Charles.

"Okay," Charles said. "Enough welcoming me. Why did you drag me out of my cozy apartment while I was engrossed in a fascinating biography of Zachary Taylor?"

Another of Charles's quirks is his interest in United States presidents. One of his irritating quirks is quoting them.

Virgil took a sip of coffee then said, "I believe it was you who invited yourself to our breaking fast."

"Whatever. So, what were you talking about on the message machine? Something about a boat, a body?"

Virgil gave Charles an abbreviated version of his morning and the eventful walk to the boat landing. He also shared how he'd seen the victim in local bars but hadn't had a conversation with him. Charles interrupted so many times with questions that Temple had time to bring his breakfast, return twice to refill our coffee, and would've had time left over to sing the entire soundtrack from *Hamilton*.

Charles's interrogation ended with, "How are we going to catch the killer?"

Before I could explain we didn't know if the man had been killed or if his death was accidental, share the obvious fact that regardless what had happened, it was a job for the police, without hitting my two friends in the head with the fact it was none of our business, Charles was asking me to call Chief LaMond to find out what'd happened.

"Charles, Cindy is probably at the boat landing. The last thing she needs is a call from a citizen butting into her business."

"You're right," he said, then looked at his bare wrist where normal humans wear a watch. "So, you'll call her in a half hour?" He nodded, then stuffed a bite of French toast in his mouth.

Virgil looked at Charles and said, "If I may be so bold, why don't you call the Chief?"

Go Virgil, go.

"Simple, my aspiring detective friend. The Chief thinks I'm a worthless, nosy, ignoramus. For reasons that make no sense, she thinks Chris is trustworthy, helpful, and her close friend. She tells him stuff she wouldn't divulge to her priest, that is if she was Catholic, which she isn't. She'll tell him what we need to know."

Days after we first met, Virgil nicknamed Charles and me a crimefighting duo. That wasn't bad enough, and incorrect, I might add, but he said his aspiration was to join the group making us the crimefighting trio.

"Guys, I'll call the Chief this afternoon. By then she should have the man's identity, may even know cause of death."

"Sounds like a plan," Virgil said.

"Not a good one," Charles added. "It'll have to do."

———

I'd told Charles I'd call the Chief this afternoon. If history was any indication, no later than a few seconds after noon, he'd be calling to see what I learned. I'm not a big fan of telephone conversations, so instead of waiting for Charles's call, I took my second walk of the day to see if Cindy was in her office. The Folly Beach Department of Public Safety was in the salmon-colored City Hall. The main entrance to City Hall faced Center Street but the Public Safety entrance was around the corner on West Cooper Avenue and faced the Surf Bar. I took the elevator to the Chief's floor where I lucked out. Cindy was at her desk flipping through a manila folder. She scribbled something on the folder then added it to a pile of folders that must've been a foot high. I tapped on the door.

The Chief looked up, frowned, pointed her pen at me, then said, "You better be here to give me airline tickets to Rome or I'm going to have you arrested for harassing an overworked, underpaid public servant."

Cindy was in her mid-fifties, five-foot-three, with curly, dark hair, and an irreverent sense of humor. I didn't bring airline tickets to anywhere, so I hoped it was her attempt at humor.

"Good morning, Cindy. Have a few minutes?"

She frowned. "Of course. Why wouldn't I have time to ignore my chiefly duties I'm six-months behind on to spend time with a worthless retired geezer who has nothing better to do than pester me?"

I took that as a hint to move a pile of folders off a guest chair and replace them with my rear. I'd known Cindy since she moved to Folly nearly ten years ago to join the police department. She was promoted to Director of Public Safety six years later. I consider her and her husband, Larry, two of my best friends. I think the feeling is mutual, despite some, okay, many of her comments.

"I'm guessing you didn't bring me airline tickets, so what did I do to deserve this visit?"

"I hear there was an incident near the boat ramp this morning."

"There was."

"Want to tell me about it?"

She tapped her pen on the desk then pointed it at me. "No."

"Why not?"

"Did you see that nice, big, arched sign over the entry to the building, the one that says Folly Beach Public Safety?"

"I did."

"Do you happen to work in the building behind that nice, big sign?"

"No."

"Does that give you a hint why I don't want to tell you anything about this morning?"

"Yes."

She continued tapping the pen on the desk. "Why are you asking about something I'm not going to tell you about?"

"I was talking to Virgil Debonnet—"

Cindy interrupted, "Would that be the Virgil who discovered the body I'm not going to tell you about?"

I nodded.

"Why were you talking to him?"

"He called. He was traumatized, wanted to talk to someone. That's all."

"So, it wasn't because he wanted you to help him catch the

killer, you know, like the last time you teamed up with Virgil, the time you nearly got yourself killed."

This was not the time to drop Charles's name in the conversation, especially adding that Charles wanted to play detective—again.

"He was upset, wanted to talk. I don't want to take more of your valuable time. Good luck solving whatever happened." I started to rise.

"I've never known you to give up that fast. Don't tell me you're getting too old to be nosy."

I sat back down, smiled, and repeated, "Want to tell me about this morning?"

"Damn, you're good. Tricked me into telling you. As I'm sure you know, a body was found in a jon boat stuck in the grasses along the Folly River. What you probably don't know is the body belonged to one Walter L. Thurmond, age fifty-four, former resident of a James Island condo complex, current resident of either heaven or hell, not sure which."

"How'd you find out who he was?"

"Excellent detective work, years of investigative experience."

"And?"

"Driver's license in a wallet in his pocket."

"Excellent work, no wonder you're Chief."

"Smart ass," Cindy said then smiled.

"Yep. Do you know anything about him other than his name?"

"First time I saw him was this morning. One of my guys thinks he'd seen him coming out of a couple of local drinking establishments near closing time. He wasn't falling-over drunk or causing a ruckus, so there was no reason to stop him."

"Cause of death?"

"Chris, you know that'll be up to the medical examiner to cypher. I'm just a lowly cop. If I had to guess, it could have something to do with the knife rammed in his back."

"Does the lowly cop have any idea who put it there?"

"Not a clue. Fortunately, it ain't my job to figure out. The Sheriff's Office has that pleasure."

The Folly Beach Department of Public Safety is not equipped to investigate major crimes and defers to the Charleston County Sheriff's Office.

"Who caught the case?" I asked, realizing how strange it was that a retired bureaucrat from a healthcare company in Kentucky would think to ask that question.

"Adair."

I'd known Detective Kenneth Adair from a few years back when he accused a friend of mine of killing a student.

I said, "Anything else you can tell me?"

"Yes."

"And that is?"

"If I learn that you, or your buddy Charles, or your new buddy Virgil are butting in police business, I will not have you arrested."

I smiled. "Good."

Cindy returned my smile, before saying, "I'll line-up a firing squad and reduce our beach community's population by one, two, or three pests."

I'd overstayed my welcome.

CHAPTER THREE

The temperature was in the low-seventies, average for this time of year, so instead of heading home after leaving Cindy's office, I began the seven-block walk to Charles's apartment. I smiled when I realized I'd walked more today than most days, and it wasn't yet noon. Charles lived in an old apartment building at the end of Sandbar Lane. The building once housed one of Folly's more popular restaurants with an outstanding view of sunsets over the Folly River. His Toyota Venza was parked in the gravel lot in front of his unit; his classic 1961 Schwinn bicycle chained to a post beside his door.

I started to knock when my phone rang. Charles's name appeared on the screen, so it must be a few seconds after noon.

"Well, what'd you learn?"

"Open your door."

"You learned I should open my door?"

I hit end call, then waited to see his straggly face in the

doorway. The wait was brief.

"Why'd you hang up?"

"Guess."

"Because you're at the door."

"Good guess."

"I see you didn't come bearing gifts, so why the visit?"

"Thought telling you in person was better than sharing what I'd learned over the phone."

He motioned me in. "What are you waiting for?"

Charles claims to have read every mystery novel written since Gutenberg invented the printing press, plus countless other books both fiction and nonfiction. A glance around his apartment would support that claim. Floor-to-ceiling wooden bookshelves made of stacked concrete blocks and irregular pine boards covered three walls in the living room. I couldn't see them from my vantage point but knew shelves were on four walls in the bedroom, two walls in the kitchen, and one in the bathroom. Books overflowed each shelf. He plopped down in a worn, navy blue velour recliner.

There were two stacks of books on the floor and more on the only other chair in the room. I moved the books off the wicker rocking chair and sat.

"You know this ain't a full-service restaurant, so if you want anything, you know where the kitchen is."

"I'm fine." I pointed at the book that was open on the small table by his recliner. "Finish the Zachary Taylor biography?"

He looked at the book. "Nah. It's in the kitchen. This is one of Clive Cussler's novels where the bad guys try a thousand ways to kill the hero. Fail every time."

"How many books are you reading at one time?"

"Thomas Jefferson said, 'I cannot live without books.' He agrees with me on that."

I suspect it was the other way around, but I didn't see anything positive by sharing that thought.

"Do you know Walter Thurmond?"

"Can't he live without books either?"

"Don't know. His living ended this morning."

"In a jon boat?"

"That would be the one. Know him?"

"Met him one day outside Taco Boy. He was standing in front of the entry looking lost so I asked if I could help him find something. He told me he was waiting for a client."

"What kind of client?"

"Just guessing, but probably human."

I sighed. "Did you learn anything else about him?"

"Had on a suit. Looked out of place over here. Had snooty airs about him. That's all. Did Cindy tell you he was the man in the boat?"

"Yes."

"Do I have to drag it out of you? What else did she say?"

"Lived in a condo on James Island, and oh yeah, had a knife sticking in his back."

Charles nodded. "Suppose that's what killed him."

"No wonder you think you're a private detective."

"Don't think, know."

"Whatever."

"She say anything else?"

"Said you, Virgil, and I would be the subject of a firing squad if we meddled in police business."

"No can do. Only Mississippi, Oklahoma, and Utah allow firing squads."

I wondered how he knew that but didn't want an extended monologue about it. "She wants us to leave policing to the police."

"Have you told Virgil?"

A trick question if I'd ever heard one. If I said yes, Charles would pound me with enough grief to fill a garbage truck. He had to be first to hear anything. If I said no, he'd glare at me and ask why not.

"You're the first to know."

"Good. So, when are we going to tell him?"

"Why do we need to tell him?"

He shook his head. "You already forget? He found the body. He's one of us. He needs to know."

Dare I ask what he means by *one of us*? No, but he did have a point about Virgil finding the body, besides, he called us to let us know what he'd found.

"Why don't you call him now?"

Charles smiled. "If you insist."

He called, but to no avail. Virgil didn't answer, nor did a message machine. Charles hit end call and stared at the phone like it was part of a conspiracy to keep him from talking with Virgil.

Charles was quick to get over his irritation, then began rehashing everything Virgil had said about finding the body. It was almost as if by repeating everything, the identity of the killer would magically appear in the narrative. If it did, neither of us heard it. He decided he'd try to call Virgil later, then let me know if he learns anything new.

As I headed out the door, Charles said, "Let me know when you figure out how to catch the killer?"

I didn't respond.

CHAPTER FOUR

On the way home, I stopped at Barb's Books, a used bookstore located on Center Street. The store's namesake, Barbara Deanelli, and I've dated a few years. She moved to Folly from Pennsylvania, after a contentious divorce from her husband who was also her law partner. Her brother, more accurately, half brother is Dude Slone, owner of the surf shop on Folly.

Barb was standing behind the counter munching on a sandwich. She was sixty-seven-years-old, but looks younger, my height, runner thin, with short black hair. She wiped a crumb off her lip before giving me one of her captivating smiles.

"What brings you in? I know it's not to buy anything."

She was right. My reading is limited to newspapers and restaurant menus.

"I came to see the lovely bookstore owner."

"I hope that's all, since I don't have any food." She stepped out from behind the counter and kissed my cheek. "I do have soft drinks in back, if you're interested."

I said I was and followed her to the small office in back of the store. She grabbed a Diet Pepsi from the refrigerator, handed it to me, then took the chair from behind her contemporary desk and rolled it to where she could see if anyone entered the store.

I sat in the other chair, took a sip, and asked about business.

"Slow, but it's early. Why do I have the feeling you didn't stop in to see the bookstore owner or to see how busy she'd been?"

"You'd be partially wrong. I did stop to see you. Now that I'm here, did you hear about the body found at the boat ramp this morning?"

"Dude called to tell me, or that's what I think he was saying. With him, I never know."

Dude and Barb shared a father, different mothers, and vocabularies as different as a tree to a turnip. Barb had been trained as an attorney while Dude had never met a sentence he couldn't mangle. He'd never settle for ten words if one would almost do.

"What'd he tell you?"

"Something like, 'Dead bod be floatin' in mini boat where boats slip in river.'"

"Was that it?"

"He added, 'No be knowin' name.'"

I smiled. "I think he has a future writing for the newspaper."

"You be wrong," Barb said in a passable Dude imitation.

"If you're interested, I can add a little more to the report?"

She smiled. "Me be curious."

"Your friend and mine, Virgil Debonnet, found the body. The victim was in a small boat stuck in the tall grasses near the boat ramp."

Virgil has been a regular in Barb's Books since he moved to Folly. His financial woes prevented him from buying anything, but he enjoyed spending time with the owner.

"Poor man, that had to be traumatic. He likes to walk early, so I suspect he'll think twice before doing that anytime soon."

"When he called, he was shaken. I met him for breakfast. I think he's okay."

"Any idea what happened?"

"He was stabbed."

Her eyes narrowed, she took another sip from her drink, then said, "Virgil didn't call to get you involved, did he?"

To lie or not to lie, that is the question.

"He expressed interest in finding out who killed the man. I think he was just talking. He knows it's in the capable hands of the Sheriff's Office."

"I hope you're right. Any idea who it is?"

"Walter Thurmond, according to Chief Lamond."

Barb shook her head. "You're kidding?"

"Know him?"

"He's a regular."

"What do you know about him?"

The bell over the door rang before she answered. Barb went to greet the potential customer, but I remained seated and thought how small a world it was on Folly. Occasionally, someone refers to the island as Mayberry on the ocean. It's easy to see similarities.

Barb returned saying she didn't have what the customer was looking for.

I repeated, "What do you know about Thurmond?"

"Not a lot. Think he lives off-island, although he's in at least twice a week. He buys spy novels. He gets everything I get in by Ken Follett, Tom Clancy, or Robert Ludlum. That's about all I know about him."

"Any idea what he does for a living?"

"Interesting you should ask. He dresses well, looks distinguished, and is relatively young. Mid-fifties, I'd guess. What's interesting is he's in during the week, during work hours for most people, so he must not have regular hours. When he first started coming in, I enquired about his profession. He said businessman, then changed the subject."

"Don't guess you know what business?"

"He never went down that road. To tell the truth, he reminded me of some of the businessmen we defended, often referred to as white-collar criminals. To be honest, some were, but they still deserved an aggressive defense."

"How was he like them?"

She laughed. "Oozed charm, bright-white teeth always smiling, but you could tell there was something else going on under his flawless exterior. It's hard to put into words."

"Did he mention a family?"

"Not really. He didn't wear a wedding ring, but that doesn't mean he wasn't married. He paid cash. He always had a wad of cash in his pocket. That's getting rarer with everyone using plastic."

"If he lived off-island, somewhere on James Island, according to Cindy, any idea why he was over here? Could he have had a job on Folly?"

"Possibly, but I didn't get that impression."

"Charles told me he ran into him once in front of Taco Boy."

"Whoa," Barb said, "when were you talking to Charles about him?"

"He met Virgil and me at the Dog."

"Tell me again how you aren't getting involved."

I told her I didn't have any plan to. Not a denial, but close.

"Yeah, right. Okay, back to Charles. What did he say about Thurmond?"

"Charles introduced himself to Thurmond then asked if he could help him. Thurmond said he was meeting a client."

Another potential customer arrived, interrupting our conversation. This one stayed longer, buying several books, before Barb returned.

"Where were we?" she said.

"I was telling you about Thurmond meeting a client."

"Glad you mentioned a client. The last time Thurmond was in, suppose it was the middle of last week, we were talking when he looked at his watch then said he had to meet with someone named Ryan Sparks. The way he said it was like I should know who Sparks is. I had no idea. Do you know him?"

"Doesn't ring a bell, but I know someone who probably would."

"Your friend whose mission is to meet every living resident of the universe plus their pets."

"Charles."

CHAPTER FIVE

I headed home after leaving Barb helping a customer find a Susan Boyer novel. As soon as I walked in the door, I realized I was hungry. I used my culinary skills to fix a peanut butter sandwich then to prove I wasn't totally inept in the kitchen, sliced an apple I bought the day before at Bert's Market, my next-door neighbor. I took my meal to the screened-in porch to watch the cars drive past my cottage.

After finishing my gourmet lunch, I called Charles to see if he knew Ryan Sparks.

He answered with, "Figured out how we're going to catch the killer?"

I ignored his opening. "You know Ryan Sparks?"

"Did he stab Walter Thurmond?"

"No idea. Do you know him?"

"Not really. I hear he was a professional baseball player. He ain't anymore. Lives on a boat docked at Sunset Cay

Marina. I've never met him. All that comes from rumors going around."

"Know anyone who may know more about him?"

"Check with Sean. He lives on a boat, so he may. What about Sparks?"

"Barb told me she heard Walter Thurmond talking about having a meeting with him."

"How does Barb know Thurmond?"

"He was a regular customer."

"Does she know who killed him?"

"Don't you think if she did, I would've led with that?"

"So, she doesn't know who killed him?"

That didn't deserve a response. "I'll see if Sean knows Sparks," I said, then hung up, something my friends often did to me. It felt good.

Sean Aker is a local attorney I've known for a decade. He helped me with the paperwork required to start my photo gallery, a business that went the way of many small enterprises. I closed it and it's now a long-ago memory. After that, Charles and I helped clear Sean who'd been accused of killing his law partner. That cemented our friendship.

It was still mid-afternoon, so I called his office to see if he was available. Marlene Ryle, his receptionist who'd worked in the office since it opened, said he was in his office with the door closed, which she interpreted as his taking a nap. I said I'd be right over, and for her not to wake him so he wouldn't run out before I got there.

Sean's office was on the second floor of a building adjacent to City Hall. One of several Folly Beach gift shops occupied the first floor. I thought about the first time I'd visited the office and the colorful surfboard on the wall above the first-floor entry. A fire had nearly destroyed the building, so the entry and the entire second floor had been rebuilt. The surfboard was a fatality of the conflagration.

Marlene greeted me with a smile as did her pet Shih Tze sitting on her lap. She, Marlene, not the dog, noted Sean was awake waiting for me in his office. The lawyer reinforced being awake when he met me at the door. He was approaching fifty, a couple of inches taller than I am, weighed approximately fifty pounds less than I weigh, with short, curly black hair. Gray was beginning to appear around his ears.

"What legal trouble have you got yourself in now?" he said.

I shook his hand. "None I know of."

"Social visit?"

"Partially."

"Sounds interesting. Come in, have a seat. That way Marlene will think I'm working."

Over Sean's door there was a wood cutout of a pie-sized parachute with SEAN printed in bright red, green, and blue on the canopy. It'd replaced a similar cutout that'd been destroyed by the fire. In addition to being an attorney, Sean was a surfer, scuba diver, and skydiver. He has more energy, and more courage, or stupidity, than anyone I know.

The top of his desk was neat, organized, which either indicated he was highly competent or didn't have any work. We shared a brief update on our lives since we'd talked a year or so ago. He said work consumed his life; I said retirement took up most of my time.

"Okay," he said, "with that out of the way, what's the non-social reason for your visit?"

"Do you know Ryan Sparks?"

"Why would I?"

"I heard he lives on his boat on the river. You live on a boat, so I thought you might know him."

"You live in a house, right?"

I nodded.

"Do you know everyone who lives in houses?"

"You don't know him?"

"Just pulling your chain. Yes, I know Ryan. Lots of people do. We don't have many celebrities living here."

"Celebrities?"

"For kids who dreamed of being a major league baseball player when they grew up, anyone who had that opportunity is considered a celebrity."

"That what you wanted to be?"

He chuckled. "That, a fireman, or a rock star." He hesitated, looked at the ceiling like he was reliving his early years, then returned to the present. "Practicing law came in somewhere lower than being the guy who cleans septic tanks."

"What do you know about Ryan?"

"Guess I've talked to him more than a lot of others since we both live on the river. Most of the time his boat is docked at Sunset Cay Marina. I'm anchored about two miles up this way. It's easier to get to work in my dinghy. I leave my car behind the office."

"What do you mean most of the time he's docked at Sunset Cay?"

"He doesn't have a car, so whenever he comes to restaurants or visits his sister and brother-in-law, he motors up here near where I'm anchored then paddles ashore in a kayak. That's when I talk to him most. Seems like a nice guy."

"Sean, if he played major league baseball, why wouldn't he have a car?"

"Torn rotator cuff. He was a pitcher, made it to Triple-A ball before the injury. It ended his career, or at least that's the story he tells anyone who'll listen. Why the interest?"

"Did you hear about the body found by the boat ramp this morning?"

He smiled. "My gossip machine Marlene told me, but she didn't know anything more than it was a man with a knife in his back."

"I thought with everything going on, you would've seen the commotion from your boat."

He smiled again. "I would have if I was on the boat. I spent the night with, umm, a friend on East Hudson. Didn't know anything unusual happened until Marlene told me." Sean had been divorced several years. I don't know the details, but he'd confided his wife had a good reason for kicking him out. I didn't need to know more. "Know who the man was?"

"Walter Thurmond. You know him?"

"Don't think so. He live on Folly?"

"James Island. Charles Fowler said he met Thurmond once in front of a restaurant. Thurmond said he was waiting to meet a client. Barb told me he was a customer and the last time she saw him he shared that he was meeting Ryan Sparks."

Sean slowly nodded his head, then said, "Ah, it's coming clearer. Charles plus you by default are nosing into what happened to Thurmond."

"Curious," I said. "You mentioned Ryan had a sister over here. Know who she is?"

He smiled. "Glad you're only curious, not nosing around.

No, to answer your question. He said her name was Megan, her husband Kevin, but that's all I know."

I thanked him before saying I didn't want to take more of his valuable time. He laughed then said it was a welcomed change from talking about exciting topics like business incorporations, drafting wills, and figuring out how to get DUI charges reduced for some of his sobriety-challenged clients.

CHAPTER SIX

What a day, I thought as I returned to the porch to watch cars heading home from work. The fog-filled morning beginning with a call from Virgil telling me about a murder, followed by spending time with Charles, always an adventure, a visit to Chief LaMond, then visiting Barb's Books, before talking with Sean Aker. I hate to admit it, but each day I'm feeling my nearly seventy years hanging around this planet. Muscles I didn't know I had ache. My fingers remind me daily that arthritis has taken up residence. And, don't ask about my aching back. With that said, one thing hasn't changed much: my appetite. All that's left in the house to eat are a few slices of bread, peanut butter, plus the apple core left from lunch.

A two-block walk to Rita's Seaside Grill should meet my hunger needs. The popular restaurant sits on a prime spot of Folly Beach real estate. It's across a street from the Folly Beach Fishing Pier, across another street from the iconic Sand

Dollar Social Club, and catty-corner to the Tides, the island's nine-story beachfront hotel.

The temperature was still in the low seventies so given the choice, I told the hostess I'd prefer being on the patio rather than inside. A singer was setting up his equipment, so I chose a table as far from the speakers as possible. I wasn't the only person wanting to eat in a quieter section. Cindy and Larry LaMond were at a table in the back corner of the patio.

Cindy saw me, shook her head, then said, "Lord, what'd I do to deserve this?"

Instead of the Lord, Larry responded, "Chris, care to join us?"

Cindy smacked his arm.

"Thanks," I said. "I don't want to interrupt your peaceful dinner."

Cindy slid the vacant chair out beside her. "You already have, so sit your ample butt down."

I took her up on the generous offer, although I would've worded it differently.

"My lovely wife had a rough day, so I thought she deserved a night out."

Cindy tapped his arm, easier this time. "Hell, I deserve a trip to Paris, the one in France, not Tennessee, and a diamond tiara, but I wasn't going to turn down a nice meal."

I'd known Larry long before Cindy moved to Folly. He owned Pewter Hardware, a tiny hardware store located next to the Folly Beach Post Office. He was two inches shorter than his wife, thirty-plus pounds lighter, and ten years older. He'd often been asked if he was a jockey. He hated horses, so saying the *j* word in his presence was a serious faux pas.

"Honey, you deserve much more than that," Larry said, followed by his best smile.

Ashley, the LaMonds' server, returned to ask what I wanted to drink. I told her white wine. Cindy and Larry said they were okay. After she left, I asked Cindy if they'd ordered yet. She said no, that she was trying to unwind with a beer before eating.

Larry took a sip of his martini, then said, "Did you hear about the body at the boat ramp?"

"I heard—"

"Crap, Larry, he not only heard, he came to the office to pester me about it before I had time to take my morning nap."

"I should've known," Larry said. "You know the man?"

"No, Cindy told me he wasn't from here."

"Guys, that's enough. Larry, remember the reason we're here? Hint, it isn't to talk about work, especially a homicide."

Ashley returned with my drink before Larry told Cindy if he remembered why they were here. Cindy said they were ready, then ordered burgers for each of them. I told Ashley to make it three.

"How's business?" I asked Larry, not because I wanted to know, but to move the discussion away from the early-morning discovery.

"Picking up after the winter lull."

The singer began his first number, so I leaned closer to hear Larry over the music. He, Larry, not the singer, was saying something about the increasing price of pine mulch. I didn't understand all he was saying but realized I didn't care. I didn't pursue it.

"Larry," Cindy said, "I'm sure Chris is fascinated with the

economics of pine mulch, but let's not talk about work, yours or mine. Remember, we're here to relax."

The performer began a cover of John Fogerty's hit "Centerfield." Larry mouthed, "Put me in coach, I'm ready to play."

I said, "Did you play baseball?"

"Nah, I was a football and basketball star," he said then laughed.

Considering his diminutive size, I hoped he was laughing at the absurdity of his comment. He was often defensive about his size, so I wondered how many martini's he'd had.

His laughter faded. "Actually, I did play baseball in high school. I was fast in those days, and not too shabby with the bat. Why?"

"Fogerty's song reminded me about something Sean Aker said about someone who lives over here playing professional baseball."

Cindy said, "Who?"

"Ryan Sparks. Either of you know him?"

Larry said, "Lives on a sailboat."

Cindy turned to her husband. "How do you know?"

"He buys cleaning supplies from me. What did Sean say about him?"

"He played pro ball before tearing his rotator cuff."

Cindy said, "How'd he end up here?"

Larry said, "Megan and Kevin Goodman, his sister and brother-in-law, live out East Ashley Avenue."

Cindy stared at Larry. "How do you know all that?"

"Sweetie, things break, people need to fix them, they come in the store. Most pay with credit cards so I see their names. I know tons of people here, not like you who only get to know the criminals, drunks, derelicts."

She smiled. "Like Chris."

Our burgers arrived before I could defend my non-criminal, etc., status.

The way Cindy and Larry stuffed the first bite of burger in their mouths, they must've been as hungry as I was. The singer had left his baseball-themed music and slowed down the pace with a cover of Billy Joel's "Just the Way You Are."

Two bites and three sips later, Larry said, "Why'd you ask about Ryan?"

"I was talking with Barb Deanelli. She said Walter Thurmond told her he was meeting with Ryan. I didn't know Ryan, so I was curious about who he was."

Cindy said, "Whoa. Why were you talking to Barb about Thurmond?"

"I was telling her about his death. She said he was a regular. She also knows Virgil, so I thought she'd want to know he'd found the body."

"What's that have to do with Ryan whatever his name is?"

"Probably nothing. We were just talking."

"It sounds like buttin' in police business."

To deny or not to deny.

I didn't have to choose. Larry said, "Ryan seems like a nice guy. I feel sorry for him. He had his life mapped out. It all revolved around baseball, so now he doesn't know what to do. He told me he's like his sailboat, both his boat and his life are adrift."

"What about his sister and her husband?"

Cindy sighed as she leaned back in her chair.

"I see Kevin more than Megan. From what he says, I gather that they have a small house, bought it a few years ago, but are making improvements, adding on, major remodeling. He hinted he inherited a chunk of money and is using it to fix up the house."

I said, "Does he work over here?"

"No. He's an aircraft assembler at Boeing although he's sick of his job and wants to get into real estate. Megan is a computer software developer with a company headquartered out of state, but she works from home."

Cindy leaned forward. "And why do you want to know that?"

Larry answered before I could. "Sweetie, we're just talking, nothing more. Isn't that right, Chris?'

"Sure."

Cindy rolled her eyes.

The musician began his rendition of "When a Man Loves a Woman," and I changed the topic to the weather, something Cindy couldn't accuse me of meddling with.

CHAPTER SEVEN

I answered the phone a few minutes after sunrise to hear Virgil say, "Christopher, you'll never guess who I'm with."

I was beginning to feel I'm in the movie *Groundhog Day*.

"Queen Elizabeth." Maybe a smart aleck answer each time he asks a question I would have no way of knowing the answer to would break him of the grating habit.

"Your guessing continues to suck. Don't say it, I don't want you to guess again. Hop over to the Dog. The answer will be sitting with me."

I told him I'd be there in twenty minutes then continued my exercise streak by walking. It was another foggy morning, but nothing compared to yesterday. Virgil was on the front patio talking to someone I didn't know. Virgil had on the same outfit he wore yesterday. Each man was nibbling on a bagel with cream cheese, one of the least expensive items on the menu. I didn't know the other man but knew Virgil's budget.

"Thanks for coming. I was telling Ryan about you."

Virgil's table mate, Ryan Sparks, I assumed, stood to shake my hand. He was at least six-foot-two, trim, with short black hair. He was also irritatingly young, mid-twenties, I'd guess.

"Pleased to me you," he said. "Virgil tells me you're a private detective. I've never met one."

He still hasn't, I thought as I gave Virgil a nasty look.

"Not really. A few friends and I've lucked out, helped the police a couple of times. I hear you are or were a professional baseball player."

He laughed. "See, you're a detective to know that."

Virgil said, "Chris, along with Charles Fowler, a friend of ours, and I solved two murders a few months back. I suppose it was before you got here. We found out that—"

To lead the conversation away from me being a detective, I said, "Ryan, how do you know Virgil?"

"I met him last night at The Washout. We were sitting at the bar and started talking. He told me he found the body at the river. Can you believe that? I took an interest since I live on my boat."

Virgil turned to me and said, "Isn't that an amazing coincidence? Running into each other, learning that Ryan lives on a boat, me finding the body."

It would've been amazing if it had been an accidental encounter. With Virgil being an aspiring private detective, I had my suspicions about the randomness of their running into each other.

"I was talking to Sean Aker yesterday. He told me he knew you since both of you live on the river. He told me about you playing ball."

Amber Lewis arrived at the table to set a mug of coffee in

front of me. I'd known Amber since I arrived on Folly. She and I had dated for a while then had remained friends.

"Want anything to eat, Chris?"

"How about French toast?" I said.

"Wow, I never would've guessed. You only order it every time you're here."

"Miss Amber," Virgil said although she wasn't talking to him, "your charm, wondrous personality, and amazing memory never cease to amaze me."

She said, "Your sweet-tongue way with words never ceases to amaze me. Unless you gentlemen wish to order something else, I'll place Chris's heart-healthy order."

I'd known Amber long enough to detect sarcasm. Virgil's smile told me he didn't know her that well.

Ryan watched Amber go then said, "Unfortunately, my baseball career came to a screeching halt last year. I was playing for the Charlotte Knights, a Triple-A farm team of the Chicago White Sox. I tore the rotator cuff in my pitching arm." He shook his head. "Ended my dream of making the majors."

I asked, "Don't players often recover from that injury?"

He sighed. "Yes, but the doc said mine was worse than most. He used all sorts of medical terms I didn't understand to say it. Bottom line, I wasn't one of the lucky ones."

I said, "Sorry."

Virgil said, "Ryan was drafted by the White Sox after he graduated from LSU. He threw a smokin' ninety-five-miles-per-hour fast ball. If you don't know much about baseball, that's seriously swift."

"What're you doing now, Ryan?"

He laughed. "Got a degree in history. Know what jobs are

available for someone with a history degree without teacher education training?"

"Can't say I do," Virgil said.

I said, "What?"

"Hell if I know. A Starbucks barista is at the top of the job chart from what I can figure. If I had a car, I could drive for Lyft or Uber. Not much market for ride sharing a sailboat."

"How'd you end up here?" I said although Sean had told me Ryan had a sister and brother-in-law living on Folly.

'Got a sister over here. I was struggling for several months after my baseball dreams struck out, then decided it'd be good being near family. She's all I have left."

"Chris," Virgil said, "Ryan told me last night he's living on his sailboat since his sister and her husband's house is too small to live with them."

"Even if there was room, I wouldn't feel comfortable invading their space. I don't need much room. Hell, I spent two years cramped on a bus going from game to game, spending nights in tiny fleabag hotel rooms sharing space with a couple other players. My boat's large compared to that."

Virgil said, "Where do you keep your boat?"

"Most of the time at Sunset Cay Marina. I have a slip out there."

"Oh," Virgil said. "I thought I may've seen it out by the boat launch ramp yesterday morning."

Since Virgil had met Ryan for the first-time last night, I wondered how he would've known Ryan's boat from others moored nearby.

"You probably did, although I doubt you could've seen much. The fog was thick enough to slice with a machete. I moved it there a couple of days ago. Wanted to eat at Jack of

Cups which was too far to walk from the marina. When I come to town, I bring my boat in close to the boat ramp then take my kayak ashore. Walk the rest of the way."

Virgil said, "Back when I had more money than sense, I had a great, oceangoing boat. Several people could've lived on it."

"What happened to it?" Ryan said.

"Way too long a story to tell now. Maybe later."

I said, "Have you always had the boat?"

"Nah. Bought it used with my signing bonus. Thought I'd have plenty of money when I reached the majors, enough to buy a house overlooking the ocean, a wife who liked to lounge by the backyard pool, and a border collie." He smiled. "Ended up with a used sailboat, nothing else."

"Too bad," Virgil said. "Did you see anything yesterday morning when all the police and fire folks were fishing the man out of the jon boat?"

My breakfast arrived before he responded. Amber also refilled my table mates' coffee mugs.

"What was that question again?" Ryan said after Amber left to deliver a check to the table behind us.

Virgil said, "Yesterday morning. All the commotion after I saw the dead body in the boat stuck in the grass along the river."

"Virgil, I think you asked me that last night, not certain since I was a bit under the influence, you were too if my sketchy memory serves me right. Like I said then, I didn't know anything about the body until I returned to my slip at the marina. Roger, a guy I met who lives nearby, told me about it. He didn't know what happened or who it was."

Virgil said, "The victim's name was Walter Thurmond."

"Oh," Ryan said.

Virgil said, "Know him?"

"Sort of."

Virgil said, "What's that mean?"

"I talked to him a couple of times; once in Snapper Jack's, once at the Crab Shack. He is, or was, some sort of business-man. He told me he bought companies making medical equip-ment." He glanced at me. "Stuff all you baby boom folks will need now that you're old."

I tried not to take it as an insult. I failed. "Anything else about him?"

"Not really. Virgil, like I asked last night, what happened to him? When was he killed? I don't recall what you said."

"Somebody added a knife to his wardrobe," Virgil said. "Don't know when. Do you, Chris?"

Good question, I thought. "I don't know when he was killed."

Virgil said, "Ryan, did you see anyone in a boat the night before last or early yesterday morning?"

"To tell you the truth, guys, it's possible I had too much to drink. I don't remember much of anything. I must've made it back to the boat."

Virgil said, "What're you going to do now?"

"Like after I finish breakfast, or with the rest of my life?"

"Both."

"Walk to my sister's to see if they need help with the remodeling she and Kevin are doing. The rest of my life part gets harder. Tell you what I'm not going to do. Never going to throw another ninety-five-miles-per-hour fastball."

Virgil tried a couple more times to ask Ryan about anything he may have seen or heard the night or early morning when Thurmond took his last breath. Ryan either didn't know anything or if he did, he wasn't sharing. Finally, he said he'd better get to his sister's house, then looked around for Amber. I told him I'd get breakfast, for him to go ahead to his sister's. He thanked me, shook my hand with a grip that would make me feel sorry for a baseball if he squeezed it that hard, said it was nice meeting me, then exited the patio. Virgil watched him go, then said, "Nice guy, but I think there's something he's not telling us."

"Why do you say that?"

"Detective intuition."

What has Charles done to Virgil?

CHAPTER EIGHT

Virgil and I went separate directions after finishing an additional coffee refill. Unlike Virgil, I didn't have the impression Ryan had been hiding anything. I did find it interesting he'd talked twice to the victim who told him he bought companies that made medical equipment needed by aging baby boomers. Could that have had something to do with his death? Sure, but so could a million other things. I knew near nothing about the high-finance world of buying businesses but knew someone who might. My friend Bob Howard spent much of his professional life brokering commercial real estate deals, before switching to the residential side of the business, then retiring after buying a small, run-down bar in Charleston, located fewer than ten miles from Folly. I gave him a call and was surprised when he said he was on his way to Folly to meet a man about buying a six-unit apartment building.

"Thought you were out of that business."

"I'm doing a favor for a guy I made enough money from over the years to buy a vacation home in Tanzania."

"Tanzania. You going on big game hunting?"

"Damned, Chris, do you take everything I say literally? It was a metaphor for making a shit-pot full of money. I don't even know where Tanzania is. Why in the hell did you call?"

I knew I shouldn't have commented on Tanzania. I'd known Bob since my second week on Folly. He was my Realtor on both my cottage and Landrum Gallery.

"Know Walter Thurmond?"

"The guy who prides himself on being an entrepreneur? The one who's young enough to be my son, that is, if I had one? Oh yeah, how could I forget, the guy who got himself stabbed in the back the other day a few blocks from your house?"

I smiled. "That's the one."

"Where are you?"

"Home, why?"

"I'll be there in twenty-five minutes. You better have beer in your refrigerator."

I didn't have time to say I didn't. He'd hung up which gave me time to go to Bert's Market to grab a six-pack.

A half hour later, I opened the door to Bob ranting about the line of traffic trying to get on the island, the morning fog, indigestion, and probably the price of eggs in China. Yes, that's my effort at a metaphor. I ignored most of his ranting, something I learned to do years ago so I could enjoy being around him.

"Enough about my problems," he said, "where's the beer?"

Bob was in his late-seventies, six-foot-tall carrying the weight of someone much taller. His usual attire included shorts nearly year-round and an untucked, colorful Hawaiian shirt covering his super-sized belly. Today was no exception.

I escorted him to the kitchen then grabbed a Budweiser out of the refrigerator. He'd plopped down in one of the kitchen chairs and was looking around.

"Damned fine cottage I found for you. Hell, this kitchen looks as good as the day you moved in."

That was because it was the most underused room in the house. I didn't share that fact, mainly because he'd already moved on and was talking about the client he was meeting in an hour. Ten minutes later, I'd heard enough about the client's tightwad ways, the great deal Bob was getting him on the apartment building, and how Bob hadn't lost his touch as one of the greatest Realtors in the country, possibly the universe.

"What else do you know about Walter Thurmond?"

"Why do you think I know more than I told you on the phone?"

"Because you invited yourself to the house, something you've done, oh, let's say, never."

He held up the Budweiser can. "Free beer."

I smiled. "And?"

"Hell, no wonder they say there's no such thing as a free beer."

"I think it's *no such thing as a free lunch*."

"Crap, that's what I said. Beer."

"Walter Thurmond?"

Bob took two quick sips, set the empty can on the table, looked at the refrigerator, then said, "Any more?"

I handed him a second can, took the other chair, and stared at my friend as he took a long draw.

"You drive a hard bargain," he said. "Okay, Walter L. Thurmond. What do wheelchairs, walkers, hospital bed, stair lifts, shower benches, bed pans, compression socks have in common?"

"All items in increasing demand among the aging population."

"Excellent answer. Now, what's a key fact about the baby boom generation?"

"There are a bunch of us."

"A bunch like the largest generational group in the history of our great country. Well, that was until those damned millennials started coming along. Let's not worry about them yet. I'm talking about baby boomers, old people, you."

I didn't remind him he was eight years older than I am, making him a pre-baby boomer.

"Bob, you told me on the phone Thurmond bought companies that produced products for the health needs of us old folks. What didn't you share?"

"All that's well and good. Except there's a rumor going around that good old, now dead, Walter wasn't quite as pure as the driven snow, or whatever that stupid cliché is. The story is he wasn't satisfied doing the right thing. Speculation is he's, or was until his untimely demise, conning suckers into buying part of his alleged companies, then ripping them off."

"Stock fraud?"

"Nope, doesn't involve stock. That stuff's highly regulated. It's getting harder and harder for honest crooks to rip people off with stock schemes. Walter buys small underperforming companies that make the old-folk crap, allegedly turns them around, then sells them for oodles of money. The people who give him money are actual partners in the companies with Walter the con artist. The companies aren't publicly traded so there aren't regulators looking over his shoulder. It's a small operation so the feds or local governmental bigwigs don't stick their bureaucratic noses in his business. He finds co-buyers who have cash at their disposal so there aren't loans that have bank regulators snooping."

"Any idea how many people, umm, co-owners Thurmond has conned?"

"Hell Chris, I'm just a retired realtor who owns a money-pit, run-down bar. I ain't a forensic accountant or fortune teller. Just repeating a rumor."

"Have you heard names of people he may've ripped off?"

"Nope, but I can tell you one thing. I'd bet my commission on the deal I'm making this afternoon that one of the late Walter Thurmond's co-owners didn't take too kindly to being ripped off. That person would be my number one suspect for ramming a knife in Walter's back."

"Know anything else about him or his con?"

"If I didn't know better, I'd think you're drifting into snooping. Don't you think the cops, you know, those folks paid to solve crimes, are capable of figuring out what happened to Thurmond?"

"Of course, they are. I was curious, simple as that."

"You forget who you're talking to? As Abe Lincoln said, you can fool all the people some of the time, but you can't fool old Bob."

That wasn't exactly how I remembered the quote but understood what he was saying. "The body was found by Virgil Debonnet, someone I've known a few months. He was shaken after finding Thurmond, so I was interested. That's all.

Bob looked at the refrigerator then at his watch.

"Want another beer?"

"Yes, but I've got to be sober when I meet with my client. That's why I got out of the realty business. I'd better be on my way."

I thanked him for stopping by and for the information on Thurmond.

On the way to the door, he said, "I know you're not snooping, not going to try to catch the killer, not doing anything more stupid than you have in the past, but in the likely event you change your mind, I'll see what I can find about who may've lost money to Thurmond's con."

Did Bob know me better than I knew myself?

CHAPTER NINE

I awoke the next morning expecting another early-morning call accompanied by a question from Virgil. It didn't come but instead of feeling Virgil withdrawal, I was relieved my daily dose of drama had subsided. My need for food hadn't. Since all that was in the kitchen was a box of stale corn flakes with nothing to pour on them unless you count four cans of Budweiser or a bottle of chardonnay, a walk next door became my sole agenda item.

Bert's Market, the Folly landmark that never closes, sells everything from beer to bologna. A large, fluffy cinnamon roll interested me more than either beer or bologna. I was putting one in a paper sack when someone tapped me on the shoulder. I turned to see Brian Newman, Folly's long-term mayor. Brian was in his early seventies, tall, trim, confident, and oozed military, understandable since he'd retired from the Army after serving thirty years in service of our country.

We shared a couple of pleasantries before he said, "Did

you hear about the murder victim found at the river the other day?"

"Yes, Virgil Debonnet, a friend of mine, discovered the body."

"I should've known that nothing bad happens here without you knowing."

"Virgil called me that morning. He was shaken."

"As he should've been."

I set the bag containing breakfast on the counter. "Any idea what happened?"

Brian glanced at the bag then glared at me. "Yes, the gentleman was murdered. Our law enforcement authorities working with the Sheriff's Office are investigating."

His tone indicated he could easily have added, *it's none of your business so don't even think about getting involved.*

I said, "I'm certain they'll catch the person who did it."

He nodded. "They will."

"I heard the victim, I believe his name's Walter Thurmond, was running a con. I don't know details, but it could've contributed to his death."

"I'm certain the authorities will follow up all leads." He sighed. "But, in the unlikely event they're unaware of what you heard, why don't you let Chief LaMond know? Thurmond didn't live on Folly, but I heard Officer Spencer had an encounter with him. I don't know the details. It was a couple weeks ago so I doubt it had anything to do with his death."

It wasn't quite an open invitation to get involved, but to me, a crack in the door appeared. "I'll call her."

He said he had to run then repeated it was good seeing me. I said the same about seeing him. I also thanked him for suggesting I call the Chief.

After I got home, I made the call between bites of cinnamon roll.

"What now, Mr. Pain in My Posterior."

Cindy had no shortage of terms of endearment.

"I was talking to your boss a few minutes ago."

She interrupted, "What'd Larry say?"

"Your other boss, Brian Newman."

"Oh, what did he say?"

"It wasn't what he said, it was what I told him."

"You want me to guess or are you going to share?"

"Bob Howard stopped by yesterday. He—"

She interrupted, "Blustery, obscene, slovenly Bob Howard?"

"One and the same."

"Good, wanted to make sure we were talking about the Bob Howard I know."

"He was telling me he'd heard Walter Thurmond was a con artist."

I shared as much of what Bob had said that I remembered. Surprisingly, the Chief listened without interrupting, said "interesting" a couple of times. She had me repeat Bob's comments so she could take notes. I had the impression it was the first she was hearing about that side of Thurmond. She ended by saying she'd share it with Detective Adair. Truth be told, she ended by saying she'd share it, then adding I could now leave everything to the police. In other words, butt out.

I finished the cinnamon roll, then recalled what else the mayor had said, something about Officer Spencer having an encounter with Thurmond. Allen Spencer was new to the police force the year I'd moved to Folly. We'd run into each other countless times over the years. Since we'd shared being new to the oceanfront community the same year, we had similar impressions about the area. I could trust him; I believe he felt the same about me. I also had his number and a standing invitation to call if I ever needed anything.

This would be a good time to take advantage of the offer. After several rings, I was beginning to fear the call was going to roll to voicemail when he answered.

"Hey, Chris. What's up?"

"You working today?"

"Until three, why?

"I wanted to ask you about something the mayor told me."

He agreed to meet me in the gravel parking area between my house and Bert's. He'd be there in fifteen minutes unless he got a call.

Ten minutes later a late-model, silver, Folly Beach patrol car pulled in the lot, backed in a space, before Allen Spencer stepped out. Allen was roughly six-feet tall, muscular reflecting his hobbies of surfing and lifting weights. When I first met him, he was thin, but since then, he'd gained considerable weight.

We exchanged greetings before he asked what the mayor had shared.

"You had a run in with Walter Thurmond a few weeks back."

Allen's eyes narrowed, he shuffled his polished shoes in the gravel lot, then said, "Now he's dead."

I nodded.

"It wasn't much of a run in. Thurmond and another guy were in front of Lowlife Bar engaged in an argument inching close to a fistfight. I was driving by and pulled over when I saw the other guy shove Thurmond. Thought I was going to have to step between them before blows were exchanged. Each guy had been drinking, neither appeared drunk. They stepped back from each other, didn't give me any trouble. I didn't see a reason to hold them. No big deal."

"What were they arguing about?"

"Guy I didn't know, umm, name's Ben something." Allen took a small notebook out of his pocket, flipped through a few pages, before saying, "Benjamin Likard, five-foot-seven, late-50s, lives on Shadow Race Lane. Anyway, he was saying something about him and Thurmond being partners in a company. Something about Likard putting up a bunch of money, he didn't say how much, then wanting to pull some out, part of the profits or something like that. Thurmond apparently wasn't giving it to him. I don't know details, don't have any need to. All I was doing was preventing a fight."

"What did you learn about Thurmond?"

"He lives off island. That's about it, other than now he's dead."

"Anything else about Likard?"

"Seeing his address and that he drives a new Lexus, I'd say he has money. That's it."

"Think he could've had something to do with Thurmond's murder?"

"Suppose. My encounter with him was two weeks before Thurmond bit the dust. I told this to the Chief; she shared it with the Detective who caught the case. He'll follow up. Why are you interested?"

"Virgil Debonnet is a friend. He found the body. That's all."

Allen smiled. "Tell you what. You pretend you mean that, and I'll pretend I believe you."

CHAPTER TEN

I was to meet Barb for supper at Loggerhead's, the popular restaurant located directly across the street from her condo. The weather was near perfect with the temperature in the low seventies with puffy white clouds dotting the otherwise clear sky. Both locals and vacationers were taking advantage of the elevated outdoor patio when I arrived fifteen minutes before we were to meet. Ed, the restaurant's owner, met me at the top of the steps and said there was a forty-five-minute wait for an outside table. I headed to the bar to wait for Barb and a table where I spotted Virgil leaning against the bar and waving his hands around in an animated conversation with a man I didn't recognize. Virgil waved me over.

"Christopher, welcome to one of my favorite hangouts," Virgil said as he stepped back to create space for me to stand near him. "Do you know Kevin?"

Just what I needed, another of Virgil's questions. "Don't believe so."

Kevin was in his late thirties or early forties, an inch or so taller than I am, heavier, blond hair with gray mixed in.

Instead of Virgil continuing the introduction, the man stuck out his hand. "I'm Kevin Goodman. You must be Chris Landrum; Virgil was telling me about you."

I glanced at Virgil then turned to Kevin. "Something good, I hope."

Kevin chuckled. "Mostly. He said you were a private detective who worked with him on a case or two."

This time I did more than glance at Virgil, before saying, "Kevin, not really. Some of us have lucked into helping the police."

"Not exactly Virgil's version. Anyway, nice meeting you."

Virgil said, "I ran into Kevin. He's waiting for his wife who's meeting him for supper. He invited me to join them once his table is available. Want to join us?"

I thought that was rather forward of Virgil to add someone else since he was the one invited to join Kevin and his wife. But, hey, that's Virgil.

"I'm meeting Barb. We wouldn't want to intrude on Kevin's hospitality."

"Nonsense," Virgil said. "It's not a problem, is it, Kevin?"

I'd known Kevin for a whopping three minutes so couldn't tell if the smile was real when he said, "We'd love to have you. Besides, we've been waiting for a table for a half hour so it should be ready soon."

Kevin looked over my shoulder at someone approaching the bar. His smile widened, giving me the distinct impression the smile he'd given me was less sincere. I turned to see a woman heading our way. She was about the same height as Keven, thin, with black curly hair, plus at least a decade younger than the man I just met. She kissed Kevin then looked at Virgil and me before turning back to Kevin.

"Guys," Kevin said, "this is the lovely young lady I've been waiting for."

Virgil stepped closer to the latest entry to our group. "And a lovely young lass well worth the wait. I'm guessing you're Megan."

She glanced at Kevin, then said, "Don't know about the rest of that, but yes, I'm Megan, Kevin's wife."

Kevin introduced his wife to Virgil then tried to introduce me, which would have been smoother if he'd remembered my name. I filled in my name. She said it was a pleasure meeting us.

Something finally surfaced from my memory bank. "You're Ryan Sparks' sister and brother-in-law."

"We are," Megan said. "How do you know Ryan?"

Virgil jumped back in the conversation, "I introduced Chris to Ryan the other day. Your husband was kind enough to invite me, Chris, and his lady friend, Barb, to join you for supper."

"Oh," Megan said while looking around. "Barb?"

I told her Barb was at work but would join me shortly.

Kevin ordered beer for Megan then told her he and Virgil were talking about Virgil finding the body at the river. He added I was a private detective. Once again, I denied being a detective, private or otherwise. Megan didn't pursue it. Instead she took a drink of the beer the bartender had slid in front of her before commenting how wonderful it felt to be away from her computer. Kevin told us Megan was a computer software developer who works from home.

Virgil said, "That must be exciting work."

If he thought developing computer software was exciting, I wondered how many beers he'd consumed.

Megan laughed. "Exciting, not really, but the ten-second commute to work has its advantages."

The hostess interrupted our exciting talk about Megan's career to tell Kevin his table was ready. He asked if it was large enough for five since his party had expanded. She said it was, so I asked her to tell Ed to take my name off the list. She said, "No problem," one of my least-liked phrases, and we followed her to a table in the middle of the patio. Five minutes later, Barb arrived wearing one of her trademark red blouses, tan shorts, and a smile. I stood to welcome her and to introduce her to Megan and Kevin. She said she already knew Megan as one of her regular customers, but she was glad to finally meet Kevin since Megan always talked about him. Virgil was another of her regulars, so no introduction was necessary.

Becca, a server who always had a friendly smile and kind word, was quick to the table to see if we needed additional drinks. Barb ordered a glass of white wine; the rest of us had brought our drinks from the bar. With that taken care of, Barb said, "Megan, how's the remodel coming?"

"Still a mess."

Barb turned to me. "They're remodeling their house, adding a room, redoing the kitchen and dining area if I remember correctly."

Megan added, "It's only taking three times longer than they said it would and costing twice the estimate."

Kevin said, "I'm sure our new friends don't want to hear about it."

"I don't blame them," Megan said. "I get a headache

simply talking about it. At least, thanks to your mother, we're able to make the improvements we dreamed about when we moved in."

Virgil said, "Did she lend you the money?"

I cringed at such a personal question, but anyone who knows Virgil knows he has few filters on his questions, or most anything he says.

Megan gave him a sideways look.

Kevin patted her on the back, turned to Virgil, then said, "She passed away last year. Dad's been gone five years. Mom left us a tidy sum, enough to fix up the house, then some."

"What's everyone going to order," Megan said, uneasy with Kevin's comments. She looked around for our server.

Becca must've been watching. She was at the table before anyone could comment, then took our orders and headed to the kitchen.

Virgil watched her go, turned to Megan, then said, "Have you talked to your brother since I found the body?"

"He came to the house the next morning. I worry about him."

Virgil said, "Why?"

"I don't know how much you know about his baseball career, but it ended with his injury. He had such high hopes of making the majors." She shook her head. "High hopes but no back-up plan if he didn't make it. Now he's rudderless, like he's out there on the ocean floating aimlessly."

"He didn't tell me much," Virgil said, "but he seems to be handling everything okay. He reminds me of myself after I lost my fortune. It was rough, but a good attitude helped me through it."

"Don't know about that," Megan said, "Ryan's good at hiding his feelings."

"We tried to lend him some of the inheritance," Kevin said, "He wouldn't take it. Said he was fine. If he can be fine living on that little sailboat, good for him. I couldn't do it."

Our food arrived. I didn't know how hungry I was until I got a whiff of the flounder dinner Becca placed in front of me. For the next few minutes the only words spoken were from people at the table behind us. I wasn't the only hungry person in the group.

Virgil broke the silence. "Kevin, Megan, either of you know Walter Thurmond?"

Megan looked at Kevin, then at Virgil. "I did. Ran into him a couple of times in town. After staring at my computer three or four hours straight, my eyes and brain need a rest, so I walk in the yard, on nice days, walk up Center Street. I was sitting in the rocking chairs in front of Vacasa Real Estate. A guy came along and sat in the chair next to me, then started talking. Didn't know him from Adam. He asked if I was on vacation. When I told him no, he started grilling me on what I did, where I lived, if I was married, and a bunch of personal questions. Needless to say, I wasn't happy with the intrusion or the questions. I didn't hide my displeasure. He finally got up, said it was nice talking to me, then left."

"Quite rude," Virgil said. "You said you ran into him twice. What about the other time?"

"A week later, I was on the sidewalk in front of the library when he came out, nearly ran over me. He apologized for his clumsiness, then said he remembered talking to me in front of Vacasa. I was surprised when he apologized, saying he'd been inappropriate. Said he shouldn't have asked me personal questions. He apologized a second time, smiled, then said he had to go, like he thought I wanted to talk to him longer."

"Strange," I said.

"Double strange," Virgil said. "Kevin, did you know him?"

"Actually, I talked to him once."

"I didn't know that," Megan said. "When?"

"Believe it was in Bert's. We didn't talk long."

Megan said, "What'd you talk about?"

"Nothing in particular. Weather, I think."

I said, "Either of you know Ben Likard?"

Megan shook her head. Kevin said, "No. Who's he?"

"Someone I heard had an argument with Thurmond."

Barb had listened to the conversation without commenting. Finally, she said, "Let's talk about something cheerier?"

Virgil said, "Sweet Barb, excellent idea."

And we did.

Before the group broke up, Kevin said if we ever got bored, we could stop by the house to watch Megan cuss the construction workers for not going faster. Barb declined, Virgil said he was seldom bored, but had plenty of time on his hands and might take Kevin up on the offer. I said I'd keep it in mind.

CHAPTER ELEVEN

The next morning, I stepped out of bed with two thoughts. First, my sleep hadn't been interrupted with a call from Virgil. Second, I began thinking about supper last night and the conversation with Kevin and Megan, how interesting it was that both they and Ryan had talked with Walter Thurmond. It was interesting, but knowing how small a community Folly is, it wasn't unusual, especially if Thurmond was trying to recruit partners in his businesses. Regardless, both Kevin and Megan were interesting, nice people, who wanted to improve their environment on Folly and to help Ryan even though he'd declined their assistance.

A third thought came to me as I moved to the porch to watch the traffic on East Ashley Avenue. I was hungry, but there wasn't any more food in the house than yesterday. I wasn't in the mood to go to a restaurant, so my go-to option was a walk next door to grab something to tide me over until lunch.

Bert's was busier than usual. Two extended-cab pickup trucks were in front of the store with their occupants, numbering at least seven landscape workers, differentiated by their company logoed orange vests, were lined up at the coffee urn. Denise, one of my favorite employees, was helping a woman and her pet dachshund find something in the aisle near the coffee urn. Denise nodded my direction then continued aiding the women.

Omar, the store's co-owner, was behind the register bagging a customer's purchase. I was facing the coffee urn when I heard Omar say, "Morning, Mr. Likard."

I turned to see a man in his late fifties wave to Omar then head to the coolers. Hadn't Officer Spencer said someone named Likard almost got in a fight with Thurmond? What were the odds that there was more than one person meeting Spencer's description named Likard on Folly?

How do I start a conversation? In the spirit of Charles, I would simply fabricate something to open a discussion after seeing Likard get a carton of milk from the cooler. I approached, looked at the carton in his hand, then said, "Seems like I'm in here every day buying milk."

He gave me a look that screamed, "Do I know you?"

To answer the unasked question I said, "Hi, I'm Chris Landrum."

"Ben Likard," he said and shook my outstretched hand.

Likard was casually dressed in tan khakis and a green polo shirt.

I said, "I've seen you in here a couple of times, once over at Lowlife Bar. I figured you must live on Folly, so I thought I'd introduce myself. I live nearby."

He chuckled. "Didn't happen to see me at Lowlife the

night they almost threw me in jail?"

Thank you for the opening, Ben.

I faked surprise. "No, what happened?"

"Nothing, really. I was meeting a man I have business with, and, let's say, we had a disagreement." He looked at the carton in his hand then shook his head.

"You were almost arrested for having a disagreement? Glad I'm not almost arrested every time I disagree with someone."

He laughed. "Suppose it was more than a disagreement. There was shoving. I thought he was going to punch me."

"Now that's a serious disagreement. What kind of business are you two in?"

The smile on his face disappeared, he looked around like he wanted to be somewhere else. I was afraid our conversation was coming to an abrupt halt, but then he continued, "My alleged business partner buys companies manufacturing healthcare equipment. They manufacture some, import some, things like wheelchairs, walkers, stair lifts, stuff like that. He buys small, struggling companies, provides progressive management, hopefully turns them around then sells them." He smiled. "That's more than you wanted to know, I'm sure."

"No, that's interesting. Suppose that's a growing market," I said parroting what Bob Howard had shared.

He returned the milk to the cooler before continuing, "You're right about that. That's why when he offered me the chance, I partnered with him in two companies in New Hampshire. Great growth potential, he said."

I still hadn't heard anything that could get him nearly punched. "I gather things didn't go as planned."

He smiled then said, "I suppose us nearly coming to blows

gave that away?"

I nodded.

"What'd you say your name was again?"

"Chris, Chris Landrum."

"Yeah, sorry, I'm not good with names. Don't know why I'm telling you this, but no, things didn't work out as planned. I put a lot of money in these ventures, a few hundred thousand in fact. He told me I'd be getting a chunk of it back once the profits started flowing. He told me things were going great, the companies were finally in the black, so I met him a few weeks ago to ask for a mere 50K out of the companies. Know what he told me?"

I was still stuck on the word *mere* in front of 50K. "What?"

"He gave me a long, convoluted story about not being able to pull money out because they were in rapid-growth mode; demand for their products was so high they hired more employees; they were growing so fast the state taxing authorities demanded early payment on taxes, blah, blah, blah. All good things, he said. Chris, I've been around the block a time or two. Thurmond's explanations were total bullshit." He smacked the palm of his hand against the glass door to the cooler. "Total bullshit."

I was beginning to see how the near fight was possible. I also realized he used the man's name for the first time.

"Ben, that's terrible. Did you say his name was Thurmond?"

"Yeah. You're not a friend of his, are you?"

"No. I was thinking Thurmond was the name of the man found dead the other day by the river."

"Oh yeah, I heard something about a drowning." A sly grin

appeared on Ben's face. "That was him."

"That's terrible. Any idea what happened?" I asked, hoping it came across sincere.

"Only rumors. One man told me Thurmond must've been drunk then fell in the river. Out of it so much he couldn't swim. I also heard someone did to him what he did to others. Stabbed him in the back. Don't know what version is true. If he was stabbed, he got what was coming. Know the worst thing about it?"

"What?"

"I'll probably never get my money."

This is where Charles would probably ask Ben if he was the one who inserted the knife. My friend could get away with it. I couldn't, so I said, "That's too bad. You think Thurmond conned others, made someone mad enough to kill him?"

"I know I was mad enough to, but unless the drunk drowning version is what happened, someone beat me to it. They should get a trophy. To your question, I don't doubt he conned others. Don't know who though." He flashed one more smile. "Chris, my ex always told me I talk too much; share more than I have business sharing. I'm beginning to think this is one of those moments." He retrieved the milk from the cooler, then said it was good meeting me.

I didn't know what else to say except, "Sorry about the money you may've lost."

I grabbed a cinnamon roll then followed Ben to the register. We each paid. I headed home as Ben pulled out of Bert's parking lot in a new, white Lexus LS. I didn't know how much he'd invested in Thurmond's companies, but it didn't appear he was on the verge of destitution. It also appeared he would be a prime suspect in Thurmond's murder.

CHAPTER TWELVE

It's been more than a dozen years since I'd left my serene, aka boring, life as a healthcare company executive in Kentucky. During my nearly sixty years in the Bluegrass State the most dangerous thing that happened to me was riding a roller coaster. I was never a risk-taker or someone who sought danger. My biggest challenges were related to maneuvering the ever-changing landscape within the workplace bureaucracy and my role as a human resource professional.

I figured once I retired, I wouldn't even have those challenges to overcome. What could be so difficult? Here I was, living in one of the most interesting, beautiful, popular spots along the Atlantic seaboard, not having to wake up each morning thinking about work and the problems that came with it. But, almost from the day I arrived, the danger I felt riding a roller coaster sank to minuscule. I stumbled on a murder, became the target of a relentless killer, then nearly lost my life twice, all within three weeks, I might add.

To ensure I would never face boredom again, I was friended by Charles Fowler. When over the course of the years a few other people were murdered on my new island home, Charles insisted, no, demanded, that because we had a connection, however slight, with the victims, it was our calling to help the police, you know, the people who're paid to catch the bad guys. I had no interest in sticking my nose where it didn't belong, not to mention the dangers involved. Remember, my definition of danger was riding a roller coaster.

Persistence is near the top of Charles's skills. He dragged me kicking, screaming, and fighting with all my senior-citizen energy to places I never would've ventured into in my previous life. His persistence drove both of us near death on more than one occasion. On the bright side, it also brought killers to justice.

Regardless of the results, I didn't want to get involved, but then over the course of my time on Folly I realized something that had eluded me in my earlier years: the value of friend-ships. Sure, there were people I felt close to before I moved to South Carolina, but upon reflection, those were people I was friendly with, not true friends. By true friends, I'm talking about people I'd risk my life for and who would do the same for me. I know that because I have and they have. When someone close to one of them is in danger or some-thing tragic happens to someone they have some attachment to, I not only feel it's my obligation to help any way possible, but it is something I want to do.

So, when not only Charles, but my new friend Virgil decided "we" needed to find out who killed Walter L. Thur-mond, that's why I'm not objecting. It's why I'm not kicking, screaming, and fighting with all my energy to demand that catching a killer was up to the police. Period. Have I surrendered to the influence of Charles? Absolutely. Have the inner-workings of my brain become so scrambled they're convincing me it's the right thing to do? I'm the last person to understand the inner-workings of my brain, so I have to accept the fact that I agree with my friends. I agree with Charles. I agree with Virgil. Not only agree but agree enthusiastically.

Agreeing about what I'd like to do differs from what I know how to do. I'm not certain how much the police know about the murder, but all I know is Virgil found Thurmond's body in a small boat near the Folly Beach boat ramp. Cause of death, a knife in his back. I've talked with four people who've acknowledged talking to the victim: Ryan Sparks, his sister Megan, his brother-in-law Kevin, and Ben Likard. According to Bob Howard, Thurmond was allegedly a con artist. From what Ben Likard shared, it appeared Bob was right. When Thurmond was found, Ryan was within shouting distance of the body which I suppose would make him a suspect. Was there more than proximity to tie him to Thurmond's demise? Likard had reason to be angry with Thurmond. Was it reason enough to kill? Kevin talked to him once in Bert's. Was talking about the weather a reason for murder. Of course not. Thurmond had persisted in asking Megan personal questions, although he later apologized. Was that reason enough?

The reality is the murderer could be almost anyone. There's no reason to think because I met four people who had contact with him that one of them killed him. I also realized I had no idea when he was killed, or for that matter, where. I'd stir up a hornets' nest by asking, but the best way to get answers or learn more about the murder was to talk to Cindy.

———

It took thirty more minutes to garner courage to make the call. I took a deep breath, before dialing.

As a greeting, she said, "The answer is no."

"No what?" A fair question, I thought.

"No to whatever you're calling about; no to whatever you want. No, exclamation point."

"Chief, is it safe to say you're having a bad day?" I said, swallowing a chuckle.

"Damn, Citizen Chris, you're smarter than I thought, which isn't saying much."

"Sorry, Cindy. Is there anything I can do?"

"Hanging up would be a good start."

"Anything else?"

"Buying me a chocolate milkshake would be a second good place to start."

"Where and when?"

Cindy was sitting at a small, round cafe table in front of Dolce Banana Cafe. She pointed to the awning over her head that read *MILKSHAKES*. "See, they're calling my name."

Over the years, in times of stress, I'd bought the Chief coffee, soft drinks, breakfast, lunch, and more than one beer. This was the first for a dairy product. I didn't know how that ranked on her therapy for a bad day scale.

"Have you ordered?"

"Yes, I'm to tell you not to worry, they'd let you pay for mine after you order."

Five minutes later, I placed Cindy's shake in front of her and took a sip of mine. One of the things I admired about the Chief was she was so self-confident it wouldn't bother her to be seen sitting at a table on the sidewalk of Folly's busiest street while sipping a milkshake.

"Bad day?" I said as she attacked her drink like she hadn't eaten all day.

"Chris, don't dump salt in this sweet delight. Ain't the weather fantastic?"

I agreed then talked about the mild winter we'd had, all to avoid what I'd originally called about, which would fit the definition of salt in her milkshake.

She took a long sip, sighed, then said, "My superior chiefly training tells me you didn't call to watch me slurp a shake. I'm going to regret saying this, but there's no such thing as a free milkshake, so let's have it."

"I had a few questions about Thurmond's death."

"I already regret asking, and you haven't even put a question mark behind a bunch of words."

"Do you know when he was killed?"

Cindy smiled. "Probably shortly after someone stuck a knife in his back."

I rolled my eyes. "You know what I mean."

"I do, but so far today, I've had two, no three officers in my office bitching, moaning, and groaning about, well, about everything. That doesn't count one of your elected council members whose name I won't reveal storming in my office demanding I have extra patrols drive by his house all hours of the night to keep his neighbor's cat from walking on the hood of his car leaving adorable footprints. If I can't make smart aleck remarks to you, who can I?"

Friendships are sacred, I thought.

"So, when was he killed?"

She took a sip of shake then looked at me over her straw.

"The coroner said between two a.m. and when your buddy found him."

"Was he killed in the boat or somewhere else and dumped in the boat?"

"The crime scene gurus figure with the amount of blood in the boat, most likely he was killed there."

"Was it his boat?"

"Detective Adair said Thurmond appeared to live alone. There's no record of him being married, or clothing in the house that looked like it belonged to someone else. There was a laptop docking station but no laptop. Adair's folks canvassed Thurmond's neighborhood. Didn't find anyone who knew much about him. None of them happened to see a boat at the house. To answer your question, hell if I know."

"There's no way to trace its owner?"

A red pickup with two surfboards in the back tooted its horn as it passed. Cindy smiled at the driver. I could be mistaken, but it appeared that she made an obscene gesture at the truck as it passed, another reminder about the kind of day she was having.

"What was the question again?"

"Is there a way to trace the owner of the boat?"

"Nope. It's a twelve-foot Alumacraft flat-bottom jon boat. Far from rare. Sold at many big-box outdoor sports stores. It's too puny to have to be titled. There was no indication it ever had an outboard motor which if large enough would've required a title."

"Fingerprints?"

"We all have them, why?"

"Cindy, I repeat, you know what I mean."

"Chris, in case you haven't figured it out, I'm frustrated. A dead body bobbing in the river for all to see smack dab on my island and I have nothing."

"Chief, I understand, but the Sheriff's Office has the most responsibility. You can't do it all."

"Did you miss the part about Thurmond being found on my island?" She paused, took another sip of shake, then said, "No prints other than Thurmond's on the boat. What else? I doubt your well of questions hast run dry?"

"I could be wrong, but from where the boat was found, it seems unlikely the murder took place there. Too public a location."

"Most likely that's an accurate statement although since he could've been killed at three in the morning, the odds on anyone seeing anything were slim."

"Then—"

Cindy held her near-empty milkshake cup in front of my face. "Let me guess, your next question is if he wasn't stabbed there, where did the boat come from? Had it been with a larger boat? Had it floated downstream from one of the houses adjacent to the river? Had it been dropped from one of those humongous Air Force C-17 transport planes out of Joint Base Charleston? How am I doing?"

"I was going to keep it simple. Do you know where it came from?"

"I'm guessing not the C-17. Beyond that, hell if I know."

"Suspects?"

"If Adair has any, he isn't sharing."

The County Sheriff's Office and the Folly Beach Department of Public Safety were often at odds about, well, about most everything. The sharing of information was often a one-way street running from Folly to the Sheriff's Office.

"How much did Allen Spencer tell you about the altercation between Thurmond and Benjamin Likard?"

She stared at me; her fingers tapped on the metal table. "Why?"

"I had a conversation with Likard."

"Why does that not surprise me? How do you know him?"

"Introduced myself in Bert's. Officer Spencer told me about his encounter with Thurmond, so I wanted to meet him."

"So you could stick your nose where it don't belong?"

Yes, but didn't think it wise to admit that to the Chief. "Curious."

"Chris, if you weren't such a damned fossil, I'd put you on the force. Give you a cute little badge, a gun, a bullet, make you wear a uniform."

I took that as a hint to tell her what I'd learned from Likard. Only the sucking noise when her straw reached the bottom of the cup interrupted my telling what Likard had said about Thurmond, and what Bob Howard had heard about Thurmond being a con man.

Cindy finished by saying she'd pass it along to Detective Adair, adding, "Be careful. Who'd buy me drinks if you weren't around."

See, she can be sweet. More importantly, she didn't tell me to keep my nose out of police business.

CHAPTER THIRTEEN

As I was eating a stale English muffin for breakfast, the phone rang, something that's becoming an all-too-often occurrence.

"Yo, Christopher, this is your buddy, Virgil. Guess where I am? Guess what I'm doing?"

"Spain, running with the bulls."

"Wow, is that now?"

"Virgil, I have no idea. Why don't you tell me where and with whom?"

"Holy moly. You sound like my ex with her English degree."

Remind me to look at the screen before answering the phone in the morning.

"Virgil, where are you?"

"Sittin' on the picnic table at the Folly River Park. It's a gorgeous day in paradise. You ought to join us."

Which I suppose leads to his second question.

"Who's with you?"

"Thought you'd never ask. Who do you know who played professional baseball and lives on a sailboat?"

Finally, I know the answer to one of his questions. "Ryan Sparks."

"I knew if I asked enough questions, you'd get one right. You on your way over?"

Why not? "Sure."

"Good. Could you stop at Kangaroo Express and grab some donuts? Ryan says he'd like a good breakfast."

"Sure," I repeated. It'd be a waste of words to ask why they couldn't get their own breakfast since the convenience store was a block from the picnic bench.

"Maybe some coffee, too."

I hung up before Virgil requested bacon, eggs, and hash browns.

Carrying two packages of prepackaged donuts and three cups of coffee, I arrived at the Folly River Park where Virgil and Ryan were engrossed in animated conversation. Virgil interrupted the talk to thank me for the breakfast, adding he was short on money this morning. Ryan shook my hand, said it was nice seeing me again, but didn't comment on his financial status. From their vantage point on the picnic table, they could see a corner of the boat ramp parking lot where Virgil had discovered the body. I wasn't certain but thought I saw the top of the mast of a sailboat on the river.

I said, "Ryan, did you sail up here today?"

He looked toward the boat ramp, then said, "Yesterday. I spent most of it helping Kevin with his renovation. He took off this week to work on the house, thought it would speed up the contractors."

"Ryan's trying to recruit me to help," Virgil said, smiled,

then pointed to a squirrel on thc other side of the park. "Told him I was as handy with a hammer as that little fellow over there is with a chainsaw."

Ryan mumbled through a bite of donut, "That was okay. Most of what's left to do will take plumbers, electricians, and finish carpenters. Stuff I can't do."

Virgil pointed his cup at me. "Ryan and I were talking about the body I found. I called Charles to invite him over, but he didn't answer."

I'm second choice again.

I said, "Have you heard anything new about the death?"

Ryan shook his head. "Know when he was killed?"

I shared what Cindy said about it being between two a.m. and when Virgil stumbled on the body. "Do you remember anything else about that night or morning?"

"Like I think I told you before, it was foggy; I was foggy. All I remember was hearing two people talking near the parking lot. Couldn't see them though."

He hadn't said that when we first talked about that night and morning.

Virgil said, "I don't remember you saying that. What time was it?"

"Don't know for certain. Must've been closer to morning than late night."

I asked, "Why?"

"Think I may've mentioned I was a bit under the influence that night. Doubt I'd hear or remember anything, so it must've been near sunrise."

I said, "You told us you didn't hear or see any of the police activity after the body was found."

"That sounds right."

"Ryan," Virgil said, "I'm not a good detective like Chris here, but it seems strange you didn't see or hear anything." He hesitated and looked toward the boat ramp. "Your boat was not more than, what, fifty yards from where I found the guy. Sure you didn't hear the commotion? Sirens, guys yelling, fire trucks."

"Don't believe so," Ryan said then turned to me. "Virgil tells me you're good buddies with the Police Chief. Hear if they have suspects?"

"None I've heard about."

"Bet there're a bunch. From what Sis said yesterday, Thurmond got mighty nosy with her. Asked a bunch of personal questions. Even when I talked to him, it seemed he wanted something from me. When I told him I'd played pro ball he got interested, started talking about the businesses he owned, how he let others buy into them. I had the impression he was recruiting me, then when I told him I only got paid a little over two thousand bucks a month playing Triple-A ball, he lost interest. Didn't even get to tell him I only got paid that piddling monthly amount during the seven-month season."

"What happened then?" Virgil asked.

"He went from salesman to drinker." Ryan took another bite of donut, then said, "I'm not a great judge of character, but if I was to guess, I'd say old Thurmond might've been a con man."

That was consistent with what Bob Howard had said.

I said, "What did he say to make you think that?"

"Nothing specific. I mean he didn't say give me money so I can cheat you out of it. Was more the way he said things. How he bragged on how well his businesses were doing. How others who partnered with him had gotten rich. How he hinted around trying to get me to tell him how much I made playing ball. How all the big-dream conversation ended when I told him how little I made, how little I had." He looked at his watch. "Guys, I'd better get over to Megan and Kevin's to see if I can do anything. They've put a ton of money in that house." He shook his head then hopped off the table.

Virgil told him how much he enjoyed talking to him. Ryan thanked me for breakfast before heading to his sister and brother-in-law's house.

Virgil watched him go, then said, "Did you catch what he said about hearing two people at the boat ramp? He didn't tell us that the first time he talked about what happened."

Virgil paid attention better than I'd given him credit for.

"You're right."

Virgil looked in the direction Ryan had walked. "Wonder what else he didn't tell us."

"You still think he knows more than he's saying?"

"I do. I certainly do."

"Why do you think that?"

Virgil smiled. "Detective intuition."

I didn't know about that, but there was something about Ryan bothering me. If I could only figure out what it was.

CHAPTER FOURTEEN

Virgil said he needed to get back to his apartment. I said I didn't need to get anywhere, regardless, he headed home so I decided to walk across the street to where Virgil found the body. Two men were launching a fishing boat off the trailer attached to a pickup truck. A Pelican Trailblazer kayak I assumed belonged to Ryan was tied to one of the dock's support posts.

There was no evidence of anything bad happening a few days earlier. I was again reminded how quickly the world returns to normal regardless what has happened. People can be seriously impacted, possibly for life, yet to others things continue as if nothing occurred. The phone rang as I reached that depressing conclusion.

Bob Howard said, "Well, are you on your way here for lunch?"

"Should I be?"

"Yes, if you want to hear what I learned about the late

Walter L. Thurmond."

"I assume you're at Al's."

"Where else would I be?"

Enough foolishness. "See you in a half-hour," I said then tapped End Call before he responded.

Heavy traffic delayed my arrival ten minutes from the half-hour I'd told Bob. Al's Bar and Gourmet Grill was a couple of blocks off Calhoun Street, on the outskirts of downtown Charleston. The business was in a concrete-block building it shared with a Laundromat. The structure had once been painted white but that was hard to tell after decades of wear.

I was greeted by Al Washington, the bar's namesake. Bob bought the business from Al after the owner suffered several medical issues nearly costing him his life. He and Bob had become unlikely friends decades ago. Al and most of the diners were African American. Bob was as white as a marsh-mallow, about as mushy around the waist, and had a reputa-tion, well-earned, I might add, for being an equal-opportunity offender. He never hesitated to insult everyone. Al became the bar's unofficial Walmart greeter to keep conflicts between the new owner and customers to a minimum.

Al hugged me then said, "Mr. Chris, it's good seeing you. It's been too long."

"Hey, old man," bellowed Bob from "his" booth near the back of the room, "let the boy alone. He needs to get in here and spend money. How do you think I'm going to pay your salary if you don't let customers in?"

A rhetorical question, at best, since Bob wasn't paying Al anything.

"Good luck," Al whispered then let me head to Bob's table.

Sound of The Statler Brothers harmonizing on "Flowers on the Wall" flowed from the jukebox near the entry. The sound of Bob yelling for Lawrence, the part-time cook, added to the sounds. At Bob's kind request, Lawrence started fixing a cheeseburger for me, plus a double order of fries, which, most likely, Bob would consume.

I squeezed in the side of the table opposite Bob.

"About time you got here. I was having trouble saving you a space."

A glance around the room told me there were three other diners. "I appreciate you working hard to save room," I said, oozing sarcasm.

"Smart ass," the friendly proprietor said.

I grinned. "At your service."

"You're in a chipper mood."

"Why wouldn't I be? Here I am, about to eat a fantastic cheeseburger; getting to share a table with one of my best friends; and, listening to you gripe about whatever it is you'll be griping about."

Bob laughed, something rare coming from his mouth. He turned serious. "I suppose my saying I had something to tell you about Thurmond is more why you're here than those two gooey, sticky, sugar-infused reasons."

I shrugged. "Ready to share?"

The Temptations singing "My Girl" replaced The Statler Brothers. Two of the men at the other occupied table applauded. Bob held his hands over his ears. There was a constant battle between Bob's favorite classic country songs and Motown hits. That was another reason Al remained on the scene.

"As soon as that crap stops playing," he said and stared at the men at the other table.

The smell of my cheeseburger reached me before Lawrence set it in front of me. He put the double order of fries beside my plate, but Bob slid it to where he could reach them without having to lean over.

Roger Miller singing "King of the Road" followed the Temptations. Bob grinned.

"That's better," he said. "Walter L. Thurmond. Where should I begin?"

Before I could comment, he began, "I talked to two friends, yes, I have two friends. Anyway, the first man, someone I've known longer than any snotty high-school kids have been alive, runs a big-time investment firm in town. He never dealt directly with Thurmond but knew him by reputation." Bob grabbed a fry, slathered it in catsup, then said. "And the reputation ain't good. His firm refused to do business with Thurmond."

"Why?"

"Did you miss the part about knowing him by his *ain't good* reputation?"

"Go on."

"My friend, who shall remain nameless for fear of being accused of being a gossip, which he happens to be, said Thurmond contacted two of my guy's clients to get them to buy into his can't-lose businesses. The clients had plenty of money. Would've been able to put hundreds of thousands wherever they wanted. Know why they didn't go with Thurmond?"

I shook my head.

"Said he was too slick."

"What's that mean?"

"The old boy had answers for everything. Overcoming objections is key to being a good salesman, but apparently Thurmond was overcoming them long before they were expressed. Some of that's okay, but not the way he was doing it, or so they said. Granted, I don't know exactly what that meant, but it doesn't matter what I know. These potential investors have been around the block many times, knew pure bullshit when it was being flung their direction."

"Did that happen recently?"

Bob grabbed another fry before saying, "Like recent enough that one of them took offense enough to stick a knife in Thurmond's back?"

"Yes."

"Not that my friend knew about. Besides he said the potential investors were the kind of guys who wore three-piece suits in the middle of summer, would turn up their noses at McDonald's, not sully their hands by bloodying them with a knife in someone's back."

"What about the other man?"

"What other man?"

"You said you talked to two friends."

"Crap, Chris, when are you going to stop listening to everything I say?"

"It's fascinating listening to you." I smiled and took a bite of cheeseburger.

He returned the smile. "True. Anyway Mason, that's my other friend, likes his name bandied about; thinks it'll get him more business. The old boy sells computer systems design, whatever in hell that is, got himself a degree in engineering. He makes a good salary but doesn't need to. He got most of his wealth the old-fashioned way, his grandparents cheated people out of it, then went and died leaving most of it to Mason. I've known him a dozen years or so, sold him his first mansion south of Broad. He and his wife—"

"Bob, Thurmond?"

"I'm almost there." He grabbed a fry off the plate. "Looks like you need more fries." He yelled, "Lawrence, more fries for my Caucazoid friend." He then took the last fry, pointed it at me, then said, "Where was I?"

"Thurmond."

"Oh yeah, Mason's wife, the one I was going to tell you about when you interrupted me, has about as much money as her wonderful husband. They wanted to spread some of their wealth around. They ran into Thurmond at a fundraiser for dolphins, sea turtles, or some other endangered water critter. He started giving them a sales pitch. He told them the companies he bought were in New England, somewhere that was too far away to easily tour. Also gave them a slick brochure showing smiling people working in the companies; smiling partners who were getting rich after giving Thurmond money; smiling partners sailing the ocean blue on the yachts they bought with the money they made off the fantastic business deals. You get the picture."

I was beginning to get the picture as I listened to Martha and the Vandellas singing "Dancing in the Street," while watching Bob slap his hands to his ears.

Lawrence set the new plate of fries on the table, laughed at Bob, and said, "He loves Motown."

Bob uttered a profanity at Lawrence, slathered catsup on the edge of the fries, stuffed one in his mouth, then said, or I think what he said since the fry was taking up valuable speech space, "Mason said Thurmond had a slick website that not only showed everything in the brochure, but gave specific examples of his partners who've hit it rich partnering with Thurmond. This shouldn't surprise you, but the names of the suckers were nowhere to be found on the site. Thurmond said because of privacy concerns. I say because it's a complete, unadulterated con."

"It sounds like it."

"I never met the man, but hell, I think if he wasn't already dead I'd kill him myself."

"Did Mason say anything else about Thurmond?"

"Like who killed him?"

I smiled. "That'd be a good start."

"If he told me that, what would you do with all your spare retired time if you didn't have a killer to catch?"

I figured this would be a good time to change the subject. I asked him how Betty, his angelic wife who put up with him, was doing, then how Al's health was holding up. He said, "Fine and okay," before asking why I didn't ask how he was doing.

Not only was it time to change the subject but was time to leave the bar. I thanked him for the information about Thurmond and the enlightening conversation about his wife and the bar owner.

"Smart ass," he said as I headed to the front of the bar to pay Lawrence, hug Al, and listen to Patsy Cline singing "I Fall To Pieces," as I left the near dark environment of Al's into blinding sunlight.

From everything Bob said, it was becoming clear there were reasons some people could want Thurmond dead. From everything Bob said, I had no idea who.

CHAPTER FIFTEEN

"Guess where I am?" Charles said as I answered the phone on my drive home from Al's.

I'm beginning to feel like I'm on a quiz show every time I pick up the phone.

"Where?"

"Well, aren't we in a bad mood this afternoon."

"Why?"

"Every time I ask you something on the phone you give me a smart-aleck answer."

"Can't say that again."

"East Indian Avenue."

Leaping to the conclusion that was the answer to his opening question, I said, "What are you doing there?"

"Where are you?"

"In front of Harris Teeter heading home."

"Good, park by the Catholic Church. I'll meet you there."

I did what I'm getting pretty good at. I hung up on him.

Our Lady of Good Counsel is on the corner of Center
Street and East Indian Avenue, across East Indian from the
Folly River Park. I found a parking spot on the street just past
the church. Charles was standing in the post office parking lot
in front of me. He wore tan shorts, his Tilley hat, and a
midnight blue and gold University of Toledo long-sleeve T-
shirt.

He pointed his cane at me. "What took you so long?"

"Afternoon Charles," I said, ignoring his comment. "And
what might you be doing here?"

"Might be looking for stray opossums, but I'm not. Now
here's a question. Why did I have to learn about a high-
powered meeting you had with Virgil and Ryan Sparks from
Amber instead of hearing it from you?"

"Did Amber tell you Virgil called you before he called me
this morning?"

"No."

"Then I don't guess she told you Virgil was with Ryan and
wanted you to meet them."

"Oh. Someday I'm going to remember to take this phone
thingee when I leave the apartment."

Charles hasn't had a cell phone during most of the years
I'd known him, so I understood his forgetfulness about
carrying it. He was equally as forgetful about listening to his
voicemails. I still had no idea why I was joining Charles doing
whatever he was doing.

"So, why am I here?"

"Tell you in a minute. First, let's hear everything they said.
Amber gave me Virgil's version, but he's not good about
sharing details."

I gave him an abbreviated version of the *high-powered*

meeting. It took longer than necessary since he interrupted me about 1,700 times with questions ranging from who Ryan thought killed Thurmond to what Virgil was wearing. When I told him Ryan said he thought he'd heard two people talking nearby the morning Virgil found the body, he had me repeat it.

"When Ryan was talking to you and Virgil at the Dog, didn't you say he didn't see or hear anything the morning before Virgil found the body?"

"That's what he told us."

"Which is it? Did he or didn't he hear people talking?"

"Don't know."

"How're we going to find out?"

"There's no way to learn which version it was."

"You're right. Either way, he's lying about one of them. If he lies about that, he probably lied about not killing Thurmond."

Truth be told, I don't recall Ryan saying he didn't kill Thurmond, but that wasn't a leap I was ready to make with Charles. I followed him across the street tapping his cane on the pavement the entire way.

"That's always a possibility. Ready to tell me what you're doing out here?"

"Correction, what we're doing."

I remained silent. He stopped in front of the first house on the north side of East Indian then said, "Virgil found the jon boat near the boat ramp parking lot."

I nodded.

"Downstream from here."

The houses on the north side of East Indian Avenue back up to the marsh and the Folly River. I nodded again.

"Let's assume Walter Thurmond didn't become the late Walter Thurmond at the spot where Virgil found the boat."

"A possibly correct assumption."

"If not there, where did it happen? If the boat floated downstream after Thurmond was stabbed, it could've come from somewhere up here, right?" He didn't wait for me to nod. "Whose jon boat was it? Had to belong to someone, right?"

No argument there. I nodded a third time.

"After I talked to Amber, you know the Amber who told me about the meeting you should've told me about, I saw Chief LaMond. I asked her if the cops had caught the killer. She told me no, so I asked if she knew who owns the boat. Another no, she's full of noes this morning. I asked if her folks or the Sheriff's Office folks surveyed all the property owners upstream from the boat ramp to see who might've owned the boat. Bet you can guess her answer."

"No."

"No, you can't guess, or no was her answer?"

"She said no."

"Sort of."

I wondered how I could've guessed that. "What's that mean?"

"She didn't know. It was in the able hands of the Sheriff's Office. She has more faith in the Sheriff's gang than I have."

"Your plan is to go door to door asking if anyone is missing a jon boat?"

"Correction, my friend, our plan."

I'd seen the man who answered the door at the first house around town but didn't know him. Charles told me on the way up the steps he didn't know the resident either, but that didn't stop him from acting like a long-lost relative when the man frowned as he stared at us. After Charles assured him we weren't traveling missionaries or selling magazine subscriptions, the man's frown turned friendlier. The smell of something baking in the kitchen whiffed out the door, but we weren't invited in to learn what. Charles asked if the man had a jon boat. The stranger's frown returned as he said no before asking why we were asking such a stupid question. I silently agreed with him. I was tempted to say because that's what Charles does, but instead smiled and told him we were sorry to bother him.

A similar scenario was repeated at the next house. Chief LaMond and Larry's house was after that. Charles, in an unusual burst of wisdom suggested we didn't need to ring their doorbell. I agreed like I was deferring to his decision. The section of East Indian closest to the center of town ended at East Second Street so we weaved our way to East Huron where several houses faced the marsh and had long walking piers to the river. The streets changed but our luck didn't. No one answered at two of the houses, one was answered by a man both of us knew, and three more houses were occupied by people we didn't know. At two of them, I suspected we'd have received a friendlier greeting if we had been selling magazine subscriptions. In all, we found two houses occupied by people who had jon boats. I know that because they took us out back to show us. Neither boat was missing. The rest of the houses where we talked to a human were occupied by people who said they didn't have a missing boat, jon or otherwise.

Charles removed his Tilley, wiped his brow, then suggested we suspend our search for the boat's owner. I quickly agreed.

When I hinted we'd failed, Charles veered from quoting U S Presidents and said, "When someone told Thomas Edison he'd failed during his search for a lightbulb, he said, 'I have not failed. I've just found ten-thousand ways that won't work.'"

I stopped to catch my breath, then said, "Charles, to paraphrase Shakespeare, 'A failure by any other name is still a failure.'"

He pointed his cane at me. "I'm impressed you can quote, or misquote, anyone other than yourself, but today was far from a failure. You learned there's not a mob of jon boat thieves marauding the island; you met several people you didn't know; oh yeah, best of all, you spent time with me."

"What could be better," I said with more than a touch of sarcasm.

"You're right," Charles said before heading home.

I was parked near the entrance to Pewter Hardware. The store's small parking lot was empty, so I decided to stop to see Larry.

I was greeted by Brandon, Larry's only full-time employee. He was dressed in his unofficial uniform, an old T-shirt with a peace symbol peeking out from under his tan Pewter Hardware shirt.

"Yo, Chris, what can we do for you today?"

"Was nearby so thought I'd see if Larry was around."

"He's always around, haven't you figured that out? He's out back wrestling with a window air conditioner some guy brought back. Something about it being too big for the window." He wiped grease off his hands with a well-worn shop towel. "Wouldn't you think the dummy would've measured the window before buying the unit?"

Larry came though the back door before Brandon could complain more about the customer.

Larry smiled when he saw me with Brandon. "Hey, Chris, want to buy a slightly dented, never used window air conditioner? Give you a good deal."

I declined the generous offer then followed Larry to the register where he said, "If not to buy an air conditioner, what brings you in?"

"I was with Charles asking around if anyone was missing a jon boat."

"Like the one that dead guy was in?"

"Yes. Have any of your customers said anything about missing one?"

"No. I assume you two detective-wannabes are nosing where your noses don't belong."

I smiled. "Guilty as charged."

"I'll leave it to Cindy to tell you to butt out. Any luck?"

"Afraid not."

"Remember me telling you I know Kevin and Megan, the Goodmans?"

"Ryan Sparks's sister and brother-in-law."

He nodded. "Megan was in yesterday. Kevin sent her to get drywall compound. Anyway, she said she was worried about her brother."

"Why?"

"She thinks he's more torn up by the death of the guy than he's letting on."

"I didn't think he knew him more than from a couple of conversations in a bar. Why was the death getting to him?"

"I know," Brandon said.

I hadn't noticed him listening to the conversation.

Larry said, "Care to share?"

"I was talking to him the day after the body was found. He told me he'd been thinking about borrowing money from his sis to become part owner of a company that makes stuff for old folks, no offense Chris. That ended when the guy turned up dead."

Larry looked at his employee. "Brandon, where'd you see Ryan?"

"In here. You were at the post office."

I said, "He say anything else?"

"Not really. I could tell he was bothered so I didn't pursue it. It's his business, not mine."

Larry added, "So you don't know if he talked to his sister about the money?"

"His business, not mine," Brandon repeated.

I wondered why Ryan hadn't mentioned to me that he wanted to partner in one of Thurmond's companies.

CHAPTER SIXTEEN

Brandon's thinking Ryan was taking Thurmond's death harder than he let on reminded me that Ryan's sister had said something similar when we had supper with them at Loggerhead's. I also remembered Kevin inviting me to stop by their house to watch Megan cuss the construction workers. This might be a good time to take him up on the offer.

My house was closer to the Goodman's residence than where I'd parked near the Catholic Church, so I drove home then walked three blocks to their place on East Ashley Avenue. It was easy to find. There was a dumpster in the side yard, a circular saw in the front yard, a rusting pickup truck and a Swenson Plumbing van in the drive. The exterior of the house showed signs of surviving multiple hurricanes. It was one of the properties Bob Howard had showed me when I was looking for a house.

The front door was partially open, so I knocked on the doorframe. I could hear men talking inside. The smell of fresh sawdust permeated the entry. Megan was quick to respond to my knock.

"Oh, hi, Chris. Thought you were another construction worker coming to disrupt my work. Come on in. Watch where you step."

Megan wore jogging shorts, a multi-colored Folly Beach T-shirt, and was barefoot.

I followed her to the den she'd converted to an office. Two computer monitors dominated the landscape on a contemporary L-shaped glass-topped desk. A black, high-tech looking, ergonomic, high-back mesh task chair was pushed up to the desk.

She smiled when she saw me glance at her bare feet. "Office dress-down day," she said, then laughed. "As is every day. I love working from home, that is when the house isn't filled with stinky, sweaty plumbers, carpenters, electricians, or whoever else is making racket doing something here."

"Megan, I don't want to disrupt your work. Kevin told me at supper to stop by any time to see what you're doing to the house. I can come back another time."

"Don't be silly. You don't stink; besides I need a break. Have a seat." She pointed to the much-lower-tech folding chair that'd be at home at a card table. "I don't encourage Kevin to spend much time in here while I'm working, so that's the best seat he gets. Would you like something to drink? I've got beer, wine, Pepsi, an overabundance of water thanks to the plumber finally getting the water line moved in the kitchen."

"Again, I don't want to intrude."

"Nonsense, my crack, in-house, in this house, HR department says I get breaks." She smiled. "Get them whenever I want. Now, what're you drinking?"

"Pepsi," I said to make it simple for her.

While she was gone, I looked around. There was a thin layer of drywall dust covering the top of the lone filing cabinet in the corner as well as on the floor in each corner of the room. A bottle of Windex and a roll of paper towels were on a small table next to the desk.

She returned, handed me the drink, sat in the desk chair, and said, "Sorry about the construction. We're almost getting used to everything being in disarray."

The clink of metal striking metal came from the kitchen followed by a man mumbling something. Megan looked toward the kitchen. "Plumbers, gotta love them, gotta hate them."

"When you and Kevin were talking the other night, I didn't realize how much you were doing to the house. You'd have no way of knowing, but when I was looking for a house, my Realtor showed me this one."

"Was quite a mess, I bet. We lived with it for nine years before we started fixing it up. It's terrible to say, but it took Kevin's mom dying for us to have the wherewithal to do all this, and by all this, I mean a new kitchen from floor to ceiling, knocking out the wall between the kitchen and dining room, next week they'll be finishing the sunroom out back." She hesitated, chuckled, then said, "It's going to be nice to live in if all the disruptions don't have me living in a padded cell before it's finished."

"Looks like it's going to be fantastic," I said, not knowing what else to add.

"It better be." She chuckled once more. "I'd hate to go

loony for no good reason. It's no telling how much it's going to cost. Thank goodness Kevin takes care of the money." Her smile faded. "Now, I have a sneaky suspicion you didn't drop by to hear me ramble on about the house."

I took a sip of Pepsi to gather my thoughts. "You found me out." I smiled, hoping she would follow suit. "When we were talking at Loggerhead's, you mentioned your encounters with Walter Thurmond."

Her expression leaned more toward inquisitive rather than the smile I'd hoped for before she said, "Yes. What about it?"

"You said he was stepping in personal territory, asking questions you thought were inappropriate for someone you'd just met."

She took a sip of water from her overabundance, then said, "It wasn't like he was scary or anything like that. The more I thought about it, he came across as a salesman trying to prequalify me for whatever he was hawking."

"Do you remember if he said anything about why he was prequalifying you for whatever he was selling? Did he mention owning businesses and trying to get partners to go in with him?"

Another clanking sound came from the kitchen. Megan glared toward the kitchen, shook her head, then said, "What was that again?"

I repeated the questions.

"Not to me," she said, turning back to me.

"To someone else?"

"Kevin said he told him something about it."

During our previous meeting, Kevin said he'd run into Thurmond once, but nothing was said about his businesses.

"What did Kevin say?"

"Thurmond was looking for people to go in with him. Something like some people on Folly had already joined him. That's all, why?"

"My understanding is that the police are looking at people who gave Thurmond money. They're possible suspects. I thought he may've mentioned names."

"Not to me. If you want. I'll check with Kevin and let you know if names were mentioned."

"That'd be great."

"Kevin said your friend Virgil told him you were a private detective. You trying to catch Thurmond's killer?"

"Virgil exaggerated. I'm no detective. I'm asking because I'm friends with the Chief. She's having a difficult time getting names of people who'd given Thurmond money."

"Identified anyone?"

Do I tell her about Ben Likard? If I did, what would it accomplish?

"Not really, but I have confidence the police will figure it out."

"I know my brother hopes they do, and soon. Did you know he was on his boat anchored near where they found the body? He said if it wasn't for the dense fog, he could've seen the man killed, could've seen the killer."

It was unlikely that he could've seen Thurmond killed or the killer since the odds were he was killed somewhere other than where the boat ended up. There was no reason to share that with Megan.

"What else did Ryan say about Thurmond?"

She took another sip of water, then said, "He came by after he learned of the murder. He doesn't get shook easily. He spent years standing on pitcher's mounds facing some of the best hitters in the game. I don't mean to brag on my brother, heck, yes, I do mean to. Regardless, he was fearless, had to be to get as far as he did in the pros. You'll never know how bad I feel about his shoulder knocking him out of his dream." She took another sip, slowly shook her head, then said, "My point is he never let anything bother him, but when he came through the door that day, he was shaking. Never saw him like that."

"Ryan told me Thurmond talked to him a couple of times. I guess Thurmond told him about the businesses he had, businesses that made things for seniors. Did your brother mention anything like that?"

Megan looked toward the door to the kitchen, chuckled, then said, "Ryan said he thought Thurmond was fishing for information that'd tell him if my brother had money. He hinted that someone who had such a nice sailboat, someone who'd played professional ball was fixed for life. Fixed for life, right." She frowned and shook her head. "Even when Ryan was playing, he barely made minimum wage, and that was during baseball season, the rest of the year zilch. He told me he wasn't about to tell that to Thurmond. My brother has a great deal of pride. His bad luck smacked him hard. He tries to not let it show, but it hurt. He wasn't about to tell Thurmond anything about his finances. They'd just met."

"What'd he say to Thurmond?"

She smiled. "Don't know for sure. Do know he didn't tell the man he had to live on that sailboat because he didn't have money to live anywhere else. Beyond that, Ryan didn't say." Her smile faded. "To tell the truth, Ryan was so upset, I doubt he could remember what else he and Thurmond talked about." She looked at her watch.

I took the hint. "Megan, I'll let you get back to work."

A smile returned to her face. "Yeah, my crack HR department will be writing me up if I goof off any longer. I'm glad you stopped by. It's nice seeing someone coming in the door who isn't charging by the hour."

I took an index card from my back pocket, wrote my phone number on it, and gave it to her. "If you don't mind, let me know if Kevin or Ryan say anything else about Thurmond."

She looked at the card, smiled, then said, "Deal."

CHAPTER SEVENTEEN

The next morning began with a trip next door to grab something for breakfast. On the way over, I told myself someday I'd learn to fix breakfast at home. I also knew I was more likely to hike the Himalayas than do food prep in my kitchen.

Those thoughts faded when I saw Ben Likard exiting his Lexus. He noticed me at the same time.

He smiled. "Hey, umm."

"Chris," I said.

"Right, Chris. Sorry, I'm bad with names."

He'd said the same thing the first time we met. He was casually dressed, the same as last time.

"That's okay, me too."

He reminded me he was Ben, which I did remember since he was one of my top suspects in Thurmond's murder.

He nodded then pointed the direction I'd come from. "Think you told me you lived nearby. You walk over?"

"Yeah. I live on the other side of the parking lot."

"Convenient. Interesting I ran into you," he said as I followed him in the store.

"Interesting?"

"Yeah. When we were talking the other day, you were asking about my, umm, disagreement with Walter Thurmond. Since then, I've heard a couple of things. Someone told me you were a private detective looking into who killed him."

I followed him to the coffee urn. "Not really. A friend of mine found Thurmond's body so I was curious about what happened. Anything beyond that is in the capable hands of the police. Where'd you hear I was a private detective?"

"Don't remember the guy's name. He was at the bar at Snapper Jack's spouting off to a man with him about the murder, wondering if the killer would be caught. The only reason I was eavesdropping was because Thurmond had my money. That'd make anyone interested, wouldn't it?"

I nodded but wondered if it was more than curiosity.

He drew a cup of coffee then said, "Anyway, he was talking about how you were a detective, how you've caught killers. I thought it was curious since I'd recently met you."

"Interesting, but not true. I'm no detective. You said you heard a couple of things. What's the other one?"

He smiled. "If my ex listened as good as you do, we'd still be married. The rumor's going around that a hitman killed Thurmond. The story is the dead guy owed a bundle of money to some connected guys, you know, like mob connected. They're from up north, maybe New Jersey, now that's my guess, they didn't say where. I suppose he failed to pay them what they were owed. We all know the mob doesn't take kindly to people who don't meet their obligations. Now Thurmond's dead."

"Do you remember who told you?"

"Nope. I'm not good with names, you know."

He's also not good with remembering he's told me that, three times. "Where'd you hear it?"

He nodded. "I do remember that. Was at the inside bar at Rita's where I overheard three guys talking. I got the impression two of them were visiting from out of state. The local guy was doing most of the talking like he was trying to impress the outsiders that he knew about a killing. That's all I remember, but figured since you were interested in Thurmond, you'd want to know."

We stepped away from the coffee urn. One thing you don't do on Folly is get in the way of workers focused like a laser-guided missile on getting their morning caffeine. Ben followed me to the cabinet holding fresh-baked cinnamon Danish, my Bert's breakfast of choice. I grabbed a Danish then waited to see what Ben was going to do.

He looked around, before saying, "Think I'll have one of those."

While he was getting his Danish, I said, "Did the men say anything else about Thurmond?"

"If they did, I didn't hear it. It's loud in there, you know."

———

I sat on my porch eating the Danish, drinking coffee from Bert's, all while wondering about my conversation with Ben. It was curious how he sought me out to tell me what he'd heard, not about my being a private detective, but what he shared about the rumor. Had he really heard people talking about the murder? If so, were they saying a hitman was responsible for Thurmond's death? Had the mob initiated the hit? I wouldn't rule it out, but it seemed unlikely. The manner of death seemed more personal than a mob-ordered killing. I found it convenient that Likard overheard a conversation raising the idea that the death had nothing to do with anyone here but blaming it on a problem involving someone who lived hundreds of miles away.

It seemed more likely the killer lived much closer. From everything I know, Ben Likard had more reason to want Thurmond dead than anyone. His coming up with the hitman story could be an attempt to deflect suspicion. Or, was I looking for explanations around every corner and Likard was around the nearest corner?

Regardless of his motivation, I needed to let Cindy know what he'd said. She answered the phone with, "Chief LaMond, may I help you?"

It wasn't an insult, so I knew she had someone with her, someone who didn't know about our friendship. I asked her to give me a call when she had time. She said she would, but it'd be near lunchtime. I took that as a hint I was going to get the opportunity to buy her lunch.

My hunch was proved accurate when she called at eleven to tell me she'd meet me at Planet Follywood in a half hour.

Located on Center Street, Planet Follywood was one of the island's longest-tenured restaurants. Its rustic environment and friendly staff made it a favorite of many locals plus vacationers who wanted a true beach-dining experience.

The weather was perfect, but I didn't know if Cindy wanted to sit in or outside, so I met her at the door. She said a good place for her to hide from pestering constituents was on the patio behind the building. We ordered at the bar and told the server where to find us when the food was ready. We were the only people who wanted to hide, so the outdoor area was empty. We took a table near the back of the patio in front of a raised stage for entertainers who performed regularly. This was not one of those times.

Cindy leaned back. "Okay, you're buying, but I'm not stupid enough to think it's not going to cost me. What do you want?"

"Chief, why do you think I want something other than a pleasant lunch with one of my favorite people?"

"Chris, I'm from East Tennessee. Back a hundred-fifty years ago, a bunch of snooty northerners came to where I grew up. They saw us as a bunch of ignorant hillbillies, too stupid to tell a good deal from a load of cow manure. They thought because we couldn't see what was under the ground where we were planting crops, we never would've known about stuff like coal, gas, other minerals. I know you're not a big fan of history, so I'll shorten the lesson. Some of my kin did fall for the crooks who ripped them off, but know what most of them did?"

"What?" I said, although I had a hunch I knew.

"Filled them viper-tongued, thievin', crooked scoundrels with enough buckshot to sink the Titanic, that is if the iceberg didn't do it first."

I coughed back a chuckle. "There's no doubt you inherited a lot of wisdom."

She leaned forward in the chair. "Enough to know you're not sitting across from me so you can gander at my beautiful smile, listen to my keen wit, or soak in my charm."

"Those are bonuses, Chief."

Allison, our server, arrived with our lunch, interrupting Cindy dragging out of me the reason I wanted to meet her.

We thanked Allison, then Cindy said, "So, why are we here?"

"I was talking to Ben Likard in Bert's this morning."

Cindy took a bite of her sandwich, a sip of her drink, then said, "And why should I care?"

I told her what Ben had said about a hitman. I omitted the part about my being a private detective. I wasn't as wise as the lady from East Tennessee but knew how she would react if I shared that bit of information.

"Ben didn't know who the guys were?"

"That's what he said."

"It's possible I missed the importance of that information somewhere in your telling it. What in the hell am I supposed to do with a rumor from unknown sources?"

"It's not much, but—"

"Not much," she interrupted. "How about a no-see-ums-sized speck of nothing?"

I shared my thought that Ben could've been deflecting suspicion.

"That's tinier than a no-see-ums-sized speck of nothing."

"I know."

She sighed. "I'll pass it along to Detective Adair. Maybe he can swing something in front of Likard's face to hypnotize him so he can remember who the guys were or get some information larger than a speck of nothing."

"Sorry he didn't get more from them."

"Me too, this is way too frustrating for this old gal."

"You're not that old."

She smiled. "Chris, you need to work on your sweet talking techniques. Now here's a question, do you know Martin Eastman?"

"Doesn't ring a bell. He live here?"

"East Ashley Avenue, a handful of houses before the entrance to the Preserve."

Lighthouse Inlet Heritage Preserve was at the end of East Ashley Avenue, a few miles from where we were seated.

"What about him?"

"He called the office late yesterday afternoon. He got home a couple of hours earlier from visiting his mother in Pennsylvania. He's been gone ten days. Want to guess why he called?"

Why does everyone think I get my kicks from guessing things I have no way of knowing?

"Why don't you tell me?"

"When he boarded the plane to head to his mother's house, he had a shiny aluminum jon boat nesting under his back deck. When he got home yesterday, guess what he didn't have?"

"A jon boat under his deck."

"Congratulations, you win my check."

"Sure he wasn't here when the murder took place?"

She took another bite of sandwich before saying, "Probably. A woman in Pennsylvania told me she was his mother and he was with her the entire time. I haven't verified it, but he says he has airline documents showing he made the trip."

"I don't suppose he has security cameras at his house or nosy neighbors who saw someone take the boat?"

"You don't suppose correctly. No cameras and the neighbors can't see his patio from their house. Don't ask, they didn't see anyone in his drive while he was away."

"Are you certain it's his boat?"

"Certain, no, but what are the odds of a jon boat disappearing then a body turning up in one within the same week being a coincidence?"

"Near zero."

"I agree. He'd coming by later today to see if he can identify it some way other than saying it looks like his."

"What now?"

"Suppose we'll have to start looking for a hitman who goes all the way to the end of the longest street on Folly to steal a boat so he can put Mr. Thurmond in it before putting a knife in his back."

CHAPTER EIGHTEEN

The next morning, like several others lately, began with a question. This time it was Cindy LaMond who responded to my, "Hello," as I answered the phone, with, "Do you know Ronald Honeycutt, goes by Ron?"

"Did someone steal his jon boat?"

"That boat's done sailed. Do you know him?"

"No. Who's he?"

"Remember I told you Detective Adair found a docking station with nothing docked to it in Thurmond's condo?"

"Vaguely."

"That's the most I can expect from someone your advanced age. Regardless, it appears Ron Honeycutt took Thurmond's laptop."

"Who is he and how do you know he took the laptop?"

"The how we know is simple. One of Thurmond's paranoid neighbors has more cameras around the exterior of his property than are around Buckingham Palace. Courtesy of the paranoid neighbor, we have a nice, full-color image of Ron lugging a laptop computer out of Thurmond's condo the day the body was found. Adair arrested him last night."

"Who is he?"

"You taking impatient pills from Charles? Chill, I'm getting there."

"No, but—"

"Enough. Ronald Honeycutt is a resident of our island. He lives in a beach house on West Ashley. From what Adair told me, Ron considers himself an entrepreneur. I consider him a thief, but hey, that's for a jury to determine. Anyway, according to what he told Adair, he founded a T-shirt printing company, you know, the kind that puts those stupid sayings on millions of made-in-China T-shirts. He then started an off-brand movie rental business, sort of like Blockbuster. Long story shorter, both enterprises went belly-up."

"Why'd he steal the laptop?"

"Adair said Honeycutt was a chatty Cathy when he was talking about his businesses. Once Adair uttered the word laptop, Honeycutt zipped his lips after saying he wanted a lawyer to do his talking."

"Does Adair think Honeycutt killed Thurmond?"

"Absolutely, but that gets into the pesky realm of proof, of which there's none so far, according to Adair."

"Did Honeycutt know Thurmond?"

"Did you miss the part about a lawyer?"

"I thought he may've said something about knowing him while he was being a chatty Cathy."

"You thought wrong."

"What happens now?"

"He'll be arraigned today. The judge will hear about the

video of Honeycutt walking out of the condo with Thurmond's laptop. Honeycutt will get an innocent *who me?* look on his face and plead not guilty. No one will believe him, but the law says he's innocent until proven guilty. The judge will set a bail hearing date when the video star's lawyer will tell how Honeycutt isn't a threat to anyone, how he's bordering on sainthood. The harried judge will take into consideration how overcrowded jails are, then grant bail."

"In the meantime, Detective Adair and your office will look for evidence that Honeycutt killed Thurmond."

"Gosh, why didn't I think of that?"

"Chief, I have confidence you'll get it sorted out."

"Wish I had your confidence. Anyway, since you're always nosing in everything happening here, I wanted to see if you knew Honeycutt."

"You're confusing me with Charles."

"That's what friends are for."

"Whatever."

"Good luck finding evidence against Honeycutt, or whomever killed Thurmond."

"Enough wasting time talking to you. Gotta get back to finding evidence so we can stick Honeycutt back in the pokey for misuse of cutlery."

———

It'd rained overnight, but the sky was now clear, the temperature mild, so a walk to the Lost Dog Cafe for a hot breakfast sounded better than a Danish from Bert's. I felt the pounds dropping off my body as I walked the nearly empty Center Street sidewalk while enjoying the sunshine illuminating colorful storefronts on the west side of the street. Mornings were without doubt my favorite time of day.

Unlike the empty Center Street sidewalks, there was a crowd at the Dog. The front and side patios were full. A couple along with their English Setter was seated at the entry waiting for an outside table. Fortunately, there was a vacant table inside. I was seated then greeted by Amber who was quick to the table with a steaming mug of coffee, her endearing smile, and a pat on my back, more reason that morning was my favorite time of day. She took my French toast order, then asked if I knew anything more about Thurmond's murder. I asked why she was curious.

"Virgil was in yesterday talking about how shook he was after finding the body. He said he wouldn't be able to relax until whoever did it was behind bars. He's afraid the killer will come after him."

"Why does he think that?"

"Exactly what I asked. You know how Virgil is always trying to act all happy like, positive about everything even if he doesn't have reason to be?"

I took a sip then nodded.

"He acted surprised I'd heard what he said then asked him about it. It was like he was talking to himself."

One of Amber's most endearing traits is unlike many people, she listens to what others say.

"What'd he say?"

"He laughed, tried to joke it away by saying he was teasing, or something like that. He wasn't joking. If you ask me, he's worried." Amber looked around the crowded room. "I'd better get back to work."

I understood how traumatic it would've been for Virgil to

find Thurmond's body, but wondered what gave him the impression the killer would come after him. Did Virgil think the killer may've seen him? Did Virgil know something the killer feared? Amber was right, Virgil is one of the most positive people I know. If I'd owned a home along Charleston's famed Battery, was wealthy, then lost it all to end up living in a tiny, rundown apartment, the last thing I'd be was cheerful, seemingly content with whatever I had left. I couldn't do it, but from everything I knew about him, Virgil was. After Amber returned with my breakfast, I called Virgil, who answered with a cheerful, "Hey, Christopher, great day, isn't it?"

See, I told you.

I agreed it was a great day, then asked where he was. He told me his manservant had the day off so he was at the West Hudson Laundry doing, well, what you'd expect at a laundry. I told him I was at the Dog and if he would be at the laundry a little longer, I'd stop over.

"It's pretty exciting here. My undies going around and around. Think your heart can handle the excitement?"

I told him I thought it could, smiled, then enjoyed breakfast.

CHAPTER NINETEEN

The West Hudson Laundry is a coral-colored building one street over from the Dog. From my few times in the building, I remembered it being clean, neat, and inviting. The building was empty but one of the dryers was going, to quote Virgil, *around and around*. My friend was seated on a wooden deck on the side of the structure. He was wearing the same or near duplicate, long-sleeve, button-down, white dress shirt with frayed cuffs he'd worn most every time I'd seen him. He also had on navy blue chinos, his ever-present sunglasses, and Guccis.

He smiled. "Figured with all your detective skills you'd find me out here. Told you it was a great day, didn't I?"

I skipped the argument that I wasn't a detective but agreed about the day.

He said, "What did this fine establishment and I do to earn your presence?"

"I was talking to Amber who said you were in yesterday.

She thought you were down, a rare condition from the Virgil I know, so I was checking if you were okay."

"Miss Amber is extraordinarily perceptive, scary perceptive."

He hesitated, looked at the deck's floor, then at the door to the laundromat. I waited for him to continue.

He didn't, so I said, "Something bothering you?"

"Remember when I talked to you the morning I found the late Walter Thurmond?"

"It would've been hard to forget."

"Remember I told you we needed to find out who killed him?"

That also would've been hard to forget. "I remember."

"Think I spoke too soon. Christopher, I'm not *bricky*."

"*Bricky?*"

"Sorry, that's another of my ex's Victorian terms. Means brave, fearless."

Virgil's ex wife has a degree in English, more accurately English Literature. He occasionally throws out a word or phrase of hers. He said she used them to feel superior to everyone else. Why he used them, I had no idea.

"Oh," I said. "Why say that?"

"What could I possibly offer to help catch someone the police are unable to find with their skills and expansive resources?"

That hadn't stopped him a few months ago when faced with a similar, or more difficult situation. There was something else bothering him.

"Virgil, I'm not saying you should get involved, but why do you think you don't have anything to offer?"

"I didn't know the dead guy. Why should I care about who offed him?"

"I seem to remember when we first met how much you wanted to join up with Charles in his imaginary detective agency."

"Do you also remember how it nearly got me killed?"

"I do."

"When we met, I was floundering, didn't know what I was doing. I was adrift in the tumultuous sea of life. I'd lost everything." He looked toward the parking lot then shook his head.

That was true.

"What's different now?"

"Gee, that's one heck of a way to cheer someone up. Nothing's different. I still don't have a job, don't have a lady to tell me how wonderful I am, don't own much more than what you see on my back or in those machines in there." He nodded toward the door. "I don't have a purpose for being alive."

"Virgil, you have friends, good friends. There're people who would do anything for you, me included. You have your health. You have a great personality. You're one of the most positive people I know."

He chuckled as he patted me on the back. "You sticking with that last statement?"

I smiled then amended, "Most positive, most of the time."

"That's better." He shook his head like he was either shaking water out of his slicked-back black hair or shaking bad thoughts out of his head. "I don't suppose you called to invite yourself to watch me do laundry or to listen to me bewail my pitiful life."

True, but it reinforced what Amber had said about something bothering my friend.

"You're not off by much. I did want to find out what's bothering you."

"I appreciate that, I really do." He hesitated, flicked a fly off his sleeve, then looked over at me. "Could be a bout of feeling sorry for myself or."

I waited while another fly found its way to Virgil's arm, then flew away when he swatted at it. He didn't complete his thought, so I said, "Or what?"

"I ran into Ryan Sparks the other night at Planet Follywood. He'd been there awhile, sitting at the bar, crying in his beer, beers. He slurred every fifth word. Anyway, I plopped myself on the stool next to him. He remembered me from our talk out at the River Park and offered to buy me a drink. My pockets were devoid of legal tender, so I accepted with a smile. Seems he'd been working at his sister and bro-in-law's house all day, said he was at the bar to unwind." Virgil smiled. "The boy was mighty unwound when I arrived." Virgil jumped up. "Don't run away. Gotta check on my clothes. That's my entire wardrobe in there so I wouldn't want someone absconding with it."

I didn't run away. I was too busy wondering what his conversation with Ryan had to do with his mood, if anything.

"Where was I?" Virgil said as he returned to the seat attached to the railing around the porch.

"Talking with Ryan at Planet Follywood."

"It wasn't long before I ran out of meaningless chitchat, so I asked if he knew anything else about Thurmond's murder. He about jumped off the stool. He looked at me and barked, 'Why would I?' I was taken aback. I told him I was wondering because his boat was near where I found the body. I added that he told us he'd heard two people talking near where the rowboat was stuck in the weeds, so I figured he'd pay attention to any rumors going around."

"What'd he say?"

"Chris, it wasn't what he said. Soon as I finished digging myself out of a hole by explaining why I'd asked about the murder, he changed the subject as quick as a hummingbird flaps its wings. That boy nearly gave me whiplash."

"Think it's because he was traumatized by the body being found close to his boat?"

"That's one possibility." Virgil shook his head.

"Or?"

"The *or* is what got me thinking, got me worrying. What if I was sitting in a bar beside the person who stuck the knife in Thurmond's back?"

"Why think that?"

"That's why I'm thinking I have no business nosing in things that should be solved by the police. I wouldn't have a clue how to figure who killed him. Sure, Ryan is bothered by something about the murder. That's obvious. What's not clear is why. Who am I to think I'm so all-knowing I can tell the difference between him being bothered by being close to where Thurmond was or him being bothered by me asking questions?"

"Remember when we first talked about talking with Ryan?"

"Chris, I'm rudderless, not losing my memory. What about it?"

"You thought Ryan knew something he wasn't sharing."

"Yes, so?"

"You still think that?"

"Yes."

"Do you think he killed Thurmond?"

"Yes. I also have a feeling he thinks I think he did. See why I'm worried?"

"Think so."

Fortunately, Virgil smiled. "Okay, enough about thinking. Besides, there's nothing else I can say about Ryan."

"The police are doing everything possible to learn who killed Thurmond. That's why I called. Chief LaMond told me they arrested someone who stole Thurmond's laptop the day after you found the body."

"The theft was related to Thurmond's murder? Did the same person kill him? I hope. I hope."

"Their working theory is it's the same person, but there's no proof."

"Who is it?"

"Ronald Honeycutt."

Virgil leaned my direction. "Ron?"

"You know him?"

"Sort of."

I motioned for him to elaborate.

"Don't know him well. Spent a few hours beside him on barstools around town."

"What do you know about him?"

"Little outside the four walls of the bar. Inside, he's a heavy drinker. Most times he was *powdering hair*."

"Doing what?"

"Victorian term; means getting drunk."

I, and obviously Virgil, would've been better off if he'd

married someone who majored is anything but English Literature with way too much interest in Victorian phrases.

"Got it. He was a heavy drinker. Anything else?"

"I wouldn't trust him farther than I could throw one of
those washing machines in there."

"Why not?"

"Don't get me wrong, he's nice enough to me. Hell, he
always picked up my bar tab, something I appreciate since
they're too heavy for me to lift, if you get my drift. Why didn't
I trust him? Hmm, let me think of how to say it. He's slicker
than Wesson oil on glass." Virgil nodded like that said it all.

It didn't. "In what way?"

"Ever met someone who could sweet talk a shark out of
biting off his leg? Someone who complimented everything you
did?"

"That why you didn't trust him?"

"Chris, I had the impression his charming ways, his
compliments were as thin as that piece of glass with the oil
on it."

"Insincere?"

"That covers it."

"I don't suppose he mentioned knowing Thurmond?"

"Not that I recall, although a few of the nights we were
bending elbows, I may've been, well, may've been soused. I
wouldn't have remembered if a pterodactyl landed on the bar.
He may've mentioned the dead guy, but if he did." Virgil
shrugged. "Do the police really think he killed Thurmond?"

"Yes, but thinking and proving are different things. Do
you know Martin Eastman?"

"Don't think so. Who's he?"

"Thurmond was in his jon boat."

"Ah ha, he must be the killer. Case closed."

"That could've been true if he wasn't visiting his mother in Pennsylvania when Thurmond was killed."

"Did he lend his boat to someone?"

"Good thought, but no. He reported it stolen as soon as he returned to Folly."

"Guess that'd be classified in police terms as a dead end."

At lease he didn't offer a Victorian term for it.

"Afraid so."

"What can we do to help the constabulary?"

Was this the same Virgil who told me fifteen minutes ago he'd spoken too soon about wanting to find Thurmond's killer?

"You sure you want to get involved?"

"Don't have anything better to do. There's only so long I can be entertained watching my laundry going around and around."

"If you're sure you want to help, the best thing we can do is keep our ears open."

"That I can do."

CHAPTER TWENTY

The biggest surprise I had the next seven days was receiving zero phone calls from Virgil, Charles, or someone telling me I could consolidate my credit card debt by calling an 800 number. The streak ended with a call from Charles asking why I hadn't invited him to breakfast, lunch, or supper recently. I told him I would correct that horrific oversight if he'd meet me tomorrow at the Dog for breakfast. He gave no indication he understood how much sarcasm was included in the words *horrific oversight*.

The first words out of Charles's mouth as I approached his table on the restaurant's front patio were, "Guess what I heard yesterday?"

"Good morning, Charles," were the first out of my mouth, a futile attempt to bring civility to conversations.

"Well, are you going to guess?"

I rest my case.

"No."

Amber arrived before Charles could tell me I was no fun. She kissed the top of my head, set a mug of coffee in front of me, then said, "What can I get you this morning. Wait, no, let me guess, French toast?"

"Amber, that's a good—"

Charles interrupted, "At least someone's guessing this morning."

Amber ignored him and continued looking my way, so I told her she'd guessed correctly. She headed inside to place my order.

"What did you hear yesterday?" I said then took a sip of coffee.

"Ron Honeycutt was arrested for breaking in the dead guys condo."

I thought I'd shared that with him after Cindy told me. If I hadn't, I'd be in for a ton of grief since he considers it a declaration of war if I don't tell him something within seconds of hearing it. Of course, he doesn't need to know I knew about the arrest.

"Who's Ron Honeycutt?"

"Lives a couple of blocks out West Ashley, early fifties, chubby, owned a few businesses, don't think he does anymore."

"How do you know him?"

"Dusty."

"Ron's dusty?"

"No, Dusty is Honeycutt's pug." Charles wrinkled up his face, imitating the face of a pug, or so I assumed. "So ugly it's cute."

One of Charles's goals is to befriend every dog, most cats,

and possibly all pet rodents on Folly. As a byproduct, he gets to know their owners.

"Did Dusty tell you Honeycutt had been arrested?"

Charles rolled his eyes, smiled, then said, "No."

Okay, let's back up, I thought.

"First, how do you know about Ron Honeycutt? Second, how did you learn he'd been arrested?"

"I talked to Honeycutt in front of the Sand Dollar a few weeks ago. He brings Dusty to the big city from his house in rural Folly. Ron told me Dusty likes to visit people and sniff around other dogs people bring to town. I don't have a dog, but Dusty visited with me anyway. While I was talking to Dusty, Ron asked how long I'd been living here, where I lived, what I did for a living, and a few other questions. To be honest, I liked Dusty, but Ron was too nosy for me."

Charles saying someone was too nosy fit in the pot calling the kettle black category.

"Any idea why he was so curious?"

"Not then. When I heard he'd been arrested for breaking into a condo, I began wondering if he was nosing in my business to see if I had a house worth breaking into." Charles laughed. "If that was on his mind, he and Dusty were sniffing up the wrong fire hydrant."

"How'd you learn he was arrested?"

"Gabbing with Officer Spencer. Honeycutt was arrested several days ago, but is already out on bail. That's good, or I'd worry about what'd happen with Dusty."

"Did Spencer tell you anything else?"

Amber arrived with my breakfast, refreshed our coffee, then told us to flag her down if we needed anything.

Charles watched her leave, looked around like he wanted to see if anyone was listening, then said, "He told me to keep this under my hat. Since he knows you, I'm sure he won't mind me sharing. The Sheriff's Office thinks Honeycutt stabbed Thurmond, then took his computer to keep the cops from finding evidence on it that'd tie him to the crime. That makes sense."

Chief LaMond's city pickup truck pulled in a space in front of the restaurant. She saw us looking at her, shook her head, then walked to the patio's side entrance on her way to our table.

"Morning, Chief," Charles said, proving he could make civil comments.

"Was until I saw you two vagrants sitting here. Who's going to buy me coffee?"

Charles was quick to point at me as Cindy joined us. I crossed my fingers and hoped she didn't say anything to indicate she'd already told me about Honeycutt.

Charles said, "Chief, what a coincidence. We were just talking about one of your officers."

Cindy stared at him. "What'd he do wrong?"

Charles said, "It could've been a she."

Cindy shook her head. "My she officers don't do anything wrong."

"Neither did the one I'm talking about. I was telling Chris Officer Spencer was doing a fine job keeping our island safe.

Not exactly how I remember the conversation, but it was Charles's story.

Cindy continued to stare at Charles. "And?"

"I asked him the latest on the boat man's murder. I was certain your office, with the assistance of the Sheriff's Office, was getting close to nabbing the perp."

Cindy looked at me, then turned to Charles, "I suppose I shouldn't be surprised to get a load of camel crap along with my coffee when you two are involved."

I chose not to remind her I hadn't said a word. Charles chose not to comment on her poetic addition to her coffee. Instead, he said, "Okay, you got me. Spencer didn't say you were close to catching the killer, but he did tell me about Dusty's dad being arrested."

Amber set a mug of coffee in front of Cindy then headed to the table behind us to see if its occupants needed anything.

Cindy took a sip, tapped her fingers on the table, then said, "In my quest for edification, I must ask, who the hell is Dusty?"

I leaned back in the chair and waited for Charles to edify. Buying Cindy's coffee was well worth the entertainment value.

Charles did his pug imitation before telling Cindy what, not who, Dusty was and the name of his owner.

"Remind me why Officer Spencer was sharing this with you."

Charles smiled. "I suppose because he was doing his part to improve community relations with your citizenry. You should be proud."

She tapped her fingers harder on the table. "I should be in my office doing whatever crap a good chief should be doing, rather than putting up with two old farts."

Once again, I didn't remind her I hadn't said a word.

"Chief," Charles said not letting Cindy's comment deter him, "now that we're talking about Ron's arrest, did you learn anything from the laptop he rudely removed from a dead man's condo?"

"Charles, first we're not talking about the arrest. Second,

it's going to take more than a cup of coffee for me to put up with your pestering."

"That's okay, let's grab Amber so you can order anything you want. Chris will be glad to put it on his tab."

Amber heard part of Charles's comment and returned to ask Cindy if she wanted something to eat. She decided on a bagel with cream cheese. I'd gotten off easy.

"Charles, the answer is no," Cindy said before taking another sip.

"No what?" my friend said.

Cindy smiled. "If you paid attention to what you said, you'd know what."

I decided it was time to enter the conversation. "Charles, you asked if the police learned anything from the laptop."

Cindy pointed at me, then said, "Glad someone listens to Charles. Like I said, the answer is no."

Charles asked, "Why not?"

"Because it wasn't found in the search of his house and his high-priced legal counsel said his client doesn't have the laptop, claims his client is innocent, never had the laptop, claims if the police thought Honeycutt did anything wrong, they'd, umm, we'd have to prove it in court. End of story."

Charles looked at me, then turned to Cindy. "Don't you have Honeycutt leaving Thurmond's house carrying the laptop on tape, video, or whatever you call stuff recorded on home security cameras?"

"Yep. Lesson of the day. Never let facts get in the way of a defense attorney defensing."

Amber returned with the bagel and asked Cindy if she needed anything else.

"Earplugs, so I don't have to listen to more from these two."

Amber said, "Sorry, Chief, they're not on the menu."

Amber left as Cindy moaned about the missing menu item.

I said, "Have you or the Sheriff's Office learned if there's any connection between Honeycutt and Thurmond?"

"Nothing definitive. Both men appeared to operate in the gray area between legal and illegal, or at least Honeycutt did in years gone by. He'd been convicted six years ago of running a Ponzi scheme. He spent time at public expense in the hoosegow. It wasn't one of those large Ponzi schemes like Bernie Madoff, so he didn't get many years of rent-free living. Then there were the charges of embezzlement before his Ponzi-related incarceration. He walked on those charges. Now to Thurmond. The more we learn about his activities, the more is coming to light about his scam conning people into buying into his companies, who then find they could have invested more wisely in the lottery where there was at least a chance of winning, even if that chance was like one in a gazillion."

"Nothing ties the two together?"

"Not yet."

I said, "Does anyone think it was a coincidence that Honeycutt broke into Thurmond's condo the day his body was found?"

"Nope."

CHAPTER TWENTY-ONE

I left the Dog after Cindy repeated she needed to get to the office, thanked me for breakfast, thanked Charles for giving her indigestion, then drove off. Charles thanked me for buying his breakfast, something I didn't know I was doing until Amber handed me the check with his charges on it. I thanked the god of good luck Cindy didn't mention to Charles she'd already told me about Honeycutt's arrest. With multiple thanks out of the way, I headed home.

No sooner had I opened the door than the phone rang.

"Brother Chris, this is Preacher Burl. Did I catch you at a bad time?"

Finally, someone who knows how to start a phone conversation. I'd met Burl Ives Costello five years ago after he moved here from Indiana to start First Light Church. His arrival on Folly not only brought a new house of worship, which wasn't a house since most services were held on the beach, it brought a cloud of darkness which included a murder. The consensus was the new minister was responsible. As should be obvious from his being on the phone, the suspicions were ill-founded. Burl was now a well-respected member of the community. I also count him among my friends.

"It's a perfect time, Preacher," I said and waited for the reason for the call.

"Good. Could I impose on you to spare this old preacher man a few minutes of your time?"

"Gee, retirement's keeping me awfully busy, but for you I could spare a few minutes."

He chuckled. "Good. I'll make it easy on you. I could meet you at your domicile. Name the time."

"Anytime this morning."

We agreed he'd stop by the house, or in his words my domicile in an hour.

Good to his word, an admirable trait for a minister, his aging, Dodge Grand Caravan pulled in my drive an hour after our brief phone conversation.

I met him at the door where he greeted me with a handshake plus a man hug. Burl was in his mid-fifties, five-foot-five tall, shaped like a football, portly in polite terms.

"Brother Chris, thank you for meeting me on short notice." His milk-chocolate colored mustache reminded me of a woolly bear caterpillar.

I ushered him in then asked if he wanted coffee. He said yes but only if it wasn't any trouble. Knowing his penchant for coffee, I'd fixed a pot before he arrived. He followed me to the kitchen where I poured his drink. Against my better judgment, I fixed myself one, probably my seventh cup of the day, then joined him at the table.

"Brother Chris," he said after taking a sip, "I've missed you at church."

I was an irregular attender at best.

"I do need to get there more often."

"God and I would appreciate it," he said, then took another sip.

Time to change the subject. "What did I do to earn a visit?"

Burl smiled. "It wasn't to shame you into attending services."

I returned the smile and waited.

He rubbed his hand through the few hairs remaining on his comb-over, then ran a finger over his mustache. "I'm faced with a dilemma."

I waited for the clearly nervous minister to continue. When he didn't, I mustered all my psychology training techniques combined with years working in HR, and said, "Dilemma?"

"One of my regular attendees is Ronald Honeycutt. Are you familiar with him?"

"Interesting you should ask. I was talking with Chief LaMond earlier today who told me Mr. Honeycutt had been arrested."

"Ah, then you understand my dilemma."

"Not really. What about him?"

Burl rubbed his mustache again, took another sip, then said, "As you are aware, my calling is to minister to all. It's not for me to judge the behavior, past and present, of those who come for spiritual guidance. As a result, I attract some who, how shall I say it, some who have questionable pasts. I refuse to turn anyone away."

"I understand. That's one of the things I admire about you and First Light."

"I've known you for what, four years?"

"Almost five."

"My, how time flies. I know you to be a level-headed arbiter in difficult situations. You can see both sides of a dispute, unlike many who are blinded by their beliefs, be they founded or unfounded."

"Thanks."

Burl smiled. "If you were conversing with the chief, I suspect you know Mr. Honeycutt has a history dating back years, a history that involves behavior considered criminal by societal standards."

I nodded as I wondered when Burl would arrive at the dilemma.

"The day before yesterday, Brother Ron came to share he'd been arrested. He, of course, didn't come to confess to committing a crime but to share what had occurred. According to what he told me, he'd been accused of breaking into someone's house, something about removing some form of computer. I listened without revealing my thoughts concerning his guilt or innocence, not that difficult, I might add, since I didn't have feelings either way."

"Did he say anything else?"

"I had the impression he was feeling trapped. He felt he had nowhere to turn. Sure, he had a lawyer, which would provide helpful in dealing with the criminal justice system. More than anything, he needed someone to talk to; someone who would listen without passing judgement."

I repeated, "Did he say anything else?"

"He said the condo he'd been accused of entering illegally

belonged to the gentleman found murdered near the boat ramp."

"Did he know the man who was killed?"

"I asked him. Brother Chris, this is part of my problem. He said he did, but when I expressed sympathy, saying I was sorry for the loss of his friend, he sluffed it off saying they weren't friends. He mumbled something about them being business partners, then acted like he didn't really say that. He started fidgeting, acting nervous, if you know what I mean."

I did if it was like how Burl was acting but didn't share that observation. I nodded for him to continue.

"I've given a great deal of thought to what he shared. If pressed, I wouldn't be able to swear on the book I preach from that he said they were business partners. I think that's what he said, but I'm not certain. Also, as you are aware, the last few years, I've been ensconced in situations no one should ever encounter so perhaps I'm being paranoid about learning things that appear to touch on murder. So, here's my dilemma. If Brother Ron was in fact business partners with the poor gentleman who lost his life, is that something I should bring to the attention of law enforcement? He didn't tell me he was confiding something he didn't want shared, nor did he say I could."

"I don't know what the Sheriff's Office knows about the relationship between Honeycutt and Thurmond, but Chief LaMond was unaware of a connection between the two other than the break-in at Thurmond's condo. There's also a theory he stole the laptop to keep the police from connecting the two men. Without the computer, that'll be difficult to prove. If you're uncomfortable taking what you know to the police, I could tell Cindy I heard the two were business partners. The police are already thinking they knew each other. It may give her something else tying them together."

"Brother Ron is already in trouble. I don't want to needlessly add to his difficulties."

"It wouldn't—"

"On the other hand," he interrupted, "if by chance he's responsible for Thurmond's death, I don't see harm in you sharing what I told you with the Chief. Brother Ron didn't leave me with the impression his words should remain confidential. I'm not even certain he said what I thought he said."

"I'll let the Chief know."

"No, allow me to think about it first."

"Okay, but please don't take long. If Ron was involved, the sooner the police know, the better. If I go to Cindy, I'll ask her to keep your name out of it. All this information is doing is giving the police the possible connection. Nothing more."

"I suppose I wouldn't have come to you if I wanted what I learned to remain untold. It'd be best for you to let the Chief know."

"Are you certain?"

"Certain, no. Necessary, probably."

"I'll tell her this afternoon."

He took another sip then stared in the half-empty mug.

"Preacher, while you're here, do you happen to know Ben Likard?"

"The name doesn't ring a bell. Why?"

"He's someone who was in partnership with Thurmond. I heard the two men were arguing so I wondered if you knew him."

"I assume he's a suspect in Thurmond's murder."

"Yes."

"Then maybe my concerns over Brother Ron are for naught."

"Possibly. Do you know Kevin and Megan Goodman?"

"Ah, people I am familiar with. They're not suspects, are they?"

"No. I met them and Megan's brother recently. Megan's brother lives on a sailboat at Sunset Cay Marina. His boat was anchored near where Thurmond's body was found. As you can imagine, he was shaken over the discovery. You may know her brother, Ryan Sparks."

"I haven't had the pleasure, but I've heard Megan talk about him. If I'm not mistaken, he plays baseball."

"He played but was injured. How do you know the Goodmans?"

"I ran into them in Pewter Hardware. They were buying wood paneling. Larry introduced me to them since he knew I'd done carpentry back in the day. They're remodeling their house. I empathized with the problems they were having with contractors. Nice couple."

"How'd Ryan come up in the conversation?"

"Megan said her brother was helping. She's proud of him, was bragging on how good a ballplayer he was. She didn't mention his injury." Burl smiled. "Anyone else you want to ask about?"

I told him no, then he said he'd bothered me enough. I said I'd share with Cindy what he'd said about Ron.

I walked him to the door where he stopped. "Brother Chris, do you think I'm doing the right thing?"

"Yes, if Ron is the killer, the police need to know. If he's not, no harm done."

CHAPTER TWENTY-TWO

After Preacher Burl left, I poured another cup of coffee, probably a mistake since it would be cup number nine or ten, took a deep breath, then called Cindy, only to be rewarded with her voicemail. I asked her to call when she had a spare minute. I realized after hanging up that it was best I got a machine rather than her live voice. Now I'll have time to figure out what to tell her. What had Burl shared that'd be helpful to the police? Honeycutt told him he knew the deceased. Did the police know that? From what the Chief had said, Honeycutt's lawyer cut off all communication between his client and the police, so it's possible the connection between the men would be new to them. What about Honeycutt's comment he and Thurmond were business partners? If true, it'd be something the police needed to know. Then again, Burl wasn't certain that was what Honeycutt had told him. Regardless, knowing that potential connection would be critical for the police if they still considered Honeycutt as the prime suspect in Thurmond's murder.

Cindy returned my call an hour later, beginning the conversation with something about having to spend most of the morning with two disgruntled council members. From comments she'd made over the years, there were few things she dreaded more than dealing with gripes, pet peeves, and rants by elected officials who assumed the chief was their personal enforcer of whatever was on their mind. Her bemoaning would eventually run out of steam then she'd ask why I called.

This morning it took longer than usual, but she finally said, "Did you call to make my morning worse than it already is?"

"I hope not."

"Then continue."

I told her Preacher Burl had visited. She told me that it'd take more than a visit from a preacher to save my soul. I agreed then shared what he'd said about Honeycutt. She asked how certain Burl was about Honeycutt saying he and Thurmond were business partners. I told her Burl wasn't sure but left no doubt they knew each other.

"That's more than we knew before you called," Cindy said. "Guess your call broke my streak of hearing crappy things since I got here three hours ago."

That was her way of thanking me without having to humble herself by verbalizing it. She added, "I'll let Adair know. He called late yesterday to say he'd learned more about Thurmond's businesses. He owned a company in Rhode Island. Did being the key word. It was on the verge of bankruptcy a year ago. He unloaded it and made a profit of zero dollars."

"What kind of company was it?"

"Manufactured wheelchairs, not normal ones but those that are narrow so they can be used on airplanes, trains, or anywhere where traditional wheelchairs are too wide to go."

"Why did the company fail? I would've thought there'd be a growing need for that kind of chair."

"Did you forget that I'm from the mountains of Tennessee and a lowly old police chief in a tiny town? I know as much about manufacturing wheelchairs as I do about how aard-varks' brains work."

"What about the companies he was seeking partners for?"

"According to Adair, they were all in his head and on his brochure. Without his computer, the folks in the Sheriff's Office who know much more about it than me, have little to go on."

"Speaking of partners with Thurmond, has Detective Adair talked with Ben Likard? He had a motive to kill Thurmond."

"Detective Chris, Adair had a pleasant sit-down with Likard."

"Don't suppose he confessed to inserting the knife in Thurmond's back."

"If he did, Adair forgot to mention it. What he did say was Likard was royally pissed at Thurmond."

"Enough to kill him?"

"Could be."

"Did he have an alibi for when Thurmond was stabbed?"

"Said he was asleep. To answer your next question, he was a cuddled up all by his lonesome self in his king-size bed."

"Next to Honeycutt, is he Adair's prime suspect?"

"He's on the top three list, at least until we can find Thurmond's laptop to see who else may've invested in the phantom companies."

"Who else is in the top three?"

"Ryan Sparks, and of course, Ron Honeycutt."

"Why is Ryan a suspect?"

"First, he was fewer than a hundred feet from where the body was found. He knew Thurmond, possibly even wanted to invest in Thurmond's companies. When I first talked to him, he said he didn't hear or see anything the night Thurmond exited this world. The next time, he said he heard two people talking near the shore that morning. You told me he said the same thing to you. Hold on." I heard a muffled voice in the background, then Cindy said, "Tell the dummy I'll be right there. Sorry Chris, the powers that be want to have a face-to-face, like now. Suppose I'm in trouble again. Talk to you later." She ended the call before I wished her luck.

I spent most of the afternoon thinking about what Cindy had said. I'd met and had conversations, some brief at best, with her three suspects. I suppose an argument could be made for each of them being guilty, but I couldn't keep from thinking if Thurmond was as big a con artist as had been suggested, there must be other "partners" or potential "partners" in his imaginary companies beyond the three living on Folly. Any of them could've had reason to want the man dead. Unless some of them came forward on their own, it appeared the only way for the police to learn their identities would be from Thurmond's computer—Thurmond's missing computer, the computer Ron Honeycutt stole from Thurmond's condo.

It didn't matter to the police what I thought, but if asked,

Honeycutt would be at the top of my suspect list. A close second would be Ben Likard. He was the only one of the three who admitted having a legitimate gripe with the con artist. He was the only suspect who admitted joining in a partnership with Thurmond, admitted to giving him hundreds of thousands of dollars, and then when he asked for some of his profits was rejected. That made a solid motive, in my opinion, again, the opinion that didn't mean anything to the police.

If I had to put Ryan Sparks on the list, he'd be a distant third. Granted, his sailboat was anchored close to where Thurmond was found, but there wasn't anything to connect him to the jon boat. Yes, he claimed to not hear or see anything the night or morning of Thurmond's demise, then said he'd heard two people talking near or on shore that morning. He hadn't given the con artist any money, didn't have any to give, so what motive would he have to kill him?

Finally, I came back to my initial thought. There could be countless others who had motive to stab the con artist. Was it possible one or more of them could live on my island? Sure, but wasn't it a greater possibility that most of the others lived elsewhere? One thing I'd learned over the years was my wanting something to be true seldom made it so.

CHAPTER TWENTY-THREE

It was still warm with sunset less than an hour away, so I decided to walk a block to Center Street. Folly Beach was blessed with several restaurants featuring live music, with most of the music venues along Center Street. In addition to having several music venues, the island was blessed with several musicians who shared their talents with diners, drinkers, and because most entertainers were set up outside, with anyone passing by. One of my guilty pleasures was walking up the street listening to the music, stopping at locations where I either knew the entertainer or enjoyed the genre of music being played. I say guilty pleasure because whenever I look around the crowded streets or busy restaurants, I know many of the people must go to work the next day, and even those on vacation will have to return home to their work or school routines. I, on the other hand, have nowhere I need to be in the morning. Living at the beach is a continuous vacation.

The calendar indicated it was early spring, but the vacation season had expanded dramatically since I arrived a decade ago. I was far from the only person enjoying tonight's music. I'd listened to a bluegrass duo as I leaned against the wall separating the Washout's dining area from its parking lot, before crossing the street to head toward the beachfront Tides Hotel. I stopped at the Crab Shack's outdoor dining area to listen to Teresa Parrish, aka Sweet T, one of my favorite singers, when I heard my name. Ryan Sparks was seated at a small, bar height wooden table beside the hostess station at the sidewalk. He was wearing a gray and black Chicago White Sox T-shirt, black shorts, and red tennis shoes.

Ryan pointed his beer bottle at me, smiled, then said, "Care to join me?" He pointed the bottle at the bar stool on the other side of the table.

"Sure," I said then slid on the stool.

Sweet T was singing "Mom's Fifth Marriage," a song she'd written and swears it is true, Ryan tapped the bottle on the table in time with the music, as I looked around to see if a server was nearby. Kathy, a server who'd worked at the restaurant for several years, was quick to the table. "White wine," she said, proving I'd spent way too much time at the Crab Shack.

I nodded.

Ryan looked at the singer, then at me, before saying, "Did you know I wanted to be a picker and singer when I was in high school?"

I wondered how he thought I'd know that.

"What happened?"

"Never could learn how to play the guitar, besides, my

choir teacher said I had the voice of a bullfrog." He laughed, took a sip of beer, then said, "Kicked the hell out of my dream. The good news was that playing baseball didn't require playing guitar or singing."

Kathy set my drink on the table then asked if I wanted something to eat. I glanced at Ryan, at the pile of cracked peanut shells in front of him, then told Kathy to give us a few minutes.

"You hungry?"

"Umm, yeah, but umm, I'm a little short on cash."

"My treat."

"You don't have to do that."

"I know. Let's order something." I nodded toward Kathy who was watching us from the other side of the patio.

She returned with a smile and menus. I ordered a flounder crunch sandwich, fries, and coleslaw. Ryan went with the BBQ pork sandwich, and Sweet T went with the second verse of "Smile, Smile, Smile," another self-penned song.

The smell of fried fish permeated the air. A motorcycle sped past the restaurant disturbing the peaceful evening with a roar that'd make a 757's jet engine jealous. Ryan watched the sound-polluting bike pass, then said, "Come here often?"

"Not often."

"It seems like I've been on the road since graduating from college. Never got to settle anywhere longer than a few weeks. Playing ball, traveling from city to city, seeing new things, experiencing all parts of the country was great." He chuckled. "The long bus rides from city to city was the pits. That's one of the reasons I was looking forward to playing in the majors. Flying instead of bouncing over streets for hundreds of miles, had a nice ring to it." He laughed. "So did the big bucks I'd be earning."

"Sorry it ended the way it did."

He took a sip of beer, leaned back on the stool, then said, "Me too .... me too."

Neither of us spoke for a few minutes as we listened to Sweet T sing "Jolene."

Kathy arrived with our food and asked if we needed anything else. Ryan looked at me, then said, "Another beer."

He focused on his sandwich until saying, "Hear they arrested someone for breaking in the dead guy's condo. Know anything about it?"

"Not much. The guy arrested was Ron Honeycutt."

"That's what I heard. Also heard he killed Thurmond. I talked to him a time or two, you know."

No, I didn't. "Honeycutt?"

"Yeah. Met him one night over at that Irish restaurant, Saint something."

"St. James Gate," I said, imitating Charles penchant for accuracy.

"That's it. He was talking to, of all people, Walter Thurmond, you know, the dead guy. Thurmond had tried to get me to go in with him on one of his medical equipment companies. Of course, that was before he found out I was broke. Suppose he felt sorry for me and bought me a drink. I wasn't too proud to turn down the offer. That's when he introduced me to Honeycutt. That was the first thing I thought of when I heard Honeycutt was arrested for breaking in Thurmond's place. Doesn't surprise me he killed Thurmond."

"Why?"

"Nothing bad was said between the two, but I could tell

they'd been arguing before I showed up. You've heard the saying about shooting daggers with your eyes?"

I nodded.

"That's what Honeycutt was doing to Thurmond. Nothing said, but daggers were flying."

"Any idea why?"

"When I got there, they changed into their big-boy pants and pretended to be civilized, friendly." He took another draw from his beer, then said, "I don't blame Thurmond if he was mad at Honeycutt."

"Why?"

"I ran into Honeycutt the next morning across the street there." He pointed at the small, sandy parking lot on the other side of Center Street. "He put his arm around me like we'd been buds forever. Said something like he'd bet I'd like to invest some of my money in something that'd double my investment in a couple of years. Now, I'm no financial whiz, but know returns like that are as common as a polar bear over here. I tried to say no. He wasn't having any of it. He started to rile me enough that I had to get rude to get him to back off."

"Did he?"

"For a little while. The next morning, he caught me as I came ashore in my kayak down at the boat ramp. I was on my way to my sister's house to help Kevin with the remodel. He was walking that little ugly dog of his. He came on stronger than he did the night before. Let's just say, I'm not the least surprised he killed Thurmond. Not the least. That man's evil to the bone."

"Know anything that'd help the police with their investigation?"

"Not really."

I couldn't think of anything else to ask about Thurmond or Honeycutt, so I said, "How are Kevin and Megan coming with the remodeling?"

"Slow as molasses."

"That kind of project always takes longer than people think."

"They thought it would take a little longer, but nothing like this. Sis said a little longer was up three weeks ago. They're frustrated."

"You anchoring here overnight or taking your boat back to the Marina?"

He smiled. "Keeping it right where it is. Piloting a sailboat while under the influence isn't something I want to be charged with."

We stayed another hour, listened to music and watched the steady stream of people walk by the restaurant.

Ryan said, "This is something I could get used to."

I told him I knew what he meant.

CHAPTER TWENTY-FOUR

The next morning, I was interrupted by a call from Charles. "Got a question, you coming with us?"

I sighed and said, "I've got two questions. Who is us and where are you going?"

"Me and Virgil. He used to be a photographer back when he was rich and had an expensive camera. We're going to walk around taking pictures. He'll use my camera when he sees something he wants to shoot. Thought you'd want to tag along."

When I first moved to Folly, I'd spent hours walking the streets with Charles. He wanted me to teach him photography. While he learned a lot from our adventures, the most enjoyable part of our walks was talking about anything that came to mind. With Charles, that covered countless topics.

"Where do you want to meet?"

"How about in front of City Hall. We're a few minutes from there."

They were easy to spot. Virgil had on the long-sleeve, white dress shirt he wore on a regular basis, gray dress slacks, his resoled Guccis, and his ever-present sunglasses. Charles wore a long-sleeve, red and black T-shirt with Louisville Cardinals on the front, tan shorts that he wore on most every photo walking adventure, and his Tilley. The camera strap was over his shoulder, his cane tapping the sidewalk as they headed my direction.

Charles began with, "Was telling Virgil how we used to do this all the time; how you had the gallery where you sold your photos; how I was your executive sales manager. The good old days."

Virgil said, "Wish I had that good a friend when I had my camera. Que sera, sera."

"You've got us now," Charles said. "What could be better."

"Excellent point, my friend. Excellent point."

Enough bonding, I thought. "Are we headed to the beach?"

Charles put his right arm out like it was a turn signal. "Nah. Everyone takes photos at the ocean. Sand, sunshine, water, yellow beach umbrellas. Overdone. I think we'll head out West Cooper, shoot some of the neat stuff people put in their front yard. Pick up trash along the way."

West Cooper ran perpendicular to Center Street, so we headed away from the center of town through a residential area. Virgil looked at me, so I figured he was wondering why. I simply smiled.

Charles had a penchant for photographing discarded candy wrappers, plastic anything along the road, and cigarette butts. Why, you may ask? Short answer, no clue. Slightly longer answer, because he's Charles. On the bright side, he also picks up the photo subjects and deposits them in nearby trash containers.

A couple of blocks later, Charles found something he said he couldn't resist shooting. Most photographers would've managed to resist shooting a vehicle-flattened Milk Duds box.

"Charles," Virgil said as he watched my friend bending over to get the best angle on the fascinating subject. "You have a unique eye for seeing what others miss."

Charles thanked him like Virgil had awarded him a Pulitzer Prize for photography. I'd forgotten how little it took to make Charles happy.

A couple of blocks later, we reached the spot where West Cooper dead ends at a children's playground. Apparently, Charles ran out of trash to photograph so he took a few photos of three young children playing on a slide. Virgil borrowed Charles's camera to photograph the children from three different angles. I didn't photograph anything but enjoyed watching the fun the kids and my friends were having.

We turned left on Fifth Street West, then headed back toward town on West Ashley Avenue. Charles bent over to photograph a Skittles wrapper.

As he was framing the shot, Virgil said, "Chris, I've been thinking about you know what."

I assumed he was referring to the body. I nodded.

"I might be wrong, since I'm not as good a detective as you guys. I keep thinking there's something off about Ryan. I think he's the killer."

"What makes you think that?"

"Like I told you before, it's only a feeling. Each time I talk to him—"

"That's Dusty," Charles interrupted.

I heard a dog barking coming from a large, two-story, elevated house backing up to the ocean.

Virgil said, "Charles, what's Dusty?"

"Don't you hear him barking?"

Virgil stopped, tilted his head toward the house, then said, "Yeah, I hear a dog. Why do you think it's what again?"

Charles said, "Dusty, Ron Honeycutt's dog."

"You know Dusty's bark?"

I smiled. "Charles is a dog whisperer. If he says it's Dusty, put money on it."

Charles had turned into the drive before I finished telling Virgil about Charles's dog whispering skills.

I said, "Where are you going?"

"To visit my friend."

Virgil said, "Ron?"

"No, Dusty," Charles said like it was the most logical thing in the world.

Virgil pointed to a late-model, red Mercedes convertible in the drive. "Is that Ron's car?"

I said I didn't know, and Charles shook his head as he walked up the steps to the elevated front door.

Virgil stopped at the bottom of the stairs and said, "Is he really going to knock on the door to ask if he can see Dusty?"

I nodded. "You'll get used to it the more you're around him."

By now Dusty, or the dog Charles assumed was Dusty, must've known someone was nearby. The bark intensified; paws scratched at the door. Charles rang the doorbell which only drew more barks.

Instead of patiently waiting for someone to answer,

Charles, being Charles, turned the knob and inched the door open.

"Look fellas, it's open."

I said, "Don't you think you should wait until—"

He pushed the door open a few more inches and Dusty wiggled out, Charles knelt to pet his canine friend, and Dusty started licking Charles's face. Virgil and I remained at the bottom of the steps.

Charles lifted Dusty, pushed the door the rest of the way open. "Hey, Ron, it's Charles." There was no answer, so Charles repeated it louder.

I said, "Charles, no one's here. Why don't you put Dusty inside and let's go?"

Charles was mumbling something to Dusty that sounded like a cross between baby talk and Hungarian. He looked at Virgil and me at the bottom of the stairs. "Give me a minute. Gotta make sure he has water."

Before I could tell him how absurd that sounded, Charles was in the house with Dusty cradled in his arm.

Virgil looked at me, rolled his eyes, then said, "You've been friends how many years?"

I started to answer when Charles screamed, "Get in here!"

I had a hunch he wasn't distraught because Dusty was out of water. We were quick to the top of the stairs and through the front door. I heard Charles talking to Dusty in the back of the house. We followed the sound of his voice through a large family room to the kitchen. The view of the ocean and the beach out the expansive kitchen windows was fantastic. The view didn't hold my attention nearly as much as did Ron Honeycutt's body lying in a puddle of dried blood on the polished tile floor. Unlike Walter Thurmond, a knife was stuck in Honeycutt's chest.

CHAPTER TWENTY-FIVE

Before I could tell him not to touch anything, Virgil yanked open the French door leading to the deck and leaned over the railing as he lost his breakfast. Charles leaned on the granite counter, put his hand over Dusty's eyes, then shook his head. I stepped out the front door to see the address, dialed 911, and told the dispatcher where we were, what we'd found, then returned to the kitchen. Virgil was still on the deck staring at the ocean. Charles delicately tiptoed out of the room avoiding the puddle of blood and Dusty's bloody footprints.

I told Virgil we'd be in the family room waiting for the first responders. He didn't say anything but acknowledged hearing with a sharp nod.

The sound of sirens began heading our way from the center of town. One of Folly's fire engines arrived first. Most of the beach's firefighters doubled as EMTs and two of them were out and heading up the stairs as soon as the truck stopped. I met them at the door but didn't slow them down by telling them their medical skills weren't needed. I pointed toward the kitchen as Virgil joined us in the family room.

Officer Trula Bishop arrived next. Her patrol car skidded to a halt behind the fire engine in the oversized crushed shell drive. I'd known Bishop since she joined the force five years ago.

"Mr. Chris, don't tell me you found yourself another dead body."

"Afraid so, Trula."

She saw Charles and Virgil sitting in the family room. "Ah, Mr. Virgil, we meet again. You know you're hanging around bad influences."

She didn't wait for a response, said for us to stay put, then headed in the kitchen. Another officer I didn't know barged in the front door, hand on his holstered handgun's grip, as he looked around like he'd find an armed killer waiting to ambush him. I pointed to the kitchen. He took the hint and headed that way.

One of the EMTs walked past us while talking on his handheld radio telling someone to cancel the ambulance, to call the coroner instead. Trula was next to exit the kitchen. She took a chair opposite the three of us.

"Okay, guys, spill it."

Virgil and Charles looked at me, designating me as the spokesperson. I shared what brought us to the house. Charles interrupted to tell her that Dusty had invited us in. She knew Charles enough not to challenge his statement. She asked if we'd touched anything. I said only the front door and French doors out of the kitchen. She jotted everything I said in a notebook she pulled out of her back pocket. She asked if this was the first time any of us had been in the house. We each said yes.

The front door swung open. Chief LaMond stepped in, saw us on the couch, rolled her eyes, then said, "Officer Bishop, what have they stumbled on now?"

Trula gave a police-speak summary of the events before Cindy headed to the kitchen. A moment later, she stuck her head back in the living room. "Officer Bishop, call Detective Adair at the Sheriff's Office and suggest he may want to tool on over."

After another ten minutes, Dusty began whimpering so Charles told Bishop his canine friend needed to go outside, had things to do. Bishop told Charles to take him out, but not to go far. A few more minutes later, Cindy returned to the living room, as did Charles and Dusty.

"Fellas, I know you've already told Officer Bishop what happened, but go over it again."

We repeated our story, but Virgil surprised me when he said, "The knife in his chest is a seven-inch Wusthof Classic filet knife."

Cindy glared at him. "What in the hell is a Wusthof? Oh yeah, how do you know?"

"Had a set like it back when I was rich. It cost over two-thousand bucks. My ex said it was *butter upon bacon* when I bought it."

Cindy said, "Huh?"

"Victorian slang for an extravagance."

The chief glanced at me, rolled her eyes, then said, "Did you pull it out of his chest, measure the blade, then stick it back in?"

Virgil said, "Nope. The seven-inch filet knife is missing

from the set on the counter. Just guessing it's the one stuck in him."

Bishop wrote it all down while Cindy stared at him.

The officer I didn't know came in the living room. "Chief, anything you need me to do?"

"Drape crime-scene tape around the perimeter of the yard. Keep the riffraff out." Under her breath, she said, "Too late to keep all of it out."

He gave his boss an awkward salute, then headed out the front door.

I said, "Who's he?"

"Damian. Recent hire."

Trula said, "We call him Barney Fife behind his back."

The Chief glared at her then turned to the riffraff who'd managed to get in. "Don't suppose you know who killed him?"

"No," I said. Neither Charles nor Virgil offered a guess. "From what you said about his checkered past, there are probably several possible suspects."

"Seems to me," Virgil offered, "it had something to do with Thurmond's death. Both stabbed, some said they were in cahoots. Now don't get me wrong Chief, that's only a thought. You're the pro."

"Chief," Charles said as he rubbed Dusty's back, "Ron must've known whoever did it pretty well. It wouldn't be easy sticking a knife in someone's chest unless the person felt comfortable being near the stabber. I didn't see any defensive cuts on Ron's hands. I'd venture to guess it was because of something the two were arguing about. The killer didn't come prepared to kill Ron, since he had to borrow the murder weapon from Ron's collection."

To my surprise, Cindy said, "You're probably right."

It may not have been the first time the Chief thought Charles was right, but I'd venture it was the first time she'd told him so.

Detective Adair walked through the front door like he owned the house. He had on a navy blazer, a starched white dress shirt, gray slacks with a sharp crease, and polished black shoes. He was still in his thirties and looked more like he was going to a board of directors meeting rather than a crime scene. His eyes quickly moved from Cindy to the three of us on the couch.

"Please don't tell me you all are involved in this."

Cindy said, "They won't, but I will. They found the body."

"Good morning, Detective," Virgil said. "I'm getting a phobia about knives."

Cindy nodded to the kitchen. "Stabbing victim."

"Don't leave," he said in our direction.

Cindy watched the detective enter the kitchen. "His job just got harder. He's going to have one whale of a time getting Honeycutt to confess to killing Thurmond."

I'm sure her comment was intended to be humorous, but laughter was the last reaction that came to mind.

Charles said, "What's going to happen to Dusty?"

"I'll have our animal control officer pick him up. She may know someone who'd want to adopt him. If not, she'll notify Pet Helpers. They'll find someone. Why don't you take him?"

Charles rubbed Dusty's head. "I'd love to, but my apartment's not big enough for me to live in. It'd be unfair to stick Dusty in it."

Detective Adair returned, took the remaining chair, looked at the three of us, then said, "Okay, let's hear it. From the beginning."

Charles leaned forward on the couch. "I met Virgil this morning, he wanted to walk around with me to—"

Adair interrupted, "From your arrival here."

That cut about an hour from Charles's description of the day. After he finished, Adair asked if Virgil or I had anything to add. Virgil added his trivia about the cost of the knife set. I remained silent.

"Any idea who might've done this?"

We said no. Adair got our contact information then let us go. Cindy had to promise that she'd call animal control about Dusty before Charles agreed to leave.

I was beginning to share Virgil's phobia about knives.

CHAPTER TWENTY-SIX

I was afraid Virgil wasn't going to make the short, two-block walk to Center Street, much less to his apartment several more blocks away. He was having trouble catching his breath; he stopped twice, bent over to put his hands on his knees. I asked if he was okay but only receiving a tentative yes. I knew better. I suggested we stop at Loggerhead's, located a block before Center Street. He quickly agreed. His walk up the handicap ramp to the elevated deck couldn't have been slower if he'd been carrying a refrigerator. Charles helped him the last few steps and to the closest empty table.

A server approached, gave a caring look at Virgil who was slumped in the chair, then asked what we wanted to drink. I said water to start and she headed to the bar.

Charles glanced at me then turned to Virgil, "You okay?"

The temperature was only in the low seventies, but Virgil wiped sweat off his forehead, then in a near whisper, said,

"Guys, I've been fortunate my entire life, oh yeah, except for losing a fortune, having a wife dump me, and, I almost forgot, that car running me down a while back. But, all in all, I'm fortunate." He hesitated, looked across the street where he could see a sliver of the ocean under the four-story Oceanfront Villas condo complex, turned to me, then to Charles. "What in hell did I do to deserve running into two dead guys in a week?" He shook his head. "Not only dead but stabbed. I wasn't kidding back there when I said I was getting a phobia about knives."

The server, who said her name was Kelly, returned with our water and asked if we needed anything else. I told her to give us a few minutes.

She left, Virgil took two large gulps of water, before saying, "Guys, I'm waiting for the answer. What'd I do to deserve this?"

Charles said, "Nobody deserves finding two bodies. It just happened. Finding Honeycutt was my fault. I'm the one who insisted on seeing if Dusty had water. You didn't do anything except follow me into the house."

Virgil took a smaller gulp, wiped his brow once more, then said, "Perhaps I didn't ask my question the best way. How about this? What are the odds of me finding both dead guys, both killed the same way, and me being a simple guy hanging out on Folly, minding my own business, which ain't much, I might add?"

I didn't think that would be any easier to answer than the first way.

I said, "it could've been any of us. It's horrible, traumatic, but it was only bad luck. You were—"

Charles interrupted, "Really, really, bad luck."

I continued, "You were in the wrong place at the wrong time. Charles is right, he's the one who led us into the house."

Virgil smiled, the first time since we arrived at Honeycutt's house. "So far that doesn't make me feel better. Anyway, good try, my friends. Know what might help?"

Charles said, "What?"

"A cold brewski, except like I mentioned in the middle of telling you how fortunate a life I've led, I lost my fortune. My pockets are void of cash. Could I impose on one of you to foot the cost of my drink?"

"I've got it," Charles said. "Order anything you want."

I nearly fell off the chair at Charles's offer. If I didn't think it'd confuse Virgil more than he already was, I'd pull out my phone and video the historic moment.

Virgil smiled and waved Kelly to the table. He ordered a Budweiser. Charles did the same, while I settled for a soft drink.

Only a handful of others were seated outside, about right for early in the week. We were shaded by an umbrella and a cool breeze kept us comfortable. Under normal circumstances, this would be the perfect environment to bask in the charm of the small barrier island. No one would consider today's circumstances normal, although Virgil was breathing normally and his forehead no longer oozed perspiration. Our drinks arrived and Kelly asked if we were ready to order lunch. This time, Virgil asked her to give us a few more minutes.

"So, who killed him?" Charles said after taking a sip of beer.

His question wasn't a good way to calm Virgil.

Virgil looked up from his beer. "You mean who killed them?"

"Yeah, them," Charles said.

I said, "We're not certain the same person killed both."

"Of course we are," Charles said after taking a draw on his drink. "We know the guys knew each other, were probably in cahoots conning people out of their money, and I almost forgot, each was stabbed."

"I'm not saying the same person didn't, all I mean is we don't know for certain." I turned to Virgil. "Sure you want to have this discussion now?"

Virgil said, "Think we could order. My stomach's doing somersaults. Food may help."

That answered my question. Charles waved Kelly back. Charles and Virgil ordered hamburgers, I went with the chicken Caesar wrap, an attempt to eat healthier. Virgil requested a refill on his water.

After Kelly left, Charles said, "Of course Virgil wants to have this discussion, don't you?"

Charles was often last to take a hint.

"No," Virgil said and looked down at his drink.

Charles said, "Why don't—"

"Yes," Virgil interrupted.

"Yes, what?" Charles said.

"I don't know. No, I don't want to talk about it. But yes I do. I'm confused. I didn't know either man more than to say hi. There's no reason to be involved. Sure, I know I said we should figure out who killed Thurmond. That was back when he was the only dead guy." He turned to me and smiled. "Chris, I told you I changed my mind and wanted nothing to do with it. Remember?"

I nodded.

"Then wishy-washy me bounced back into rah-rah let's catch a bad guy mode."

"I remember."

Charles said, "What's your point?"

"I don't know."

Charles said, "You don't know what your point is, or you don't know if you want to get involved?"

Virgil leaned forward in his chair. "You got me there. I don't even know what your question means. "What I meant to say or think I meant to say was it's the cops' job catching whoever killed them. After Thurmond was murdered, I felt an obligation, I guess obligation is the right word, to see if I could do something to help them. That's what I told Chris. I didn't know what I could do, just knew I had to do something."

Kelly arrived with our food, interrupting Virgil's sort of explanation. He took a bite of burger, leaned back in his chair, then looked either at the sky or the overhead umbrella. "You guys remember where I was in my story, my mini-saga?"

"You told Chris you had to do something."

"Right, then changed my mind. Why in the world does a, umm, retired stock market analyst think he can do what the police can't?" Virgil smiled. "I feel like I'm playing Ping-Pong with myself." The smile faded. "Then before you went to fetch Dusty, I flipped again. Wanted to catch the bad guy."

"So, after I saved poor Dusty from dying from dehydration, you reflipped. Two dead was more than you could handle, but if I remember right, after that you said yes. That mean you want to talk about it? Want to see if we can help the cops?"

Virgil sighed. "Yes." He held up his hand for us to remain silent. "Let me ask something. Aren't you scared? I'm petrified. How can I know anything about catching a killer?"

I patted his arm. "Every time I've gotten myself in anything law enforcement related, I've been afraid. I don't know anything more than you do about figuring out who killed someone."

Charles jumped in. "Yeah, and Chris is a retired executive. What's he know more than you know? And, look at me, holy moly, I never worked long enough to be retired from anything. I'm shaking in my boots every time I stick my nose where it don't belong. My friend, I don't even have boots."

"Virgil, is there danger in us butting in?" I asked. "Sure. We've found that out a few times. But we're not running around accusing anyone of murder. All we're doing is asking a few questions; more importantly, we're keeping our eyes and ears open. What trouble can we get in doing that?"

Would I come to regret that statement?

CHAPTER TWENTY-SEVEN

I remained on Loggerhead's deck after Virgil left saying he'd better get home while his legs weren't shaking. Charles didn't mention shaky legs but said he had to get to the surf shop and deliver a package for Dude. Making local deliveries for Dude was one of the few, very few, ways Charles picked up cash to live on.

My legs weren't shaking, but I was more traumatized than I let on to Charles or Virgil. It wasn't every day that I came across a body with a knife in his chest, be it a seven-inch Wusthof Classic or otherwise. I wondered how long it would've been before someone discovered the body if Charles hadn't heard Dusty. From what I'd heard, Honeycutt lived alone. He didn't have a regular office so coworkers wouldn't have wondered why he missed work enough to call the police to make a wellness check.

To block the trauma of our discovery out of my mind, at least momentarily, I decided to call Preacher Burl to let him know about the death. After all, he'd told me about the connection between Honeycutt and Thurmond. There were a few more people on the patio than when I arrived, but it was quiet enough to call from the table.

Burl answered with, "Brother Chris, how may I help you?"

I resisted offering a smart-aleck response. "Is this a good time to call?"

He offered it was.

"Charles, Virgil Debonnet, and I left Ron Honeycutt's house a little while ago. I wanted to let to know we found his body."

"Oh, my Lord. Heart attack?"

"Afraid not, he'd been stabbed."

There was silence on Burl's end.

"Preacher, are you there?"

"Sorry, I was sitting down. Stabbed like poor Brother Walter?"

"Yes," I said rather than differentiating between being stabbed in the back or the chest.

"Are you okay? That had to be horrific to discover."

I told him I was, but Virgil was taking it hard.

"Do you, or do the police have any idea who may've ended Brother Ron's life?"

"Not yet."

"Do you think his death may've been prevented it I'd gone to the police as soon as Brother Ron told me about the connection between him and Brother Walter?"

"I doubt it, but don't suppose we'll ever know."

"He never mentioned any family to me, so I don't know who the next of kin may be. I'd offer spiritual assistance and support if I knew who to talk to."

"That's kind of you. I don't know of anyone either."

There was another silence, then Burl said, "After we spoke the other day about Brother Ron, I remembered a comment he made. In fact, I was going to tell you about it, but it slipped my mind until now."

"What was it?"

"Now don't get me wrong, Brother Ron didn't tell me that he was responsible for stealing the computer from Brother Walter. He said something like even if the police found the computer, there wouldn't be anything on it to implicate him in wrongdoings. At the time, I thought he meant he hadn't done anything wrong so there couldn't be anything on the computer that would indicate otherwise."

"You think he meant something different now?"

"Perhaps. It's possible he was saying there was something on the laptop that could implicate him, he stole it, then erased whatever it was. Don't take it as gospel, that's the thinking of this old preacher man, nothing more."

"That's an interesting thought."

"Did the police find the laptop?"

"I don't know. They kicked us out of the house as soon we gave our statements. I'm certain the police will do a thorough search now that he's dead."

"I feel terrible. If I'd only gone to the police as soon as I learned the men, the two deceased men knew each other, perhaps Brother Ron would still be alive."

"You have no way of knowing. Don't kick yourself for something that probably would've happened anyway. Tell you what, why don't I let Chief LaMond know what Honeycutt said about the computer. That may encourage them to search for it more than they might otherwise. Would that help?"

"It won't bring him back."

I agreed but told him it may bring them closer to finding who killed him.

Cindy would still be at the crime scene, so it wouldn't have been wise to call her. That could wait until later. I ordered another drink, set back in the chair, and listened to the singer who'd begun his set. A distraction was what I needed. Hopefully, the music will provide one.

———

Three hours later, I figured the Chief would've left the crime scene, so it'd be safer to call. I'd been home for two hours and debated calling every fifteen minutes yet put it off.

"Are you okay?" Cindy said instead of hello.

"As far as I know, why?"

"You put on a good front most of the time, but I know how sensitive you are, how much things like today bother you."

Occasionally, Cindy's perceptive, sensitive side sneaks through. She doesn't share it with many, so I was touched.

"Finding Honeycutt like that was traumatizing. I tried to hold it together to help Virgil. I've never seen him so shaken. I'm better now."

"Good, so why are you pestering me?"

That was more like the Cindy I'd become accustomed to.

"Did you or the Sheriff's Office find Thurmond's laptop at Honeycutt's house?"

"No. We also didn't find the Hope Diamond, the bones of a dinosaur, Jimmy Hoffa, or your buddy Dude's missing words. Why?"

I shared my conversation with Preacher Burl.

"Did the Preacher think Honeycutt meant he had the computer?"

"He didn't know, but thought it was a possibility, especially after hearing of Honeycutt's death."

"The Sheriff's Office guys searched it when they arrested him for the theft, but I don't know how thorough they were. I think the crime scene guys did a thorough search of the house after I left today, but I'll double check. I know they didn't find a laptop."

"Any leads on who might've stabbed him?"

"No."

"Think it was the same person who killed Thurmond?"

"Duh, don't you think both being stabbed would've given that away?"

"If that's true, then speculation that Honeycutt killed Thurmond is untrue."

"Wow. I thought it would've taken a highly trained detective to figure that out, not an old whatever you are."

"Other than insults, you have anything to add?"

"Yeah. I'm hungry, tired, my back aches, and now I have two murders on my island. Think that's enough for today, don't you?"

"Yes."

I would've told her to go home, have Larry rub her aching back, and put her feet up. I would've if she hadn't already ended the call.

CHAPTER TWENTY-EIGHT

The next morning, I awoke thinking about the murders. In addition to questioning my sanity for having those gruesome thoughts, I had more questions than answers. Cindy was convinced the same person killed both men, yet until Honeycutt's body was found, she and Detective Adair felt Honeycutt was responsible for Thurmond's demise. He had broken into Thurmond's condo the day of his murder. According to people who'd talked to Honeycutt, he'd hinted he was in a business relationship with Thurmond. Ryan had witnessed an argument between the men a few days before Thurmond's body was discovered. Speculation is easy; proof is elusive.

Without Thurmond's laptop, there didn't appear to be direct evidence connecting the two. If Thurmond had partnerships with Honeycutt, Ben Likard, or anyone else for that matter, shouldn't there be records, partnership agreements, licenses, or other legal documents cementing the relation-

ships? I'd been confused by the simple legal documents I had
to file when I was sole owner of Landrum Gallery, so I was in
no position to dig into what would most certainly be complex
legal work required to own a manufacturing company. I relied
on Sean Aker to handle my business paperwork, so if anyone
could find answers, it'd be my attorney.

My call to his office was answered by Marlene who
informed me I was in luck. Sean had just arrived and hadn't
been in the office long enough to take his morning nap. If I
hurried, she could keep him awake long enough to meet
with me.

I did, she did, and Sean met me at the door with a wide
smile.

"I hope you have billable work for me. Marlene is
hankering for a raise, but unless more people get in legal trouble, she's out of luck."

I said, "Legal work, yes, but hopefully nothing you charge
me for."

He sighed then motioned me in his office.

Marlene sighed and the Shih Tzu sitting on her lap made a
whimpering sound. She rubbed under its chin while
mumbling something about no more premium dog food.

"So, what can I do for you that's not going to make me any
money?" Sean asked as I settled in the chair in front of his
desk.

"Have you heard that Ron Honeycutt was found dead
yesterday morning?"

"Did you forget Marlene is sitting out there? She's my
newspaper, radio station, and TV news reporter."

"She tell you that Virgil Debonnet, Charles, and I are the
ones who found him?"

"Why am I not surprised?"

I assumed that meant he hadn't heard. I shared how we were drawn to Honeycutt's house by his barking dog, then what we found after entering.

"She also told me a couple of days ago Honeycutt had been arrested for stealing a laptop from Thurmond's condo. Since he didn't have the wisdom to hire me to defend him, I hadn't paid much attention. Marlene said the police thought he was Thurmond's killer."

"Yes, but that theory flew out the window yesterday."

"If the police arrest you for killing the men, will you hire me to take your case?"

"Yes, Mr. Marketer, but that's not why I'm here."

"Seriously, Chris, that had to be horrific. Are you okay?"

"Not all the way, but better than yesterday."

"What about the Charles and Virgil?"

"Charles was shaken but will be fine. He has a way of bouncing back from most difficult situations."

"True. I've noticed that. I don't know Virgil that well. How'd he take it?"

"Harder than Charles and me. He puts on a good front, but he was visibly traumatized by the discovery. You know he also found Thurmond's body?"

"That's what Marlene said. I can't imagine how finding both would affect someone. I know I'd lose it. Are you going to check on him to make sure he's okay?"

"Yes."

"Good. Let me know if there's anything I can do to help."

"That's why I'm here. As I'm sure Marlene has told you, Thurmond was allegedly conning people into going in business with him in companies importing or manufacturing equipment for the aging population."

"For people like you?"

"Rub it in, youngster."

He smiled. "Simply clarifying. Go on."

"I'd heard Ron Honeycutt was one of those people. Also, another local resident, Ben Likard, told me he was in partnership with Thurmond. He'd tried to get some of his profits out of the company. Thurmond refused."

"Next time you talk to Likard, tell him you know a good lawyer he can call when he gets arrested for killing Thurmond."

I assured him I would.

He looked at his watch. "Are we about to the reason for your visit?"

"You have another appointment?"

"Nap time."

"Sean, could you check business records to see if there actually were partnership agreements with Likard or anyone else?"

"In South Carolina, most business records are collected through the Secretary of State's office. I assume that's true in other states, but I don't know for sure. Where were these businesses located?"

"I know he had one in Rhode Island but sold it a while back. That's all I know about."

"I can do computer searches, but without more to go on, the odds of me finding anything useful are slim."

"That'd be a good start."

"Now I've got a question. Don't the police know about these alleged business dealings? They have resources that'd dwarf Marlene, her dog, and me. Doesn't it make sense they already have people digging through business records to see who may've given money to Thurmond; people who would've had good reason to stick a knife in his back?"

"Sean, that's three questions."

"Poor misguided Chris, I'm an attorney. I learned in law school why ask one question when three will do? After all, we charge by the hour."

"Yes, yes, yes." I said answering his questions and reducing his billable hours.

"Then why are you here bumming free legal work to find out something the police will get answers to much quicker than I can?"

"Two reasons. First, I don't know how high a priority the police will place on exploring these records. Second, even if they do, why would they share what they find with me? Chief LaMond might let me know what she learns, but the Sheriff's Office won't. The murder, umm, murders investigations are in their court."

"Other than this Likard guy and the late Ron Honeycutt, do you know anyone else who may've fallen prey to Thurmond's con?"

"No, but if I hear of anyone, I'll let you know."

"One more question," Sean said, "why are you sticking your nose in what's clearly police business?"

"Curiosity, that's all."

"You know I don't believe you."

I smiled. "Yep."

"Do me one favor, will you?"

"If it's easy."

"Please be careful. The sentence for killing three people is the same as for bumping off two."

"I'll be careful."

"You also might want to stay clear of knives."

I left Sean on that bit of advice.

CHAPTER TWENTY-NINE

On the way down the stairs from Sean's second-floor office, I remembered what Virgil told me about Ryan being irritated with Thurmond. Instead of turning toward home, I went the other direction to the parking lot at the boat ramp to see if Ryan's sailboat was nearby. It was, plus his kayak was tied to the support post so he must be in town. Most likely he'd be at his sister's house, but in the unlikely event he wasn't, I walked past a few Center Street restaurants to see if he was there. Using a term Ryan was familiar with, I struck out at The Washout, Woody's Pizza, and Planet Follywood before spotting him at the Crab Shack inched up to the small outdoor bar beside the entry.

"Perfect timing, Chris," Ryan said along with a wide smile.

"It is?"

"Absolutely, I don't like drinking by myself. They say it's a sign of alcoholism. You've saved me from that debilitating disease."

I took a seat beside Ryan, returned his smile, and said, "Glad I saved you."

He chuckled. "Know what I like most about Folly?"

"What?"

"Wherever I go there're friendly locals to talk to. Every restaurant where I park my butt there's someone who starts a conversation. When I was on the road playing ball, I never got to call one place home. I haven't been here long, but consider it home, my place to put down roots." He smiled. "Roots aren't easy to put down when you live on a boat."

"There's no shortage of friendly people here."

A grackle squawked at us from its perch on the top of the building. It was agreeing with me or begging for food.

Ryan ignored the bird. "Don't get me wrong, I'm no Pollyanna. You have your share of jackasses, people who irritate the hell out of me, but they're few and far between. Overall, this is where I want to be. Know what I mean?"

What better lead in to ask about his relationship with Thurmond. "I think so, but elaborate?"

"Let me run inside and get another beer, get something for you. What wets your whistle?"

Someone wanting to buy me a drink wasn't something I was accustomed to hearing. I told him white wine would whet it. I was also surprised he offer to buy me a drink since the last time I was here talking with him, he didn't have any cash. I bought his food. The grackle continued to squawk as I wondered if Ryan had heard about Honeycutt's death. Should I bring it up or see if he mentions it?

My new friend returned, set wine in front of me, then took a long draw on his beer before saying, "What were we talking about?"

"You were saying that you were surprised by how many people talked to you, but that there were some who irritated you. You were going to tell me about some of them." Not exactly where the conversation was headed, but perhaps I could nudge him along.

"Speaking of irritating people, did you hear Ron Honeycutt was killed? Guess it was yesterday."

This wasn't the time to tell him who found the body.

"Yes. How'd you hear?"

"Megan. I was at their place helping clean up after the plumbers left. Those guys may know everything about pipes, water, and crap, pun intended, but they know as much about cleaning their mess as I know about biophysics, which is nothing. Anyway, sis had gone to Bert's to get, hell, I don't remember what, besides, it doesn't matter. She got back and told me someone in the store was talking about Honeycutt's encounter with a knife."

"Strange, isn't it?" I said, then took a sip of my drink. "Didn't you say you knew both Walter Thurmond and Ron Honeycutt? Now they're dead, both stabbed to death."

He took a slow sip of beer as he glanced at me over his beer bottle. "If I didn't know better, I'd think you're accusing me of killing them."

"Sorry," I said then smiled, hoping it was contagious. "That's not what I meant. I thought it was quite a coincidence. Don't you?"

"Suppose so although I'd bet a lot of people here knew both guys. They were business partners, or that's how the story goes. Thurmond must've talked to everyone he came across who he thought had money to try to get them to buy into one of his businesses. Hell, I came close, you know."

"I heard they were in business together but didn't know anything more than that. What'd you hear?"

"Not much more. I already told you I heard them arguing. Figured it had something to do with business. That's about all."

"You also mentioned you didn't like Honeycutt, something about the way he kept pushing to get you to invest with him."

"Yeah. At least Thurmond's business plan made sense. There's one huge market for health equipment for seniors. A market that's already big and growing exponentially. That's why it appealed to me."

He's mentioned it twice since we've been sitting here. How do I ask where he planned to get the money to buy in with Thurmond?

"You say you almost bought in one of Thurmond's companies."

He slowly shook his head. "It would've taken borrowing money from Megan and Kevin. I saw how much they were sinking in the house, so as much as I wanted to, I couldn't muster the courage to ask. After what happened to Thurmond, I thank my lucky stars I didn't. Don't know what would've happened to the money now that he's dead."

"Good point."

Ryan looked at a couple walking past on the sidewalk, then turned to me. "Thurmond and Honeycutt, two of a kind." He nodded twice then continued, "The more I've thought about it, the more I realize they were a lot alike."

"In what way?"

"I'm thinking they were con men. Don't know if they were in a con together, but from the way they acted, what they said, I saw similarities. Let me ask you, do you know anyone who bought in one of Thurmond's companies and made money?"

"No."

"Bet the same's true for Honeycutt."

"Could be, but I don't know anyone who did business with him."

"It wouldn't take a big lead off first base for me to think someone would want both of those men dead." He smiled. "Hell, no lead necessary, they're both dead."

"True."

"Let me ask something. You claim you don't, but enough people have told me you help the police solve crimes. They claim you're a detective."

"Ryan, I'm not—"

He waved his near empty beer bottle in my face. "Haven't asked my question yet."

I motioned for him to continue.

"Who killed them?"

One of the prime suspects was sitting in front of me, but now wasn't time to share that tidbit.

"Ryan, if I knew the answer, I'd have already told the police. I know the lead detective on the case. He's good. It's a matter of time before he makes an arrest."

"Think the same person killed both guys?"

Did he miss the me not knowing part?

"Your guess is as good as mine."

"I'd go with yes."

"You're probably right."

"Know something else?"

I shrugged.

"It ain't me."

I nodded but didn't tell him I agreed. I didn't have bad feelings about Ryan, but Virgil did, so I didn't want to discount the possibility that Ryan was guilty. My reluctance to point a finger at him came down to motive. What would Ryan have gained? Sure, his boat was anchored near where Thurmond's body was found, but the police believe there's a good chance the con artist was killed upstream and the jon boat floated to its destination near Ryan's sailboat. If Ryan had invested in one of Thurmond's companies and learned he was conned out of the investment, he would've had a motive, but nothing indicated he gave Thurmond anything. Yes, he didn't like Honeycutt, but there wasn't anything to indicate he gave him anything either. If Ryan had a strong motive, I couldn't see what it was.

CHAPTER THIRTY

Cindy LaMond called the next morning with a question. She asked what time I was going to meet her for breakfast, subtext, buying her breakfast.

I thought about asking why I wanted to buy her breakfast but knew there was a good reason for the invitation, one she wouldn't share over the phone.

"How about now?"

"Then you're late. I'm sitting at a table on the Dog's patio."

Some comments don't deserve a response. "See you in ten minutes."

Good to her word, Cindy was munching on a slice of bacon on the restaurant's front patio. She smiled, pointed to her plate, and said, "Thanks for breakfast."

I thanked her for the opportunity as an attentive server arrived and took my order for coffee and French toast.

Cindy watched the server go, then said, "How's Virgil?"

"Fine, I guess. Why?"

"Could be because when you were at Honeycutt's he barfed over the back railing. Then, when you were leaving, I didn't think he was going to make it down the steps, much less to his apartment."

"It shook him, but by the time he left us, he felt better."

"How are you doing?"

"I've had much better days. I'm okay now."

Cindy slowly shook her head. "You sure?"

"Yes. Thanks for asking."

"No need to thank me. If you kicked the bucket, who'd be stupid enough to buy me breakfast?"

Speaking of breakfast, the server arrived with my order and a refill on Cindy's coffee.

I watched her take a sip and said, "Any update on the murder?"

"That's why I called. After you told me what Preacher Burl said about Honeycutt saying nobody would find anything about him on Thurmond's laptop, I checked with Detective Adair to see how thorough a search his guys made at Honeycutt's house." She looked at my breakfast. "He waffled some before confessing they did a routine search but didn't dig deep into anything that wasn't related to Honeycutt's knifing. I reminded him Honeycutt had stolen the laptop from Thurmond so there was a chance it was at Honeycutt's house. He then reminded me they'd searched his house when he was arrested. I repeated that it could still be there."

"What'd he say?"

"He tried to hide it, but he was perturbed that this lowly city cop was suggesting how he should do his job. He left it at that, until I got a call from him last night." She took a bite of eggs, sat back in the chair, and looked at the cloudy sky.

"Are you waiting for me to beg you to tell me why he called?"

She grinned. "Yes."

"Consider yourself begged."

"Better. After a return visit, guess what his crack crime scene techs didn't find in the house?"

"The laptop."

"Excellent guess."

"There's more or I wouldn't be buying your breakfast."

"Another excellent guess."

"And?"

"Guess what the same crime scene techs found in the spare tire well of Honeycutt's red Mercedes convertible?"

"The laptop."

"Holy horseradish, Chris, you should go on one of those TV quiz shows."

"Is there more, or do I have to beg again?"

"There's more but it's not worth begging for. Adair said the laptop looked like a herd of elephants had run over it. His techs, not the crime scene crew, but the IT tech gurus said they couldn't pull anything from it. It's a worthless hunk of whatever laptops are made of. Sorry."

"They learn anything else?"

"They learned that this paperless society is going to be the bane of law enforcement. They didn't find a single sheet of paper, other than on a roll by the toilet, a few crumpled up real estate fact sheets, and a six-month old automotive magazine in the house or car that would hint at any wrongdoings or business relationship between the dead guys. There wasn't anything at Thurmond's condo either."

"Couldn't the killer have taken evidence from the house and condo?"

"Sure, but normally someone would've left something: unopened junk mail, utility bills, scraps of paper that would've had nothing to do with whatever reason the men were killed. Adair believes, and I tend to agree, that both men did all their work, legal and illegal, in bits and bytes, which made an excellent reason the laptop was stolen from Thurmond's condo."

"If I'd taken the laptop, demolished it beyond the chance of retrieving anything off it, I would've thrown it in the ocean or put it in a trash container far from my house. Why would Honeycutt have hidden the worthless piece of electronics in his trunk?"

"Good question, why don't you ask him?" She snapped her fingers. "Whoops, not possible without the help of a medium. I don't know."

"Still think Honeycutt killed Thurmond?"

"I did until you found Honeycutt in the kitchen. That sort of stabbed my theory."

"Suspects?"

"Two weak ones: Ben Likard and Ryan Sparks. Both have the same alibi for the time of death of both men. They claim they were asleep, but not with each other."

"I understand why Likard is on the list since he lost money to Thurmond, but do you really think Ryan is a suspect?"

"No great reasons, but yes, I do." She held up her forefinger. "First, he's already told us he didn't like either man." She added a second finger. "Next, he first said he hadn't heard or seen anything near the time Thurmond was killed, then lo and behold, he claims to have heard two people talking near where the body was found."

"Cindy, I—"

"Hang on, I have one finger to go." She then held up a third finger. "Finally, his boat was what, a hundred feet from where Virgil discovered the jon boat." She motioned for me to speak.

"Not liking either man isn't a reason to kill them. I know several people I don't like, yet it wouldn't enter my mind to do them in."

"You're not Ryan."

"True, now about Ryan first saying he didn't hear or see anything then remembering he heard voices. I can see that happening without indicating anything bad. He had to be traumatized learning the body was found that close to his sailboat."

"I agree, yet I can also see him conveniently remembering hearing voices to deflect suspicion away from himself, a variation on *the other dude did it* defense, the other voice did it."

Again, I couldn't argue with her logic. "How about him being close to where the jon boat was found, so was Virgil, yet he's not a suspect. I thought Thurmond was killed somewhere upstream then the boat floated down river to where Virgil found it."

"That could be the case. It makes as much sense believing the boat was tied to Ryan's sailboat where he was killed, and the boat set adrift taking it to where it got stuck."

"But the jon boat came from a house way out Ashley Avenue and Ryan doesn't have a way of getting there to steal it."

Cindy shrugged. "Then, there's that."

"You don't know if any of these theories are true, do you?"

"All I know for certain is I got a free breakfast." She pointed at her plate. "That doesn't solve the crime but filled my stomach."

"Is there anything to tie Thurmond and Honeycutt together?"

"Speculation they were in cahoots with whatever scheme Thurmond was running on unsuspecting suckers he conned into going into partnership with him on nonexistent businesses. No paper trail or computer trail to prove it. I did learn one thing about Honeycutt that's interesting, although it doesn't help find his killer."

"What?"

She held her empty red mug up. Instead of waiting for the server to appear, I took the subtle hint then took both mugs inside for refills. When I returned, Cindy had leaned back in her chair with her eyes closed. When I clinked her mug on the table in front of her, her eyes popped open.

"This is the first time I've managed to relax since the killings began. Thanks for listening."

I let her uncharacteristically kind words go without a smart-aleck comment. Instead, I said, "I'm glad." I waited for her to say something. She didn't, so I added, "What did you find interesting about Honeycutt?"

"I was telling the truth about the techs not finding paper in the house. They did find the Mercedes registration in the car's glove box. It's leased. A couple of phone calls, and I learned he was also leasing the house. I wouldn't be surprised if he didn't lease the crowns on his shiny, smiling, teeth. That doesn't prove anything, but suspect that his life was a total front, a front for hit-and-run conning."

"Hit-and-run conning?"

"Yeah, he moves here, cons as many people as he can, pulls up stakes, moves somewhere else, starts over."

"In other words, someone he conned in the past, someone from nowhere around here, could've found him and stuck a knife in his chest."

"Opening up the suspect pool to an infinite number of people."

"On the other hand, Honeycutt could've been working with Thurmond. They had a disagreement over something. Honeycutt kills Thurmond, then steals the laptop to get rid of evidence connecting the two. Someone else kills Honeycutt because of some beef you know nothing about, someone from anywhere in the universe. Then that someone gets in his car and drives away, far away."

"Couldn't have said it better."

CHAPTER THIRTY-ONE

Barb called late that afternoon saying, "Know what I'm in the mood for?"

I was beginning to agree with Cindy that I should be on a quiz show.

"Looking at my charming smile."

"Supper at Rita's then a moonlit walk on the beach."

Looking at my charming smile must go without saying.

"Want me to meet you there?"

She chuckled. "No, I was calling to get Charles's number so I could invite him to go with me."

"What time?"

"I've got a customer who promised to pick up some books I'm holding for him a little before seven, so I won't be getting out of here until seven or so. Why don't you get us a table and I'll get there as soon as I can?"

"Deal."

She then did something I wasn't accustomed to my friends doing. She pleasantly said, "See you there," before hanging up.

Unlike when I'd met Larry and Cindy on Rita's patio, there wasn't live music, so I took the table offered by the hostess near the front gate leading to the Center Street sidewalk. It was still before seven, so I wasn't expecting Barb to arrive for several minutes. I ordered white wine then leaned back in the chair to take in the low-seventy-degree temperature and watch the sun descending over buildings across the street. I tried to block out thoughts of the murders, especially seeing Honeycutt on his kitchen floor. Success was hard to come by, but I was making progress when Barb stuck her head out the patio door then headed my way. She was wearing tan slacks, a fire-engine red blouse, and a smile.

She kissed my cheek, looked at the table, then said, "Where's my drink?"

The server arrived, set my wine in front of me, then asked Barb what she wanted to drink. She pointed at my glass. "The same."

The server left to get Barb's drink. Barb grabbed my glass. With an uncharacteristic move, she took a sip.

I said, "Rough day?"

"As compared to defending a guilty client in court, no, but for this simple, used bookstore owner, it was a frustrating day. The customer who promised he'd be there before seven never showed. The new credit card machine touted as being foolproof, stopped working with three customers holding arms full of books to buy staring at me, then—"

The server set Barb's drink in front of her then asked if we were ready to order. Barb told her to give us a few minutes.

"Then?" I said to prompt Barb to continue with her list of frustrations.

She took a sip of wine, tilted the nearly full glass at me, then said, "Then Virgil Debonnet sauntered in. Guess what he told me?"

I was afraid I knew, so instead of guessing, I said, "What?"

A sip later, she said, "He offered that he, Charles Fowler, and the gentleman I've been dating discovered the body of Ron Honeycutt in his kitchen with a knife imbedded in his chest."

I nodded.

"Don't you find it interesting I heard the dreadful news from someone other than the gentleman I've been dating?"

Yes, I thought, and pondered how to agree with her without digging a deeper hole. It only took me a nanosecond to conclude I couldn't. "You're right, that's bad. I'm sorry. I should've called after we found him."

"Apology almost accepted. Plying me with food and drink should help." She took another sip. "Finding him had to be terrible. You okay?"

"Charles and I took it better than Virgil."

"He was nearly in tears telling me. Finding Honeycutt was bad enough, the poor man also found Thurmond. It's seldom I see Virgil without a smile and a kind comment. Today, the smile was nonexistent."

The server returned, Barb glanced at me, then ordered a burger. I said the same and the server headed to the kitchen. Barb said the night was too nice to be talking about death. She suggested we talk about something more pleasant. I agreed and we did.

By the time we finished supper, the sun had set with only a touch of color filling the sky.

Barb said, "Ready to walk on the beach?"

I told her I was looking forward to it, paid, escorted her to the exit then across the street. We took the path between the Tides Hotel's parking lot and Barb's condo building down to the beach where we walked to water's edge then turned right. We passed a handful of groups. Two were disassembling pop-up tents that had provided shade for the beachgoers during daylight; another group was four women carrying flashlights pointed at the sand in front of them; a final group was comprised of three men laughing as they stumbled through the sand. My guess is they'd been in one of the city's bars and were walking to a house along the beach. The island was safer because they were walking instead of driving.

The farther we got from Barb's building, the fewer people we saw. The sky was completely black except for countless stars over the ocean. Lights from a small boat bobbed on the waves a few hundred yards offshore.

"You sure you're okay?" Barb asked and reached for my hand as we walked.

I squeezed her hand. "I am now."

"You're still going to try to figure out who killed the men, aren't you?"

We took a few more steps before I said, "I'd like to, but I don't know how."

"Don't suppose it'd dissuade you if I said it was a job for the police."

"I know that. They have resources, experience, everything necessary to solve it."

"Yet that's not going to stop you from trying."

I whispered, "No."

Barb sighed, squeezed my hand harder, then said, "My understanding is both men were running a con. Were they working together?"

"Don't know, but they knew each other. Preacher Burl said Honeycutt told him something making him think the two were business partners, but he wasn't certain. Add to that, the police know Honeycutt stole Thurmond's laptop, so they speculate he killed him then took the laptop to keep whatever was on it hidden. That makes them think the two were connected, but how, I'm not sure anyone knows?"

"Do you think he killed him?"

"It would be the simplest explanation."

"But you question it."

"Yes. If Honeycutt killed Thurmond, who killed Honeycutt. Both men stabbed. It seems logical one person killed both men."

"Who do you know who knew Thurmond, Honeycutt, or both men?"

"Ryan Sparks knew Thurmond. They'd talked a few times and Ryan thought Thurmond was pumping him for information, most likely to see if he had money."

"That doesn't sound like reason enough to want him dead. Is he a suspect?"

"I don't believe so. Virgil thinks he is."

"Why?"

"Virgil says he has a bad feeling about Ryan, nothing specific other than Ryan telling a slightly different story about the morning Thurmond was found. At first, Ryan said he didn't hear or see anything, then he remembered hearing two people talking near where Virgil discovered the body."

"Is that the only reason Virgil suspects Ryan?"

"That plus Ryan's boat was anchored close to the body."

"Don't the police believe the boat Thurmond was in floated downstream from where he was killed? If that's true, Ryan's location would be irrelevant."

"The police aren't certain where Thurmond was killed. The most logical explanation is he was killed upstream, but there's a possibility the jon boat was at Ryan's sailboat when Thurmond was stabbed."

The temperature had dropped and the steady breeze blowing in off the ocean made it feel cooler than the actual temperature. I put my arm around Barb and pulled her close.

We walked a few more paces before she said, "One thing I remember about Thurmond was he did a lot of talking but said little. Like I told you before, he was in the store quite often. He mentioned he was a businessperson, but never went into details."

"I wonder why he didn't try to get you to buy in one of his alleged businesses."

"He probably didn't think a used bookstore owner would have the resources to buy in. Who else do you know who knew Thurmond?"

"Ben Likard. I've only talked to him in Bert's, but I'd list him as the top suspect, at least for killing Thurmond. He's the only person I know who'd been partners with Thurmond. He told me he wanted some of his profits, but Thurmond refused saying the company needed the money to expand, or other business-related reasons. Likard was angry and argued with Thurmond, the disagreement Officer Spencer told me about."

"Do you think he was angry enough to kill him?"

"Could've been. I also found it interesting Likard told me

he'd heard Thurmond's murder was a professional hit. It ran through my mind at the time he could've been saying that to deflect suspicion."

"Do the police know about Likard?"

"Yes."

"Did Likard know Honeycutt?"

"Don't know."

"The police will check."

"Sure."

"Then there's nothing you can do about that, is there?"

Subtle—not.

"True."

Barb leaned against my shoulder. "Ready to turn around and head back?"

"Whenever you are."

She stopped, pivoted, then pulled me around with her. Another not so subtle response, as we headed toward her condo.

I figured our conversation about the murders was over and said something about how much I enjoyed walking with her.

She agreed, then said, "Megan and Kevin knew Thurmond."

"Do you think they're suspects?"

"No. I'm simply saying they're two more people who were familiar with the man. I get the impression it's not easy riling Megan, so Thurmond must've been quite abrasive since she talked about how much he irritated her. If he was like that with others, it could've been another reason someone wanted him dead. What I'm trying to say is that there could've been countless others you don't know about who he could've pissed off, stolen money from, or a multitude of reasons to want him dead."

"Your point being I couldn't possibly know most of those people, so how could I help figure out who killed him?"

"Excellent interpretation. Add to that, how many people do you know who knew Honeycutt?"

"Ryan had conversations with him, so did Virgil. Apparently, Honeycutt was a staple at local bars which is where Ryan and Virgil met him. Ryan said he wouldn't trust him."

"Sounds like he was as unlikable as Thurmond, which again makes me think there could be numerous people who could've had a beef with him, people you wouldn't know."

"In other words, there's no way I could get a good handle on learning who killed the men since there are so many possible suspects."

"Add to that, there could be more who don't live anywhere around here."

She was right, but I still didn't want to let it go. What I also didn't want to do was ruin a beautiful walk on the beach with a wonderful lady.

"Enough about murder," I said, pulled Barb tighter, then gave her a kiss.

"That's the best idea you've had all evening," she said, smiled, then added, "Think it's time for you to escort me to my condo."

And I did. To the condo, and then inside.

CHAPTER THIRTY-TWO

The next afternoon Megan Goodman called reminding me that I'd asked her to let me know if Ryan or Kevin said anything new about Thurmond. She added that she was tired of being cooped up in the house with loud contractors and was headed to the outdoor bar at the Tides Hotel to breathe some pure ocean air. She asked if I wanted to join her, and of course I did.

I arrived to find Megan seated at the long, narrow bar where she had an unobstructed view of the ocean. She was sipping on what looked like a margarita. She saw me approach, smiled, then told me to go to the bar and get something to drink. Unlike many of my friends, she didn't tell me the bartender was holding her tab for me. I ordered white wine, paid, then took my drink to where she was seated.

"Thanks for joining me. The house is swarming with electricians. Apparently, most of our wiring was, as the electrician put it 'a fire waitin' to happen.' We had no way of knowing if that was true, so they convinced us to spend oodles more dollars replacing it." She shook her head. "Poor Kevin is freaking out over the cost. I keep telling him it'll be okay. So far, he doesn't believe me." She shook her head again. "Aren't you glad you came to hear me bitching about electrical wiring?"

"That's okay. I know how crazy costs of repairs are frustrating, especially in older homes. I've had my share as well."

She took a sip, then said, "When you were at the house the other day, I said I'd check with Kevin to see if he knew anything about Thurmond he hadn't shared. I said I'd do the same with Ryan."

I nodded.

"I don't remember how much Kevin told you about his contacts with Thurmond, but he told me Thurmond pressed him hard to become a partner in one of his businesses, a manufacturing company somewhere up north. I didn't let my husband go into details, since I knew it wouldn't happen. Thurmond knew we'd inherited money and wouldn't take no for an answer when Kevin told him he had no interest in spending it on a manufacturing company. Kevin said Thurmond got rude. I figure if he was that way with Kevin, he'd be the same with other people he was recruiting. It's no wonder someone disliked him enough to stab him."

"How'd Thurmond know about your inheritance?"

"Don't know. Maybe Ryan told him."

"Did Kevin know others who might've been approached by Thurmond?"

"I didn't know it until the other night, but Kevin told me my brother talked to him about borrowing money so he could partner with Thurmond."

"Did Kevin lend him any?"

"No. Is it true you and a couple of your friends found the body of the guy who stole Thurmond's computer?"

I wasn't ready for that abrupt transition. I took a sip of wine, then said, "Afraid so."

"Didn't the police think he killed Thurmond?"

"He was their prime suspect."

"What do they think now? Could they've been wrong and someone else killed both men?"

"Yes, they're not certain of anything. Did you know Honeycutt?"

She took another sip, looked toward the ocean, then slowly back at me. "Only by reputation. I heard he was a lot like Thurmond. Someone told me they were in cahoots."

"Who told you?"

She shook her head. "Don't recall. Think it was someone in Bert's. I've been spending more time out of the house than in it with the contractors traipsing in and out. It could also have been in one of the gift shops on Center Street."

That was about as vague as an answer could be, but I was in no position to press her.

"Did Ryan know others who may've been approached by Thurmond?"

"I tried to ask, but he gets defensive whenever I try to talk to him about Thurmond. Think he's still shaken by being so close to where the body was found." She took the last sip of her drink.

"Want another drink? It's on me."

She smiled. "That's kind of you, but I'd better head home. I'm already behind with my work. Can't afford to goof off more."

I asked if she wanted me to walk her home. She said she figured she could find it on her own but thanked me for offering. She also thanked me for joining her. She slipped off the barstool and headed to the exit.

Not being behind on anything, I returned to where I had a clear view of the ocean, then pondered whether I'd learned anything new from Megan about the murders. The more said about Ryan and his relationship with Thurmond, the more came out. Was Ryan serious about buying into one of Thurmond's companies? The first time we'd talked, he shared he felt adrift, purposeless. If he became a partner in a business, perhaps he felt it'd give him something to live for, a purpose. I realized that was amateur psychoanalyzing, but if true, it would've been a reason to pursue ownership, reason to push his brother-in-law to lend him money?

Did Kevin lend Ryan money to buy into one of Thurmond's companies? Megan said she didn't think so rather than giving a definitive no. Hadn't she said when we first met that Kevin oversaw their money? Would she have known if he lent Ryan some?

Why is it she couldn't remember who told her about Honeycutt being involved with Thurmond? That's not something a stranger comes up to you and starts spouting off about. If someone does, surely the person told would remember the source. Was Megan hiding something?

Finally, was I reaching for connections where none exist? I kept coming back to what Barb had said on our beach walk last evening. There could be countless others who may've been responsible for the deaths; others who have no connection to Folly; others I'd have no way of knowing about. In other words, leave it to the police.

None of the answers to these questions popped in my head, so I spent the next hour watching kids splashing, laughing, and screaming as they jumped in and out of the waves, and a colony of seagulls begging for food scraps from the kids' parents lounging under beach umbrellas while snacking on a bag of potato chips.

A call from Sean Aker interrupted my peaceful observation of the goings-on of those on the beach.

Sean began with, "Is this a good time to talk?"

I wasn't used to such a considerate opening. I recovered from the surprise to tell him yes.

"Remember, I told you I'd do a little research to see what I could find about Walter Thurmond's businesses and factories?"

"Yes. What'd you learn?"

"Nothing."

"Let's see if I have this right, you called to tell me nothing."

"Exactly."

"And that's it?"

"There's more to the nothing. The point is I've checked every database I have access to. I called friends who work in the Secretary of State's office, one in South Carolina, the other friend works in New Hampshire. They checked their sources with the results of zilch. There are no businesses showing ownership belonging to Thurmond, no manufacturing facilities in his name. Chris, there's nothing."

"You saying the businesses are bogus?"

"Looks that way."

"Could they be in states that your friends didn't check?"

"That's possible, but remote. My friend in New Hampshire contacted colleagues in three other New England states, all with the same results."

"Sean, how's that possible?"

"Simple, unfortunately. Anyone with access to a high-quality printer, a vivid imagination, and ill intent, can produce all sorts of official looking papers, contracts that can befuddle anyone, agreements that aren't worth the paper they're printed on. All done to make whatever they're selling look legitimate. I don't know it for a fact, but from everything my friends told me, that's what I think Thurmond was doing."

I shared what Cindy told me about the Sheriff's Office not finding paperwork in either Thurmond's condo or Honeycutt's house. I added what Megan had said about hearing the two men were in the con together.

"Chris, they were covering the bases quite well. No paperwork, no evidence of conning anyone. I admire their determination to keep whatever they were doing under the radar."

"Sean, before you express more admiration, don't forget they're dead."

"A serious hitch in their plan."

I agreed then he told me he had a client waiting, adding that Marlene had threatened to quit if he didn't start taking lawyering more seriously. He finished by saying if she quit, he'd have to get a job clerking at Harris Teeter. I wished him well.

CHAPTER THIRTY-THREE

The next day began much like the day Virgil found Walter Thurmond. Fog was so thick that from my porch, I barely saw the road in front of my house. This would be a good morning to stay home, savor a cup of coffee, and put my feet up. A call from Charles threw a wrench in those plans.

"Ready to take a photo walk?"

"Charles, have you looked outside? I doubt you can see anything to take a photo of?"

'Oh, ye of little faith. You're the expert photographer, so you should know fog photos are some of the best. Even I know that."

He had a point, besides it's always an adventure walking with my friend.

"Where and when?"

"Now, of course. I'll meet you in front of the Baptist Church. Don't be late."

As Kris Kristofferson said in "Sunday Mornin' Comin'

Down," I put on my cleanest dirty shirt which happened to be a red polo, tan shorts, Tilley hat, and grabbed my camera before heading six blocks to our meeting spot. Charles was leaning against the wrought iron Folly Beach Baptist Church sign in front of the sanctuary. He wore his tan shorts, his Tilley, and a gold and navy, long-sleeve, T-shirt with NC Wesleyan College in large letters on the front.

"Bet you can't guess their nickname," he said instead of something civil like, "Good morning. Great to see you."

I couldn't nor did I want to. I shrugged.

"They're the Battling Bishops. It's in Rocky Mount, North Carolina."

"Fascinating."

Charles smiled. "Thought you'd like knowing about it."

Enough, I thought. "Where're we headed?"

He pointed off-island. "Over the river and through the woods. Well, not through the woods, but you get the idea."

I did, then started walking past a few small businesses, the Hotel Folly, and the boat ramp's parking lot. Of our countless walks over the years, we'd seldom gone this direction. I asked Charles why he'd chosen this path, but he ignored my question as he continued walking. The sun was beginning to burn off some of the thick fog, so when we reached the Lee Westbury Bridge leading off island, I saw three or four boats anchored to our left.

The reason for going this direction became clearer when Charles pointed to one of the anchored water-crafts a hundred feet away. "That's Ryan's sailboat."

I told him I recognized it.

"I think he's been anchored over there more than he parks at Sunset Cay Marina. Wonder why?"

"So he can get to restaurants, businesses, and his sister's house. Sunset Cay is too far to walk."

Charles stopped and leaned his elbows on the bridge's railing. "It would've been pretty easy for Thurmond's jon boat to be tied to Ryan's like Ryan's kayak is now. He could've killed him and untied the little boat." He pointed to the shore. "It could've floated to where Virgil found it."

I joined Charles leaning on the railing and said, "What makes you think Ryan killed Thurmond?"

"Not saying he did; not saying he didn't. Virgil has a bad feeling, okay, maybe not bad, but a feeling Ryan isn't telling him everything. A gut reaction, he says. Don't forget, Ryan told two different stories about that morning. He didn't hear or see anything, then, out of the blue, he heard two people talking. I think that's strange." He again pointed to the shore.

"What's his motive?"

"You've got me."

"That helps. We know Ryan didn't buy into the companies Thurmond was pushing. He may not have liked him, but that's far from reason to kill. Besides, the police think Ron Honeycutt killed Thurmond. He stole the laptop from Thurmond's condo, destroyed it then stashed it in his own car."

Charles snapped his fingers, then smiled. "Forgot to tell you the good news."

Another of his patented one-hundred-eighty-degree transitions. "Good news?"

"Pet Helpers found Dusty a home. Ain't that great?"

It took me a few seconds to remember Dusty was Honeycutt's pug. "That's good news."

"Maybe the cops are right, then again, maybe they're not. I'm not marking Ryan off my suspect list. Which leads to the question, who killed Honeycutt? Is there a connection between the two men?"

I gripped the railing knowing I was about to get yelled at for not telling Charles sooner.

"I was talking to Megan Goodman yesterday afternoon. She was telling me she heard Thurmond and Honeycutt were working together on whatever scam Thurmond was running."

"Whoa, when yesterday afternoon?"

"Don't recall exactly, mid-afternoon."

"You didn't think that important enough to call me?"

"It was something she heard. She didn't know if it was true, said it was more like a rumor."

"A not important enough rumor to tell me?"

It was time to end his pouting. "I should've called."

"That's better. Think it's true?"

"It makes sense. What doesn't make sense is after she told me, she claimed she didn't know who told her. Said it may've been someone in Bert's or one of the gift shops. Does that make sense?"

"Nope. You think she told you that to keep you from thinking she may've had something to do with the murder?"

Before I responded, he started walking the rest of the way over the bridge. I followed and said, "I'm not saying that. It struck me as strange, that's all."

"So Virgil feels strange about Ryan, now you feel strange about his sister. Anything else strange?"

We reached the entrance to the four-story Turn of River condo building. Charles stopped, tapped his cane twice on the sandy berm, and said, "Know what I find strange?"

"What?"

"When we found Honeycutt's body, it scared me."

"It'd scare anyone. I know I was."

"Chris, how many bodies have I tripped over, stumbled into, or found since I've known you?"

"A few."

"This was the first time fear struck me—smacked me like a sledgehammer." He looked around, at the condo building, at the ground, everywhere but at me. "I'm getting too old for this stuff. Honest to God, I am. My friend, if it scared you, and I know it did me, why are we trying to find the killer?"

"If it wasn't for Virgil, you wouldn't catch me within a mile of anything to do with the deaths. I didn't know either victim. I didn't know Ryan, his sister, or her husband. I had no reason to stick my nose where it doesn't belong. I know I told you, but one of the first things Virgil told me after finding Thurmond's body was he had to find the killer. Actually, he didn't say he had to, it was we had to."

"So, Virgil is dictating what you and I do?"

"I'm afraid if he keeps nosing around on his own, he may be the next victim. He's a wonderful guy, but as you know, he tends to blunder into dangerous situations. He's my friend so I feel obligated doing whatever I can to keep him safe."

Charles started walking then turned in the attractive entrance to Mariner's Cay condos and marina. We passed the security gate when he stopped without warning, then whispered, "Virgil's my friend too."

That I knew, so I waited for him to continue.

"So, if Honeycutt killed Thurmond, who killed Honeycutt?'

That simple question told me he was back in the hunt. The question was simple, the answer perplexing.

"If he was involved in whatever scam Thurmond was

running, anger, revenge, a business dispute, and several other reasons could've caused someone to stick a knife in his chest."

"True," Charles said, "but without Thurmond's computer or paperwork, there's no way to know who might've been pissed enough to do it."

"We do know one person who fell for Thurmond's scam."

"Ben Likard."

I nodded.

He sighed. "Now what do we do?"

"Don't know."

What I did know was how much this was bothering him. He hadn't lifted his camera to his face since we started walking. That was a first.

We continued through Mariner's Cay complex, but Charles's head was somewhere else. Where, I didn't know, nor did he offer. After fifteen minutes of roaming around the development, Charles suggested we head back to town.

The fog had burned off before we crossed the bridge. Ryan's kayak was tied to the boat ramp entrance instead of to his boat where it'd been on our trip over. I thought about asking Charles if he wanted to walk to Megan and Kevin's house to see if Ryan was there. He didn't appear to be in the mood to interact with anyone, so I refrained from asking the question that most times would've been a no-brainer.

When we got to the Baptist Church, he said he thought a nap was in order and thanked me for joining him on the walk. When he got in this low a mood, there was little, if anything, I could do to bring him out of it. I wished him a pleasant nap and watched him slowly walk toward his apartment.

CHAPTER THIRTY-FOUR

On the way home, I glanced in each restaurant looking for Ryan. I didn't see him, but there were several other places he could've been, more than I could check; more accurately, more than I wanted to check.

The phone rang as I was opening the front door.

"Yo, Christopher, this is Virgil. You busy?"

I assured him I wasn't.

"Got a favor to ask. Say no if you don't want to. Up to you. Honest, I'll understand if you don't."

"Why don't you tell me what it is, before I answer?"

"Well, you see, my Rolls is in the shop. My scooter's brakes do a couple of things but neither of them stops it. What are the odds on me bumming a ride?"

Virgil has a Rolls like I have a Learjet. His sole means of transportation is a used scooter he bought off a resident of his apartment building.

"What are the odds on telling me where you want to go?"

He laughed. "My friend, you drive a hard bargain. I'd like to visit, hold on, let me check." I heard paper rustling in the background. "Got it, Martin Eastman's house. It's out near the end of East Ashley Avenue."

Martin Eastman, the person whose jon boat was stolen only to be found with Walter Thurmond's body in it.

"The police talked to him. He didn't know who took his boat. He wasn't in South Carolina when it was taken. What do you expect to learn?"

"My friend, I've been doing a lot of thinking about that. Seems to me he may not know who took the boat, but it's possible he knows some of the people who're suspects in one or both killings. Think the cops asked him about them?"

"I don't know."

"One way to find out, my friend."

"When do you want to go?"

"How about now?"

He was waiting in front of his run-down building when I pulled in the small parking area. His slicked-back black hair was combed. He wore what I'd grown accustomed to seeing on him, a long-sleeve, button-down white dress shirt, blue chinos, Gucci loafers, and of course, sunglasses. He looked more like he was preparing to spend the evening at an up-scale dance club rather than visiting a stranger.

"Thanks for the ride, my friend. I would've gone out there earlier if transportation was more readily available."

"How are you feeling?"

"Physically, about life in general, or on my mood scale?"

"After the trauma of finding Honeycutt."

"Near back to normal, my normal." He stared out the windshield like he was done talking about his feelings.

"You told me you didn't know Martin Eastman. What do you plan on saying?"

"Good question. I've learned a lot from shadowing your private detective friend."

He meant Charles so there was no benefit pointing out he wasn't a private detective. I motioned him to continue.

"One of the things he's taught me is not to spend time worrying about what's going to happen next. Like, when I meet Eastman, I figure what to say will pop right in my head. No need to plan. That answer your question?"

Afraid it did. We were approaching the end of East Ashley Avenue where it dead ends at the Lighthouse Inlet Heritage Preserve, commonly known as the old Coast Guard station. Virgil was glancing at a sheet of paper while looking at house numbers.

"That's it," he said as he pointed to a small, elevated, wood frame house on our left. It appeared to be wearing a fresh coat of blue paint. A late-model Toyota Tundra pickup was in the drive.

I pulled in behind the truck. "Do you know what you're going to say?"

"Not yet. Let's go meet Mr. Eastman."

The house had a porch on two sides. Virgil bounded up the steps like a collie pup going to meet his new owner. He was knocking on the door before I reached the top step.

A man in his mid-fifties, six-one or two, trim, with short, curly hair answered the door with, "May I help you?"

Virgil gave him a salesman's smile, then said, "Would you happen to be Martin Eastman?"

The man didn't return the smile. "Yes. Again, may I help you?"

Virgil told him who he was then introduced me as his good friend, Chris Landrum. If Mr. Eastman was thrilled to meet us, it didn't show through his gruff exterior.

Virgil wasn't put off by the man's lack of enthusiasm. He gave the homeowner another smile then said, "Mr. Eastman, I was a friend of Walter Thurmond. He's the man who tragically was found deceased in your jon boat in town near the boat launch ramp."

Virgil's definition of friend is different than mine.

Mr. Eastman said, "So?"

I wondered the same thing.

"I hate to bother you sir, but as you can imagine, I'm interested in what happened to my friend." He held up his hand like he was holding Mr. Eastman back. "Don't get me wrong, I know you had nothing to do with his death, but something keeps bothering me."

Eastman hadn't made any effort to invite us in, or for that matter, for us to have a seat on the porch chairs.

"When will the police let me have my boat?"

"Mr. Eastman, I'm not here at the behest of law enforcement. I'm afraid they wouldn't share that information with me. If you'd like, I'll check and get back to you. We can do that, can't we, Chris?"

I nodded and so did Eastman, but he didn't say anything, nor had he asked what'd been bothering Virgil.

Now what was Virgil going to say?

"As I was saying, I'm confused about why someone would come all the way out here to steal your boat. If he, I admit, it could be a she, wanted a small boat, there are much closer places to find one than here."

Eastman blinked; his neutral expression turned to a frown. "Are you implying I'm part of this murder?"

"Heaven's no, Mr. Eastman, I was wondering if you know any of the people the police believe may've had contact with Thurmond."

Eastman said, "What was your name again?"

"Virgil."

"Virgil, I have no way of knowing who you're talking about. Work takes me out of town more often than I'm here. I don't go to the Center Street establishments. Other than my neighbors," he hesitated then pointed to the house on each side of his. "I know few Folly residents. I can appreciate you trying to find out what happened to your friend, but I don't know how I can help."

"Mr. Eastman, do you know Ron Honeycutt?"

"Honeycutt," he said, then shook his head.

"How about Ben Likard or Ryan Sparks?"

"Never heard of them. Now, is there anything else?"

Our "friendly" conversation was ending abruptly.

Virgil nodded. "No, I think that's all. I appreciate you talking to us."

Eastman didn't say he appreciated anything as he started back inside. He stopped, turned to Virgil, then said, "Let me know what the police say about releasing my boat."

Virgil said he would. At the same time, I didn't ask him how he'd let Eastman know without bumming another ride out here.

We pulled out of the drive when Virgil asked me to pull off the road across from the house. I pulled in a sandy drive on a vacant lot. Virgil looked across the street at Eastman's house then at the house on each side of his.

"Chris, I'm nowhere the detective like Charles and you, but look where we are."

"So?"

"We're what, three miles from where I found the body. Thurmond lived off island near Harris Teeter. Honeycutt lives, umm, lived on the other side of Center Street. Then there's Ryan who lives on a boat docked five or so miles from here. Why did someone come out here to kill Thurmond or steal a boat? Wouldn't you think the killer had some connection on this part of the island, if for no other reason than to know that Eastman had a boat he could procure?"

"That makes sense."

He huffed, shook his head, then said, "Making sense don't amount to a hill of beans by itself, does it?"

"Nope."

CHAPTER THIRTY-FIVE

Barb and I'd planned to have supper, so I agreed we'd meet at her condo. She was going to choose the restaurant which was fine with me. She met me at the gate to the condo complex. She wore a red blouse and white shorts in deference to the warm evening. She gave me a peck on the lips and said she hoped I didn't mind but she'd invited Charles and Laurie Fitzsimmons, the lady he'd dated since he met her a couple of years ago. Laurie was in Barb's Books yesterday where the women had hatched the plot to have dinner together. I said it was fine then asked where we were going.

She looped her arm in mine. "Taco Boy. Laurie hasn't been there in a while, so I thought it'd be a good place to go."

The multi-level restaurant was less than a block off Center Street, an easy walk from Barb's condo. We arrived ten minutes before the time we were to meet, but I wasn't the least surprised to see Charles leaning on the railing leading to the entrance.

He hugged Barb, patted my arm, then said, "Figured you'd be late, so I got us a table on the upper level. Laurie's up there. I also thought you wouldn't be able to find us so I'm your escort."

We, of course, weren't late according to the clock, but that never influenced my friend's concept of on-time. Barb knew him well enough to ignore his comment. She thanked him for being so considerate meeting us. As an experienced trial lawyer, she said it without showing a glimmer of sarcasm.

We followed Charles to the rooftop bar and lounge, the room with the best view of the surrounding area and the ocean a block away. Since it was mid-week the restaurant was crowded, but not overflowing like on many weekend evenings.

Laurie stood when she saw us approach. She was in her late-fifties, five-foot-three, petite, with short, dark hair, and attractive with a pleasant smile. She hugged Barb, then me, before we took our seats. A server was quick to the table to take our drink orders. Charles and Laurie had beer glasses in front of them. Barb and I each ordered white wine. Noise from a couple of groups at the nearby bar was noticeable, but not loud enough to prevent us from hearing each other.

Laurie said, "I'm glad Barb suggested we eat here."

Charles and I agreed about how wise a choice she'd made.

"Chris," Laurie said, "Charles was telling me how you two found the man killed in his house the other day. That had to be terrible."

"It was."

"Charles said he shook for a day after it, and what about that poor Virgil? Charles said he didn't think the man would ever get over it."

This wasn't the conversation I wanted to have while enjoying a pleasant evening with friends.

"I saw Virgil today. He's much better. Have you decided what you're going to order?"

Laurie said, "Not yet."

The server arrived with our drinks then asked if we were ready to order. I suggested she give us more time.

Charles stared at me, then said, "Where'd you see Virgil?"

It was a mistake mentioning seeing Virgil.

"His scooter was out of commission, so he asked me to take him to see Martin Eastman. Barb, you know what you're going to order?"

She didn't answer quick enough. Charles waved his hand in my face. "The guy who owned the boat where Virgil found Thurmond?"

I resisted asking him how many other Martin Eastmans he knew. "Yes, Virgil was curious if Eastman knew any of the suspects in Thurmond's murder."

"Charles," Laurie said, "why don't we talk about something more pleasant?"

"Sure, but first, Chris was going to tell us what Eastman said."

Not really, I thought, but knew that wouldn't fly with my friend.

"He didn't know them, nor did he know why a killer chose to steal his boat. That's it."

"Another dead end," Charles said. "At that rate, how're we going to find out who killed the guys?"

Barb said, "Chris tells me it's in the capable hands of the Sheriff's Office and Folly's police department. I think they have it covered, don't you, Charles?"

"Of course, Barb. We're just asking questions. Our friend Virgil found both bodies. We owe it to him to help the police."

Laurie tapped her beer on the table hard enough to get our attention. "Charles, two years ago you and Chris didn't leave it up to the police to catch the person who killed my husband. You pushed and pushed, wouldn't give up until you figured it out."

Charles smiled, nodded, then said, "Yes, we—"

Laurie interrupted, "As a result, you came seconds from getting killed. I don't know about Barb, but don't think I could live through something like that again."

Charles said, "If we hadn't gotten involved, you might not be with us. The killer made two attempts on your life, wouldn't have stopped until he succeeded."

She gave Charles a weak smile, then said, "Doesn't mean I like it."

Charles reached across the table and took her hand. "I understand, but you know me enough to know that's what I do, that's who I am. Chris is the same way." He looked at me.

"Laurie, we know there's danger involved, but Virgil is our friend. All we're doing is asking questions. We're not going off half-cocked stalking a killer."

The server returned. We ordered even though none of us appeared certain about what we wanted. Charles had hijacked the conversation enough to where food wasn't on the top of anyone's priority list. Laurie went from not wanting Charles to be involved, to asking if he thought the men were killed by the same person.

"Good question," he said. "The police think Honeycutt killed Thurmond, mainly because of the video showing

Honeycutt stealing Thurmond's laptop from his condo the day after he was killed."

Barb said, "Didn't they find the laptop in Honeycutt's car?"

"Yes," I said.

"While that's proof of theft, it's only circumstantial evidence related to the murder," Barb said, reverting to her days as a criminal defense lawyer.

Laurie said, "Doesn't having the video and finding the computer mean less now that Honeycutt was killed the same way Thurmond was?"

"That's what I'm thinking," Charles said.

"Did they know each other?" Laurie said, forgetting her concerns about Charles looking into the deaths.

"Megan Goodman told Chris she heard they were in business together."

"Chris," Barb said, "who told her?"

"She thinks it was someone in Bert's or one of the gift shops but doesn't remember who."

"Doesn't remember who?" Laurie said, "She remembers where she heard it, but not from whom? That doesn't make sense."

"Sure don't," Charles said.

All of us agreed on that point. I told the ladies what Sean had learned about there not being a record of businesses and factories owned by Thurmond in South Carolina or in several New England states. Barb said that didn't mean much since she knew from shady businesspersons she'd defended there were ways people could hide ownership through shell companies and offshore registrations making it difficult to trace ownership. I deferred to her knowledge.

Charles had reached his limit for staying out of a conversation. He said, "Barb, do you know Ben Likard?"

"Chris asked about him when we were with Kevin and Megan at Loggerhead's. He's been in the store twice since then. Paid by credit card, remembered his name from the conversation at Loggerhead's. Chris also said Likard had an argument with Thurmond, thus making him a suspect. A suspect, I'm certain the police have talked to. Isn't that right, Chris?"

"Absolutely."

"What books did he buy?" Charles asked, not ready to leave the subject.

"They weren't on how to kill someone who ripped you off in a con." Barb smiled.

Our food arrived changing the direction of our conversation to something more palatable. Despite a couple of efforts by Charles to return to a conversation about murder, the ladies, along with my help, squashed them. All in all, it was a pleasant evening with three friends, something I suspected each of us needed more of. I know I did.

CHAPTER THIRTY-SIX

I was awakened by sun rays peeking under the blinds which meant I'd slept later than usual. A half hour later, I'd showered, fixed a pot of coffee, and was sitting at the small kitchen table rehashing bits of conversation from last night's gathering at Taco Boy. Food was good, most of the conversation pleasant, and I kept thinking how comfortable it felt having friends to enjoy the evening with. Despite efforts to push it aside, I kept coming back to the topic we'd tried to avoid most of the night: the deaths of Walter Thurmond and Ronald Honeycutt. Laurie had reinforced something that struck me as strange when I first heard it. That was how Megan remembered hearing that Thurmond and Honeycutt had been working together in the scheme to defraud potential partners in their businesses. Was it possible she'd heard it in Bert's or one of the gift shops but not remember who'd told her? I suppose so, but it seemed unlikely. Did that mean something?

Perhaps French toast would be the catalyst to my understanding. I chuckled when I realized rationalizing was something I'd come close to perfecting. Admitting my favorite breakfast item wouldn't help me clarify anything about Megan's comment, but would meet my need for food, I headed out my back door for the walk to the Dog.

The walk to breakfast was interrupted as soon as I opened the door, stepped outside, turned to shut the door, then came face to face with a knife rammed into the doorframe. I looked around to see if anyone was nearby. I didn't see anyone, then realized the knife was holding a postcard-size sheet of paper. On it, printed in large, block letters, were the words *BUTT OUT!*

I was tempted to yank the knife out of the doorframe but didn't want to disturb possible fingerprints. I returned to the kitchen, plopped down in the chair, and called Chief LaMond.

"Unless you're calling to report another murder, or you're buying me that Porsche I've been coveting, this is a recording. My office hours begin at 9:00 a.m. Leave a message and I might return your call."

This morning I didn't see any humor in her comments. "Chief, I need your help."

"What's wrong?" she said, accurately reading fear in my voice.

I told her what'd I'd found when I stepped outside.

"I'll be there in five."

Three minutes later, Cindy was at the front door in police chief mode. Instead of one of her trademark smart-aleck remarks, she said, "Hi, Chris. Where is it?"

"Thanks for coming. Back door," I said then led her through the house to the new addition to my exterior decor.

Before we got to the back door, she said, "You okay?"

"A little shook, but yes."

She stared at the knife and note. "Crap, it's not signed. How're we going to know who you've pissed off now."

Okay, at least she'd made it through the house without a smart-aleck remark.

"I'm no psychic, but if I was guessing, I'd say it's from whoever killed Thurmond and Honeycutt."

"Gee, did the knife give it away?"

I didn't think I needed to respond.

Cindy put on blue latex gloves then removed the knife by gripping its bolster instead of the handle then carefully wiggling it until it pulled free.

"The odds on finding prints are slim since there weren't any on the knife in Honeycutt's chest, but you never know. Don't you usually go in and out your front door?"

"Yes."

"When was the last time you opened your back door?"

"I took the trash out yesterday afternoon."

"The note's damp, probably last night's dew, so it wasn't added to your house in the last two or three hours." She dropped the knife with the note still attached in a clear plastic bag.

She looked in the kitchen. "Got coffee in there?"

I smiled for the first time since she'd arrived. "For you, of course."

"Thought you'd never ask."

I poured Cindy a mug, refilled mine, then we sat at the table. Cindy put the bag containing the knife and note beside her mug, sighed, then said, "Don't suppose you know who did this?"

"No."

"Why do you think the person thought you needed to butt out?"

"You know I've been asking around about Thurmond's murder, but don't think I've learned anything that'd help."

"Someone thinks you're closer than you do. Who've you talked to?"

"Ben Likard. I told you about that."

She nodded as she took a small notebook out of her pocket. "Did you learn anything about him you didn't share with me?"

"Don't think so. You're the one who told me about his near fight with Thurmond."

"Me and my big mouth. Who else?"

"Ryan Sparks."

"What motive would he have for killing Thurmond, and/or Honeycutt?"

"None I can see. He told conflicting stories about hearing something the morning Thurmond was found."

"Understandable considering the circumstances."

"Maybe, but it still seems unusual."

"Who else have you been bugging about the murders?"

"Megan and Kevin Goodman, although I wouldn't say bugging. They both knew Thurmond had talked with Ryan about the business opportunities. I don't think either of them liked him, but not enough to kill him."

"Larry told me they have enough to deal with because of their home remodel."

Cindy poured a refill in her mug, then said, "Dare I ask, anyone else?"

"Yesterday, Virgil and I visited Martin Eastman."

Cindy had raised her mug toward her face but stopped before it reached her mouth. "Why?"

I told her Virgil's idea that Eastman may've known one of the suspects which would've been how the killer knew Eastman had a boat to steal.

"Poor Virgil," Cindy said as she shook her head. "It's not enough that you and Charles can't help sticking your noses where they don't belong, you drag Virgil into your misadventures."

"We didn't drag Virgil into anything. He found both bodies. He was first to say we needed to find the killer. It's his idea."

She rolled her eyes. "I'm sure you did everything possible to discourage him."

Not really, I thought. I figured she already knew that so no need to lie to her. I shrugged.

"That's what I thought. Do me a favor."

"Anything."

She looked at my phone. "Call Charles and ask him if he's noticed anything unusual lately."

"Like a knife with a note attached sticking in his door?"

"That'd qualify. He's nosier than you, if that's possible, so why wouldn't he receive the same warning?"

I made the call, put the phone on speaker, asked the question, deflected several questions about why I would ask such a stupid thing, told him we'd talk later, then hung up. Since Cindy heard the entire conversation, I didn't have to retell his part of the talk. She asked me to do the same with Virgil. I did, received far fewer questions about why I'd asked the question than I had from Charles, received the same negative answer, then ended the call.

Cindy took another sip, looked at the knife and note. "Why do you think you received this friendly message instead of Charles or Virgil?"

"Someone must think I know more about the murders than the other guys. If I do, it's news to me."

"You're a big help." She pointed at the plastic bag. "I'll get this to Detective Adair so his techies can see if there are prints then I'll have my guys step up their patrols past here. You may want to let Charles and Virgil know what happened, reminding them they're possibly in danger."

"You don't have to suggest I tell Charles. Before you get to your office, he'll be over here pestering me about why I asked him the stupid question. Virgil will be slower, but not much."

She stood, put her coffee mug in the sink, grabbed the evidence bag, then headed to the door. Before she opened it, she hugged me, then told me to be careful. I thanked her for coming quickly. She said she did because she knew my coffee was better than what she had at the office. One more, "be careful" and she was gone.

I closed the door, took a deep breath, then told myself I would try to be more careful, but if the person who left the knife thought it'd get me to butt out, he or she was wrong, way wrong.

CHAPTER THIRTY-SEVEN

I'd given Charles too much credit. It was thirty minutes before he called.

His name appeared on the screen, so I answered with, "What took you so long?"

"You had the phone on speaker, so I figured someone was with you. I waited for them to leave. I'm practicing patience. You're not on speaker now. Are they gone?"

"Yes."

"What's going on? You've asked me stupider questions, but that was near the top."

"Meet me at Pier 101 at noon for your answer."

"Why do I have to—"

I interrupted with, "I'm buying."

"I'll be there." The phone went dead.

He may be working on patience, but phone etiquette still has a way to go. I called Virgil asking if he wanted to meet me at the restaurant at 11:30, knowing that's when Charles would arrive. I added I was buying before he asked questions that should wait until lunch.

Pier 101 was located on the deck overlooking the Folly Pier. Charles was located at the top of the stairs leaning against the metal gate when I arrived at 11:30. He wore his usual tan shorts, Tilley hat, and a long-sleeve maroon T-shirt with University of Puget Sound in white on the front.

"They're the Loggers," he said as he pointed to the school's name on the front of the shirt.

"Interesting," I said.

Virgil interrupted our discussion about the University of Puget Sound.

"Hi, gentlemen. Charles, I didn't know you'd be breaking bread with us this lovely day."

Charles pointed to the front of his shirt as he smiled at Virgil. "They're the Loggers."

"Who would've guessed?" Virgil said then turned to me. He had as much interest in the school's nickname as I had. "Anyone else joining us?"

"Just us. Shall we grab a table?"

Charles muttered something I couldn't understand, probably bemoaning our lack of interest in the Loggers, then followed us in the building. Given the choice of inside or outside seating, I told the hostess outside, without giving my guests a vote. She seated us at a table with a view of the pier, the ocean, and a restricted view of the beach.

A server arrived, told us she was Sara with no *h*, then took our drink order. Charles said tea, Virgil and I said water. I reminded Virgil I was buying and he could have anything to drink.

"I appreciate the offer, Christopher. Last night I was out

longer than I should've been. Let's say it resulted in me consuming more adult beverages than I should've. Water rarely sounds good, today's an exception."

"Enough about drinks," Charles said as he tapped his fingers on the table, "why'd you ask if anything unusual happened to me? Your call was as unusual as anything gets, but I figured that wasn't what you were talking about. And, who was with you?"

"Chief LaMond."

"Ah," Virgil said, "the *mutton shunters*."

Charles beat me to asking, "The what?"

"Victorian slang for police," he said like who wouldn't know that.

"Then why didn't you say police?"

Probably the same reason you keep inundating us with obscure school nicknames, I thought. "Either of you want to hear why she was at the house?"

"Duh," Charles said.

Virgil raised his hand.

I began telling them about my morning experience when Sara arrived with our drinks then asked if we were ready to order.

"Perhaps a few more minutes," Virgil said as he looked at his watch. It was still a few minutes until noon.

Neither Charles nor I contradicted him, so Sara said to wave her down when ready. I continued my story about my morning. Virgil listened without comment. Charles was Charles. He had to know what brand of knife, if the paper was lined or plain, and whose idea it was for me to call him. At least he was wise enough not to ask who added the knife to my house's decorations.

I finished my version of the morning's events. Charles waved Sara down to tell her he'd changed his mind. He needed a beer. Virgil said he didn't want Charles to drink alone and added another beer to the order. I had the greatest need for something stronger than water but resisted the urge.

After she left, Virgil said, "What do you know about the murders that Charles and I don't? Holy moly, I was the person who found Thurmond, plus I was with you when we found Honeycutt. Hells bells, I was the person who introduced you to Ryan Sparks. Wait, I even introduced you to Ryan's sister and her husband." He slapped his forehead. "That's not counting us going to meet the jon boat owner. I knew I should've stayed out of it from the beginning. Why didn't I listen to myself?"

"Chill, Virgil," Charles said. "Chris is the one with the knife in his door. He knows something we don't. Right, Chris?"

I was trying to think of who I'd talked to that Virgil hadn't, or for that matter, Charles hadn't."

"Right, Chris?" Charles repeated.

"Sorry, what was the question?"

He repeated what he'd said.

"If I know something, I don't know what it is."

"Ben Likard," Charles said like that solved it.

Virgil said, "What about him?"

Charles looked at me then turned his gaze to Virgil. "Have you met him?"

"No, but what—"

"I haven't either," Charles said. "Chris is the only one who's talked with him. Likard fought with Thurmond, fell for Thurmond's con, gave him oodles of dough. When he wanted some back, Thurmond said, 'no deal, Lucille.'" Charles snapped his fingers. "Chris, didn't you say Likard was pushing the story that Thurmond was bumped off by a hitman from no-telling where?"

"Yes. He also said he'd heard I was a private detective, so it's possible he had the impression I was trying to catch the killer, umm, or killers."

"There you go," Charles said, "case closed. All the Chief has to do now is put the cuffs on him."

"Charles," Virgil said, "I'm no expert, but it seems the *mutton shunters*, umm, police need more proof than that."

"Yes, but—"

Virgil interrupted, "Besides, it wasn't Likard or a hitman. Ryan did it."

I asked, "Why so certain?"

"I told you before, it's a feeling. Think the boy's been *kruger-spoofin'* to us."

Charles made a sound like a horse braying, then said, "Virgil, I have enough trouble understanding Dude, and many of the big words Chris's pal William sprinkles around. If you don't start speaking Folly English, I'll smack you in the face, or whatever a Victorian slang word is for smack in the face."

"It means lying."

Charles rolled his eyes. "Next time, say lying."

Virgil nodded. I smiled. Sara brought their beers and we each ordered cheeseburgers. Then Virgil repeated the killer is Ryan. Charles asked what Ryan had been lying about. Virgil said if he knew, he'd have the case solved. He repeated it was a feeling. I knew he'd been bothered by Ryan first saying he hadn't heard or seen anything, then changing it to having heard voices the morning Thurmond was found, but I agreed with Cindy, that didn't prove anything other than he'd been confused.

"Chris," Charles said, "you've heard Virgil and me blabber on about who we think did the killing. You're the one with the gift knife, who do you think did it?"

"It could've be any of hundreds of people. Thurmond could've ripped people off from anywhere, not simply the people we know about. Honeycutt could've done the same. Now with no paper or electronic trail to learn who they were, I don't see a way of knowing."

Virgil said, "Wow, you're a spoilsport, a downer. If you're right, our job isn't going to be easy."

"Virgil is right," Charles added. "We can't know everyone who got ripped off, so we need to concentrate on those we know about."

I didn't waste my breath pointing out the illogic of Charles's statement, but he was right about one thing. All we could focus on were the people we knew about. And, Ben Likard was the only person we knew who'd been ripped off by Thurmond.

We spent the next twenty minutes enjoying the food, the cool ocean breeze, while we talked in circles about who each of us thought was responsible. We realized we didn't even know if the same person killed both men, or if Honeycutt killed Thurmond then someone killed Honeycutt. Progress was fleeting.

Virgil ended lunch by saying all the crimefighting made him sleepy, that a nap was in order. Charles agreed and thought he'd do he same. I wondered how I'd missed the crimefighting part of lunch but thought Virgil's idea had merit. Before leaving, I suggested each of them should be careful, a killer was out there. They each said they would. I hoped they were right.

CHAPTER THIRTY-EIGHT

The nap I thought was a good idea was easier said then done. I tossed, turned, and kept imagining sounds at my back door, sounds like someone ramming a knife in the doorframe. Once I was so convinced, I got up and peeked outside. Other than a car driving past on the street behind my house, nothing was going on. No knife, no note, no confession. I'd faced danger before, even been close to death a couple of times, so why was a knife stuck in my house bothering me so much? I didn't have an answer any more than an answer to whom killed the two men.

The phone ringing prevented me from feeling more frustrated.

"Hey, Christopher, this is Virgil." He was whispering so I could barely hear him. "Didn't wake you from your nap, did I?"

"No. Why are you whispering?"

"He's walking to the bathroom. Didn't want him to hear me."

"Who's walking to the bathroom?"

"Ryan. We're at the Folly River Park. He went across the field to the restrooms."

"Virgil, what's up?"

"Think you could mosey over. We're sitting on the picnic table."

The park was about the size of a large backyard, so I wondered why he felt the need to tell me where they were. Moseying over was one of the last things I wanted to do, but was curious enough about the reason he wanted me to join them, to say I'd be there in fifteen minutes.

"Good, I need your help getting him to confess."

Was it too late to change my mind?

"Hi, Christopher," Virgil said with a faux expression of surprise on his face. Clearly, he hadn't let Ryan in on my pending visit. "Come join us."

"Hi, Virgil, Ryan," I said as I joined them on the picnic table.

"Funny," Ryan said, "Virgil was talking about you."

I looked at Virgil.

He said, "Was telling Ryan how we found Ron Honeycutt and Dusty. How you and Charles are investigating Honeycutt's death, Thurmond's too."

Thanks, Virgil. We're sitting here with the man you think committed the crimes, and you're telling him I'm meddling in the case. If he's right, I'd be lucky to only get a knife stuck in my house.

I managed a smile. "That's not quite accurate. We've asked

questions, but I have confidence the police will catch the killer."

Virgil said, "Ryan was telling me again about the day I found Thurmond. He thinks he saw someone at the shore near where the jon boat was found."

"Virgil, that's not what I said."

I looked at Virgil then at Ryan. "What'd you see?"

"Nothing, that's the point. I think I heard two voices talking, but I'm not even certain of that. It was so foggy. I couldn't see anything."

Virgil said, "Guess I misunderstood."

After what he said on the phone about tricking Ryan, I thought instead of him misunderstanding, it was Virgil's attempt to trick Ryan into saying something other than what he'd previously shared.

"Besides," Ryan said, "it doesn't matter what I saw, heard, or whatever. Word going around town is the Honeycutt guy killed Thurmond. He took his laptop. They found it in his car. That what you guys heard?"

"A lot of people think so, don't they, Christopher?"

"Yes."

Ryan tapped on the metal table. "Okay, I get that Honeycutt stabbed Thurmond. So, who killed Honeycutt?"

Virgil said, "That's what he's trying to figure out."

Let it go, Virgil. Grr.

He didn't. Virgil said, "Ryan, did you know Honeycutt?"

"Met him a time or two. Didn't trust him. He didn't tell me, but I've heard he and Thurmond were in the con together. Wouldn't surprise me."

"Christopher," Virgil said, "speaking of Thurmond, have

you talked to the Chief to see when Eastman can get his boat back?"

"Not yet."

Ryan leaned toward Virgil. "You talking about Martin Eastman?"

"Yes. Know him?"

"Not really, the other day Megan and I were talking about how nice the people were she'd met since moving here. Someone named Martin Eastman was mentioned. I think she met him in Bert's, the place where it seems a lot of people meet new folks."

It struck me strange how he remembered the name if all Megan did was say she'd met him.

"Ryan, you have a good memory. I have trouble remembering names."

"Always had a good memory. Besides, back in college I played ball with a guy named Marty Eastwick, so when Megan said Eastman, I associated it with Eastwick."

"Remember anything else Megan said about him?"

"Not really. Why, who's he?"

Virgil said, "He owns the boat Thurmond was in when I found him."

"Oh." Ryan looked at his watch. "Better be going. Megan invited me to supper. Can't pass on a home cooked meal. Good talking with you guys."

He hopped off the table with one fluid motion, something if I tried, a trip to the emergency room would be in my near future.

I watched Ryan exit the park, then said, "You still think he killed the men?"

"No doubt."

I hadn't heard anything that supported his definitive conclusion.

"Why?"

"He knew both dead guys. Didn't trust either one. We know Thurmond tried to get him to buy into his fake businesses. He thought about talking to his brother-in-law about borrowing money to give Thurmond. Then, how about him saying he knew Thurmond and Honeycutt were in cahoots. He did it."

"I may not have heard it correctly, but I thought he said he'd heard the men were working together, not he knew they were."

"Sure, that's the version he told us, but I saw how he said it. He knew."

"Anything else he said that convinced you?"

"How about him remembering Martin Eastman's name after claiming Megan only mentioned it in a list of people she'd met. There's no way he'd remember it and jump on it when you mentioned it. There's the connection with Ryan and the jon boat."

"You could be right, but didn't it make sense that he associated it with a name he was familiar with?"

"I suppose."

"Are you thinking Ryan stole the boat from Eastman's house?"

"Umm, yes."

"You think he kayaked or took his sailboat all the way out to Eastman's place, took the jon boat, somehow managed to get Thurmond in it, then stabbed him to death."

Virgil turned to watch the sun as it began sinking over the Folly River, then turned back to me. "Putting it that way, doesn't make as much sense as I thought. It's still possible."

Possible, yes; probable, no.

"You're right. It's possible."

He smiled like he's earned a merit badge for catching killers.

CHAPTER THIRTY-NINE

My phone's ringtone awakened me the next morning. Charles's name appeared on the screen, but this time he didn't start with a question.

"Get to my place."

"Charles, why—"

"Now!"

He had my attention. To get there *now*, I had to drive. My friend was waiting for me in the gravel lot in front of his building. As soon as I put the car in park, he pointed his cane at his Toyota. It appeared lopsided. It only took a second to realize it wasn't an optical illusion. I'd be lopsided too if three of my tires were flat.

"What are the odds seventy-five percent of my tires decided to deflate at the same time?"

"Zero," I said, stating the obvious.

He'd knelt beside the rear flat tire than rubbed his finger along the sidewall. "I'd put money on a knife doing this."

I wouldn't take that bet. "Have you called the police?"

"Why? Can they stick duct tape on the holes, blow the tires up?"

That was another of his questions that didn't deserve an answer. "You need to make a report. They also might find some evidence around the car."

"Better chance of them finding gold nuggets in the gravel."

There was no need to debate the merits, so I dialed Cindy who answered with. "What now?"

I gave her a ten-second recap where I was and why. She said she'd be here in fifteen minutes.

Charles had moved to the other side of the vehicle, waved me around with his cane, then said, "Wonder why the damned slasher missed a tire."

"Someone could've interrupted him. When was the last time you drove?"

"Went to Harris Teeter last night around eight. Think I would've noticed three flats. Would've been a rough ride."

"When did you see what'd been done?"

"Few minutes before I called you."

"It happened between nine last night and this morning."

He shook his head. "Yeah, unless the coroner can determine a better time of death for tires."

"Did you see any of your neighbors out here either last evening or this morning?"

"Nary a one."

I looked at the privacy fence on the other side of the parking lot. A row of palmetto trees loomed over the fence with a row of townhouses peeking through the trees.

I pointed to the townhouses. "Did you notice anyone on those balconies?"

"Nary a one."

"One more question. Did—"

"You're beginning to sound like me. I see why you think I'm so irritating asking questions all the time."

Wow, a glimmer of introspection.

"Charles, did you find a note?"

He sighed. "Nary a one."

I came close to laughing but knew it wouldn't help his mood.

Chief LaMond's pickup pulled in the lot then parked beside my vehicle. She glanced at Charles's car then turned to us standing behind it.

"Charles, want me to shoot the other tire to level the ride?"

I again held back a laugh. Charles held back a profanity.

Cindy added, "Sorry, couldn't help myself." She walked around the car then moved beside Charles and me. "Any idea who did it?"

"Yes," Charles said, "the same a-hole who stabbed Chris's house, the same guy who stabbed Thurmond, the same guy who stabbed Honeycutt."

Cindy nodded. "I was fishing more for a name."

Charles shook his head. "Then you're fishing in the wrong stream. I don't know."

Cindy looked at Charles's hands, then on the ground near the car. "Was there a note?"

Please don't say, "Nary a one."

"No."

"Witnesses?"

Charles looked at the sky. "Could've been someone in the

space shuttle. No one from around here said they saw anything."

Cindy patted Charles on the arm. "I'm sorry. This must be frustrating. I'll have my guys check with your neighbors, also the folks who live in the condos. With luck, someone may've seen whoever did this. Anything else I can do?"

Charles looked at the closest flat tire. "Have any duct tape?"

Cindy said, "Why?"

"Never mind," Charles said. "Thanks for coming."

"I'm here to serve and protect although I'm not doing either very well lately. My guys will be here in a little while."

She gave us a salute, got in her truck, and left.

"I have no doubt it was the same person who left the knife at my house. I wonder why he didn't leave a note."

"I figure he didn't need to. This happened after he left you the love letter. He knows you and I are looking at the deaths. It doesn't take a private detective to detect the two things are related. I'm now warned off as much as you were. No, correction, I'm warned off more than you. You only have a little slice in your doorframe. I've got to buy three tires."

He moved to the step leading to his door, plopped down, looked around, then said, "What have we got ourselves into?"

I shrugged.

"Chris, I suppose I should be honored the killer thinks I'm moving in on him, but that's an honor I can do without. On the other end of the scale from being honored, to tell the truth, I'm petrified." He pointed his cane at one of the flats. "He could've stuck a knife in me nearly as easy as that. I take too fondly to living. I repeat, what have we got ourselves into?"

"I don't like being a target any more than you, but it looks like we don't have a choice at this point. The way I see it, our only option is to do whatever we can to help the police. Whoever did this must think we're getting close."

"We may be getting close, but what worries me more is how close he's getting to us." He started to stand then plopped back down on the step. "This killer has a fondness for stabbing people, stabbing things. Don't know what it is about knives, but they scare the heebie-jeebies out of me. Scare me worse than a gun." He shook his head and repeated, "Worse than a gun."

I hated to see my friend so shaken. Truth be told, I was nearly as traumatized, but it wouldn't do either of us any good, sitting here having a pity party. It also wouldn't bring us any closer to finding the killer. Staring at his abused vehicle wasn't helping his mood, so I suggested we move into his apartment. He didn't say anything but continued shaking his head as he led me to his living room cluttered with books of all sizes and genres. I called AAA to figure out how to tow his car to a tire store while he bemoaned the cost of replacing the tires. So far, I'm a total failure at improving his mood—or mine.

An hour later, Charles's Toyota was being towed to a store on Folly Road, he asked for what must've been the hundredth time who the killer was, I answered for the same number of times that I didn't know, then he decided a good breakfast would solve all our problems. I didn't know about that but was certain it'd be better than watching him mumble to himself as he paced the tiny living room.

Both patio seating areas were full when we arrived at the Dog, so I was expecting a wait. The hostess said it shouldn't be too long, although any length wait was better than being in Charles's apartment. We sat on a bench in front of the entry where Charles was distracted from feeling sorry for himself by a young couple with a beagle puppy. Charles was in his element. While petting the pup, he asked the owners its name, then asked the names of the owners, where they were from, plus where they were staying while visiting Folly. I was afraid he was going to ask to see their drivers' licenses, possibly birth certificates, when the hostess told us our table was ready. The couple, Jim and Celia, along with their dog, Snoopy, didn't appear too upset when Charles apologized for having to leave for his table.

We were talking about Ben Likard and his being a suspect when Amber saw us, set two plates on the table she'd been waiting on, then headed our way.

"Morning guys, find more bodies?" she said with a smile.

"No," Charles said, not returning her smile.

She glanced at me, then back at Charles. "Get up on the wrong side of the bed this morning?"

"Sorry," Charles said. "Been a rough morning."

That was all it took. She looked around to see if anyone needed her attention. Seeing no one, she knelt in front of my friend. "What happened?"

Charles told her about his tires, then mentioned the knife left at my house. Amber asked us the same question we'd been asking each other all morning. What did we know that had someone determined to get us to step aside? We gave her the same answer: We don't know. Charles said Virgil suspected it was Ryan while I put more stock in it being Ben Likard.

Amber turned to me. "Ben Likard. He was in as soon as we opened this morning, sat right over there." She pointed to a small table behind the hostess station. "The reason I mention it is he wasn't in his normal cheery mood."

Charles said, "Cheery mood?"

Amber nodded left then right before saying, "Guess cheery isn't the right word. What I mean is he's always friendly, smiling, doesn't seem to have a care in the world. At least, that's the way he is when he's around me. Today he seemed tired, didn't say anything bad, just not like he was happy. More disheveled than usual. That make sense?"

"Yes. Did he say what was bothering him?"

"I didn't ask. I don't know how rich he is, but know he lives in a big house, drives a new Lexus, doesn't seem to ever have to go to work. Looks say he has money. I was thinking if he lost a bunch of money to Thurmond it may be bothering him more than he wants everyone to know. Maybe his finances aren't as good as he lets on."

"Could be," Charles said.

Another thought popped in my head. Likard being tired, not in a good mood, could also be because he'd left Charles's parking lot and a car with three flats.

Breakfast failed to improve Charles's mood, but it filled our stomachs.

CHAPTER FORTY

Charles said staring at his disabled car had worn him out, so he left to take a nap. It wasn't my car, so I didn't foresee a nap. A visit to Barb's books sounded like the perfect prescription to cheer me.

Two customers were in the store with Barb behind the counter selling three books to one of them. The other customer was browsing the romance section. The buyer left and Barb stepped out from behind the counter to kiss my cheek.

"What brings you in?"

"Could be to buy a book."

"That'd be a first."

I smiled. "Better not break my streak." I told her I'd come from breakfast with Charles.

"What trouble did you two conjure up?"

"Interesting you should mention trouble."

The remaining customer brought six books to the counter,

so I stepped aside while Barb completed the sale. The smiling customer left several books heavier, and Barb said, "Trouble?"

I told her about Charles's tires.

"That on top of the knife in your house. You two have made yourselves an enemy."

"Duh."

"Are Ryan Sparks and Ben Likard still your suspects?"

"Ben, definitely. Virgil thinks it's Ryan, but I still have reservations."

"Ben was in yesterday. He bought two books and when I told him I was getting Stephen King's latest later in the afternoon, he asked me to hold it for him. Said he'd pick it up this morning."

"Ask if he killed the two guys while you're selling it to him."

She shook her head. "Charles is rubbing off on you."

I smiled. "You won't ask?"

She rolled her eyes.

A young couple entered. The woman came over to us to ask if we, which I knew meant Barb, had anything on the history of Charleston. Barb told her she just got in *Wicked Charleston; The Dark Side of the Holy City*, and added, "It's by Mark Jones, a local author and historian who knows as much about Charleston as anyone."

I told Barb I'd talk to her later and let her find the book for her customer who said it sounded interesting.

I was in front of Mr. John's Beach Store when I spotted Ben Likard park his Lexus in front of Barb's Books. He looked more disheveled than the last two times I'd seen him. Before he entered Barb's, he wiped dust off the knees of his light-gray slacks. I waited a couple of minutes then headed back to the store. When I reen-tered, Ben was waiting for Barb to finish with her customer.

"Hi, Ben," I said hoping he bought my surprised look seeing him there.

"Hi, Mr. Landrum, we meet again."

"Please call me Chris," I said as we shook.

"Chris, I hear you have more reasons to visit this store than to buy books. Something about that lovely lady whose name is on the sign."

I smiled. "True. I'm glad I ran into you. I was wondering if you heard anything else about Walter Thurmond?"

His focus narrowed. "Why would I?"

"You told me in Bert's you'd bought into a couple of his companies. I thought you might've heard about others who may've done the same."

"I understand that, but why are you asking? Aren't the police charged with solving the murder? What business is it of yours?"

"You're right about it being up to the police. I was curious."

"If you ask me, it's dangerous for you to be meddling. I've heard there are two murders that could be related. Didn't Ron Honeycutt have Thurmond's computer?"

I, of course, hadn't asked, but was tempted to ask if he'd communicated the same sentiment in a note stuck in my house.

"Yes, they found the computer in Honeycutt's car. The police think either Honeycutt killed Thurmond then someone killed Honeycutt, or the same person killed both men."

"All I know is I've lost a shit-pot load of money to Thurmond and his investment con, money I'll never get back."

"I'm sorry about your loss. How well did you know Honeycutt?"

"Not at all. I've heard he was Thurmond's partner ripping people off, but I don't think I met him, or if I did, I don't remember."

"Any idea if others over here bought in Thurmond's companies?"

Barb escorted her customer to the door, then turned to us. "Hey, Ben, is this old geezer bothering you?"

Thanks, Barb.

"No. We were talking about the men who were killed."

Barb gave me a dirty look, then said, "I'm glad Chris isn't bothering you. I have the book you wanted. Let me grab it."

We both watched her head to the counter before Ben said, "What was your question again?"

"I was curious if you knew other investors in Thurmond's companies."

Likard paid for the book as three more customers entered. He and I moved to the corner of the room to stay out of their way.

"Others who fell for Thurmond's pitch. Let me think. I asked him a couple of times to give me names so I could contact them about their experiences with the companies. I thought Thurmond would be happy to give me names of happy investors. Instead, he said he couldn't divulge the names because of non-disclosure clauses in the contracts. I thought it sounded strange since I didn't recall that clause in my contract, but didn't push it. No doubt, a mistake."

"You don't know anybody else who've invested?"

"Don't know names. Thurmond told me there were two others who either lived on Folly or James Island who were part owners with him. He said I'd know who they were, but unfortunately he couldn't give me their names."

"That's all he told you?"

"Yes, well no, he said one was a celebrity. I suppose he thought that added credibility to his sales pitch."

"He didn't say what kind of celebrity?"

He shook his head. "I'd love to talk more, but I've got a busy day. We can talk later."

"Thanks for letting me know what else you knew about Thurmond," I said, realizing it was little.

He waved bye to Barb, headed to the door, hesitated, pivoted toward me, then said, "Meddling in police business can be dangerous, or so I hear."

"Good point."

Good point, indeed.

CHAPTER FORTY-ONE

The next morning, I couldn't get out of my head what Likard had said about how involving myself in police business could be dangerous. Was he concerned about my wellbeing, or on a more sinister level, was he the person who left me the note attached to the kind of weapon that'd ended Thurmond's and Honeycutt's lives? If it was the latter, why did he think Charles or I were threats? What did we know the police didn't or how were we on track to uncover his dastardly deeds? Granted, Likard lost a lot of money to Thurmond, a few hundred thousand dollars, if I remember correctly. Was that enough to kill over? Probably, but the police knew about his involvement.

I didn't know many people who had a spare few hundred thousand dollars sitting around. I wondered how big a deal that would've been to Likard. All I knew about him was he had a nice house, nice car, dressed well, and had time to spare, a possible indication he didn't have to work. How could I find out more about the man? A call to Sean Aker was a possibility.

Marlene told me Sean wasn't in the office, but he told her not to tell anyone where he was. She said she always did what her boss asked her to do, so she wasn't going to tell me he was at the Dog. I thanked her for not telling me, then walked to the breakfast spot.

I hadn't reached the parking lot when I spotted Sean on the front patio sipping coffee and reading Charleston's daily newspaper. He saw me approach, held the paper in front of his face, either to avoid me or to read something at the bottom of the page.

"Hey, Sean."

He lowered the paper, sighed, then said, "She ratted me out, didn't she?"

"I don't know what you're talking about."

"I'm a highly trained lawyer. I know how to lie. You need to work on your alternate reality skills."

I walked to the side entrance to the patio and took the chair opposite the highly trained attorney. "Got a question," I said, ignoring his helpful advice.

"Of course, you do," he said as Amber came around the corner, saw me, headed inside, returned with a mug of coffee, smiled, then set it in front of me.

Sean shook his head. "Miss Amber, he wants French toast."

Seriously! I need to expand my breakfast choices.

"Duh," she said, smiled again, then headed inside.

Sean took a sip of coffee, then said, "Question?"

"It's two now. First, do you ever do legal work?"

"I'm hurt you would ask such a question. What's question two?"

Yes, he didn't answer question one.

"How much do you know about Ben Likard?"

"I've never done work for him, but that shouldn't surprise you since you don't think I work for anyone. I know he's possibly the richest person on Folly."

"You know that how?"

"Ever hear of Likard Shipping?"

"No."

"I'm not surprised. It was huge in the early 1920s. Had more ships than the Navy. Mainly tankers. In the 50s the company sold off most of its fleet. Old man Likard was up in age and wanted to travel the world without having to think about his floating armada." He took another sip. "Story goes he got to travel the world for three weeks before dropping dead of a heart attack in France."

Amber arrived with my breakfast, asked Sean if he needed anything else. He said, "Peace and quiet."

"Too late." Amber said, then left laughing.

Sean turned back to me. "Fast forward ninety years past inheritances, births, deaths, family feuds, blah, blah, blah, to find the gentleman you asked about inheriting several hundred million dollars. He gave up the life of a high school teacher and took up the life of a zillionaire. A wise change if you want my opinion."

"How do you know all that?"

"I said I didn't do legal work for him. I didn't say he and I didn't spend three hours trapped in an airplane flying from Denver to Charleston. The boy's a talker once he gets started."

"How long ago was that?"

"Couple of years. Now I have a question."

"Shoot."

"Why are you interested?"

"He was one of the people who bought into Thurmond's companies. Several hundred thousand dollars in fact."

"You think he killed Thurmond?"

"Yes."

"Over money?"

"Yes."

"Not saying he didn't, but a few hundred thousand to someone worth more than Bulgaria's GNP would be like someone ripping you off for fifty bucks. Reason enough to kill? I don't think so. Of course, there could be other reasons."

"Like?"

"Crap, I'm just a lowly attorney with no clients. You're the detective. Figure it out." He smiled and took another sip.

I didn't need to remind him it was Charles who claimed to be the detective.

"Okay, got another question."

He sighed. "First you said you had one question, then it morphed into two, now you're upping the number. Do I look like Wikipedia?"

He didn't, but I knew he liked sharing from his limitless fount of information.

"I came to you because of your vast knowledge of many things."

"Did you already forget what I said about being a lawyer, about lying?"

"Do you know any celebrities living on Folly?"

"George Gershwin lived here a while; Blackbeard is reputed to have had a house here; umm, that's about it."

"Sean, the keyword in my question was living, not ancient history."

"Are you counting me as a celebrity?"

"No."

"Like I told you before, some would call Ryan Sparks a celebrity."

"To a baseball fan."

"Yes."

"Likard said Thurmond told him a celebrity who lived on Folly or James Island had bought into one of his businesses but wouldn't tell Likard who it was."

"Ryan would be a stretch, but like I said, some people would consider him a celebrity. You think Ryan, if he is the celebrity, killed Thurmond?"

"Not really. I'm trying to get the full picture of what Thurmond was involved in."

"You're much, much older than I am, but from my experience, you'll never get the full picture of most anything. You have to go with what you have."

"Did you have to say much, much older?"

Sean laughed. "Could've left out a much, but it was fun saying it."

On that note, I left him so he could enjoy the peace and quiet Amber couldn't deliver.

Sean might be right about someone who had *several hundred million dollars* not being angry enough about losing *only* a few hundred thousand dollars to kill Thurmond as someone—anyone—losing far fewer dollars to kill Thurmond, but I wasn't ruling it out. Sean could also be correct about

Thurmond referring to Ryan Sparks as a celebrity, but that would border on incredulous. On the other hand, since Thurmond wouldn't tell Ben Likard the names of any of those who bought into his companies, he could've exaggerated the level of fame one of his investors enjoyed or made up the entire story. In the unlikely event Ryan either had or planned to become one of the partners in Thurmond's companies, he'd lied about it. That could confirm Virgil's reluctance to eliminate him as a suspect. Making matters more frustrating, there could be countless others who fell for Thurmond's pitch; countless others I know nothing about. What I do know is there is someone who left Charles and me frightening reminders to butt out of trying to figure it out.

I stopped in Bert's on my way home to get lunch. Since my culinary skills approached the ability of hummingbird to sit peacefully through a Rolling Stones concert, I headed to the shelf holding peanut butter, grabbed a jar, then went over to the bread rack to get a loaf to complete the ingredients needed for lunch after my breakfast wears off.

It was a weekday, so I was surprised to see Kevin Goodman in the next aisle.

"Hi, Kevin, off work today?"

"Oh, hi, umm, Chris is it?"

I nodded.

"They're retooling at work so some of us got an extra day off." He chuckled. "I'm enjoying it by grocery shopping. Lucky, aren't I?" He looked in the basket he was carrying, then sighed.

I nodded a second time, smiled, then said, "How's the construction coming?"

"We can build a 787 Dreamliner, sell it to Singapore

Airlines, and have it fly thirteen months quicker than it took to finish the damned remodel."

I assumed the Boeing aircraft assembler was exaggerating but commiserated with him about the length of time remodeling takes.

"The good news is it was finished yesterday, well, almost finished. Painters are touching up places the plumbers messed up. Hallelujah!"

"That's great. Bet it looks good," I said, not knowing what else to say.

"Megan is inviting folks she's gotten to know over tomorrow night to celebrate the 'grand reveal' as she calls it. You're welcome to join us. I think it's a frivolous idea, but what Megan wants, Megan gets." He chuckled.

"Sure she wouldn't mind?"

"Are you kidding? She'd invite the entire island if she could. She'd love to see you there."

"I'll try to stop by. Thanks for the invitation."

"Good. Now all I must do is figure out how to pay for Megan's extravaganza. Women, right?"

I gave my third nod as he left to pay for his purchase.

CHAPTER FORTY-TWO

I thought Kevin was exaggerating when he used the word extravaganza to describe their "grand reveal." If he was, it wasn't far off. Cars were parked along East Ashley Avenue two blocks before I reached their house. I was glad I walked.

Megan greeted me at the door with a hug. I felt like a long-lost cousin meeting my relative for the first time.

"Glad you could make it. Kevin said he invited you. I'm glad he did since you saw some of the work before it was finished."

The smell of sawdust that'd permeated the air during my previous visit was replaced by the aroma of fresh paint and air freshener.

"I was glad I ran into him."

"Let's go to the kitchen and get you a drink."

We followed the din of voices coming from the combination kitchen/dining room. While the room may've been much larger than before the remodel, it was still packed. The aroma of popcorn replaced the smell of fresh paint.

Kevin was leaning against the island talking with Ryan. He saw me, excused himself, then came over to shake hands.

"Good to see you, Chris. What do you think?" He waved his hand around like he was pointing out the room's features.

"It looks great. When I looked at this house to buy all those years ago, I never could've pictured it looking this good."

"All the credit goes to Megan," he said as he wrapped his arm around her waist. "It was her vision."

Ryan had followed Kevin over. He gave me a subtle wave. I took a couple of steps over to give Ryan space to join the conversation.

"What do you think of Sis and Kevin's nearly new house?" He followed my gaze around the room then added, "This room's bigger than my sailboat."

Megan patted him on the back. "Not true, Ryan, but it is nice." She looked toward the entry into the kitchen, saw someone I didn't know standing there. "Better welcome our new guest."

Ryan pulled Kevin aside, leaving me standing by myself. I looked around for the drinks, then seeing bottles of wine, and a beer cooler near the sink, I headed their direction. Ryan said something about getting it back, I turned to see if he was talking to me, but he was looking at Kevin. I started to rejoin them, when Charles bounced into the room. He scanned the space, spotting me, then headed my way.

He opened with, "What are you doing here?"

I explained how Kevin had invited me.

"How come you didn't invite me to come with you?"

I could have asked him the same thing. Instead of pointing that out, I asked how he learned about the party.

"Suppose you think you're getting off the hook turning the question on me. I'm on to your tricks." He frowned, then smiled as he tapped my arm with his fist. "Kidding. I ran into Megan this morning at Bert's. She said because of my wonderful personality and ability to get along with everyone, she was inviting me."

I suspected he was kidding. "Uh-huh."

"Okay, that plus I helped her carry four beer cartons to the car."

"That's more like it."

"Okay smarty pants, what'd you do to get invited?"

"Kevin saw me and said he was inviting me because of my wonderful personality and ability to get along with everyone."

"Congratulations, sounding more like me every day."

Before our conversation could sink lower, Megan joined us. She told Charles she was glad to see him, saw our hands were empty, then reminded us about the drinks on the counter by the sink. Charles told her that was where he was headed before I stopped him. She left to greet someone in the doorway, someone I'd recently met, someone I didn't expect to see here. Martin Eastman.

I remember Ryan saying his sister casually knew Eastman, but I was surprised he was here. I was equally as surprised to see Ryan joining his sister and Eastman then warmly embrace the new arrival. Hadn't Ryan told me he hadn't met Eastman; that he'd remembered his name because it was similar to someone he'd played ball with?

"Who's the new guy?" Charles said then pointed to the trio.

"Martin Eastman. It was his boat Thurmond's body was in."

"The guy visiting his brother when Thurmond bit the dust?"

"Visiting his mother."

"Whoever. Point is he wasn't near here when Thurmond was killed. Now he's acting like he's known Ryan and Megan since like forever. Grab a glass of wine and let's go welcome him to the party."

"Looks like he's already receiving a warm welcome."

"Not from us."

Once Charles focuses on a goal, it'd take the Great Wall of China to block his route, so I grabbed a glass of wine and followed him to the three people who'd moved to the new sunroom.

Megan, Ryan, and Eastman were huddled in the corner of the addition, which, of course, didn't stop Charles from inter-rupting their muted conversation.

"Hey guys, great party," he said as he extended his hand to Eastman, "Don't believe we've met. I'm Charles Fowler."

Eastman gave him a look that reminded me of the scowl he greeted Virgil and me with when we met him at his house.

"Martin Eastman."

Charles said, "How do you know Megan and Ryan?"

"Umm, we see each other around town."

Ryan jumped in the conversation as he pointed to Charles's T-shirt. "Did you go to Georgia? I played ball against them a couple of times when I was in college."

I was making progress. I hadn't even noticed Charles was wearing a red University of Georgia shirt.

"No."

It was a shorter answer than my friend would normally give. Ryan had stepped on the flow of Charles interrogation.

"Oh," Ryan said, a typical response to many of Charles's comments.

"Shall we go get you some drinks," Megan said with a forced smile. Her comment was clearly directed to Ryan and Eastman since they were the only people in the group without drinks.

They followed her to the kitchen, leaving Charles and me to admire the new room.

"Well, that was awkward," said the man who'd butted into our host's conversation with Ryan and Martin Eastman.

I thought the same thing but was more interested in Ryan's relationship with Eastman since he'd previously told me they hadn't met. He'd shared that several days ago, so I suppose they could've met since then.

Virgil was next to arrive. He said he'd seen Ryan last night at the bar at Snapper Jack's and was invited. He asked if it was Martin Eastman he'd seen in the kitchen. I told him it was.

"Small world, isn't it?" he said and looked at the glass of wine in my hand. "Think I could get one of those?"

"Yes, yes," Charles said.

"Huh?"

"Yes, it's a small world," I translated. "Another yes to the drink. Follow us."

The expanded kitchen was more crowded than earlier, so we weaved our way around people to where Virgil poured a glass of wine then looked around. Megan, Ryan, and Eastman were nowhere to be seen.

"This reminds me of the soirees my ex held in our

mansion on the Battery back when I was rich," Virgil said. "Boring as hell. Ah, the good old days."

Charles patted Virgil on the back. "I can tell you miss it."

Virgil chuckled. "Almost as much as I miss cholera."

"Miss what?" Kevin said as he moved beside Virgil.

Charles said, "Virgil was saying how great the party is, how he missed attending great ones like this since he moved to Folly."

Charles never let the truth get in the way of a good, albeit, fabricated story.

Kevin looked around at the crowd. "Yes, free booze brings out the masses."

"Your renovations look great," I said, hoping to remind Kevin why we were here.

"The best money can buy," he said. "A lot of money," he added in a lower voice.

"Stunning," Virgil said.

My choice of *great* didn't do the renovations justice.

Two women I didn't know squeezed into the kitchen, Kevin left to greet them, and I suggested Virgil, Charles, and I move to the less-populated addition.

"Told you I was right," Virgil said as we moved away from the crowd.

Charles took a sip of beer, pointed the bottle at Virgil, then said, "Want to give us a hint about what?"

"Ryan killed Thurmond. Ryan killed Honeycutt. Those enough hints?"

"Explain," Charles said.

"I figured since you're the detective I didn't have to explain."

Charles nodded like it made sense, then said, "Checking to see how you figured it out."

Virgil pointed to the door to the kitchen. "Martin Eastman owned the boat I found Thurmond in. Ryan lied about not hearing or seeing anything when Thurmond was killed. Ryan knows Martin Eastman. Those facts add up to Ryan doing it. Open and shut case. Ryan did it."

"Okay," Charles said, "let's say you're right. Why?"

"Why he killed Thurmond? Why he killed Honeycutt?"

Charles said, "Yes."

"Hell if I know."

I suspected the three of us agreed on that point. I still didn't believe Ryan killed the men but found it interesting that Megan and Ryan knew the jon boat owner better than they let me believe. Was it simply because they ran into each other around town, or was there more?

Charles and Virgil remained at the party after I told them I had about as much fun as I could looking at the renovations and making strained conversation with people I didn't know. Charles said he was staying to see if he overheard anything that'd either reinforce Virgil's theory about Ryan being the killer, or anything to implicate someone else. Virgil said he was staying for the free booze.

CHAPTER FORTY-THREE

Charles called the next morning. Called at six o'clock!

"Know what gives me tons of pleasure?" he said to my sleepy ear.

"Pestering me."

"That, too."

I sighed. "What else?"

"Photographing the lighthouse at sunrise."

Right up there with the Folly Pier, the Morris Island Lighthouse was one of the most photographed features on or near Folly.

"Glad to hear it."

"Good. I'm parked in front of your house. Going or not?"

I hung up on him, knowing that unless I was getting in his car in the next ten minutes, he'd be pounding on the door. Truth be told, I shared his penchant for photographing the lighthouse and the windswept trees growing near the beach in the eighty-acre Preserve.

"What took you so long? It's almost sunrise." he said as I got in his Toyota.

"Good morning, Charles."

He groaned as he drove to the end of East Ashley Avenue and the entrance to the Preserve. Most times of the day, it was difficult to find somewhere to park since the former Coast Guard station property was so popular. Parking was not a problem at six-thirty.

"We beat the crowd," Charles said as he pulled off the road onto the sandy berm a few yards before the turn-around and entrance to the Preserve.

"Amazing," I said, not hiding sarcasm before grabbing my camera from the back seat.

The view of the lighthouse was a quarter mile from where we parked, so Charles headed down the deserted road left from the Coast Guard's occupancy. I caught up with him and we walked side-by-side to the end of the paved area where a sandy path descended to the beach. The sun was beginning to peek over the horizon.

"Good, we beat the sun, despite your lazy pace getting out of the house," Charles said as he stabilized his camera on the large boulders leading into the water to get a longer exposure.

I smiled remembering how little he knew about photography when we first met. Now taking photos ranked up there with getting to know everyone and their pets and collecting one of every college T-shirt printed.

He'd taken roughly a thousand images as if it was the first time he'd seen the lighthouse, then sat on one of the large rocks. I finished taking a dozen images then joined him on the adjacent boulder.

He tilted his Tilley back then said, "So, what did we learn yesterday about who killed the guys?"

I suspected we were approaching the real reason he wanted to get together this morning.

"I didn't learn it at the party, but it reinforced what Virgil had said before."

"That he's hung up on Ryan being the killer?"

I nodded.

"Think it's possible?"

"Suppose so, although I can't see a motive. Thurmond may've approached Ryan to be his partner in one of the manufacturing plants, but Ryan didn't have any money and told that to Thurmond. The only thing Virgil keeps coming back to is Ryan was close to where the body was found, and Ryan told conflicting stories about what he heard that morning."

Charles hopped up then headed close to water's edge then toward a copse of dead trees that've been bleached, smoothed, and battered by the sun, sand, and wind. While the area has no formal name, it'd often been referred to as Boneyard Beach. Charles stepped over one of the trees dotting the beach then looked back toward the lighthouse.

He took two more photos then said, "You still think it's Ben Likard, don't you?"

"He's the only person I know who had a strong motive."

"Motive don't mean murder unless there's proof. How're we going to get it?"

He knew I didn't know so there was no need to say it. When we arrived, we were the only people on the beach for as far as we could see. That was no longer the case. A couple with three kids were playing on the rocks. Two couples, probably in their sixties, were strolling near where the water slapped the shore. And, while dogs were prohibited in the Preserve, there was no one to monitor the rule, so two men were watching dogs the size of small horses running in and out of the surf while chasing a tennis ball.

Charles went to introduce himself to the dogs and I leaned against another of the fallen trees. Like the tide rolling in then inching out, something tugged on my memory. I still didn't think Ryan was the killer but found it interesting Likard told me a celebrity had bought into one of Thurmond's companies. While I wouldn't consider a former minor league baseball player a celebrity, others might. Then, when asked how Ryan knew Martin Eastman, he sluffed it off as he'd heard Megan mention the name. Was that enough to remember a man's name? For me it wouldn't have been. Then Martin Eastman appears at yesterday's party. In fact, it was another reason Virgil pointed to Ryan as the killer. Eastman appeared to know Megan and Ryan more than from seeing each other around town, for Ryan having never met him.

Was I too quick to eliminate Ryan as the killer?

When Virgil and I met Eastman at his house, we asked if he knew the two dead men. We didn't ask about Ryan, his sister or his brother-in-law. I wondered how he'd react to questions about how well he knew them.

Charles smiled as he came back from playing with the dogs. "That's Harper and Jules, named after the writers Harper Lee and Jules Verne. Ain't that great?"

It didn't take much to entertain my friend. I said, "Sure is," to not dampen his enthusiasm.

"Ready to head back to civilization?"

"Whenever you are," I said.

"Think I've run out of photo ops."

He turned around at the end of the road then drove toward town.

"Pull over," I said as I pointed to an empty space in front of Martin Eastman's house.

To my surprise, Charles pulled over without questions.

There were no vehicles in the drive, but I didn't know if anyone else lived there, so, for the second time in a week, I climbed the stairs to Eastman's porch then knocked. No one answered, so I knocked two more times, then headed to the car. At the bottom of the steps, I noticed the house on the left had a For Sale sign in the yard; the house on the other side of Eastman's had a swing in the yard, a silver minivan in the drive.

I headed toward the house with the vehicle. Charles grabbed my arm. "Before we go pestering whoever lives there, how about telling me what we're doing?"

I stopped at the bottom of the steps to the occupied house. "I'm having trouble wrapping my arms around why someone took Eastman's jon boat and killed Thurmond in it. No one we know who knew Thurmond lived anywhere near here."

"But—"

I interrupted whatever Charles was going to say. "Follow my lead."

He saluted. "Yes, sir."

A young woman carrying a whimpering toddler on her hip answered the door. She wore tattered shorts, a Pink t-shirt with food stains on the front, ruffled hair, and a look best described as exhausted.

She looked at Charles then at me. "Yes?"

"Sorry to bother you," I said. "I'm Chris and this is

Charles. We're looking into the theft of your neighbor's jon boat a couple of weeks ago."

Her gaze narrowed. "I didn't take it."

"No, of course not. I wondered if you saw anyone near Mr. Eastman's yard around that time. I think he was away visiting his mother."

"The police already asked me and my husband the same thing."

"I understand, but we thought you might've remembered something after the police questioned you."

"Nope."

Charles stepped closer to the door. "Mrs., umm, sorry, I didn't catch your name."

"Denise, Denise Richardson."

"Ms. Richardson, do you know Ryan Sparks?"

She shook her head.

"How about Megan or Kevin Goodman?"

She took a deep breath, then said, "Don't think so."

Charles smiled. "Only two more. How about Ben Likard?"

She shook her head as the child she's was carrying pulled her hair. Denise swatted the hand away, then said, "Last name?"

"Ron Honeycutt? He has an adorable pug named Dusty."

Denise looked at Charles like he was a pug. "No."

"Ms. Richardson," I said, "how well do you know Martin Eastman?"

"Sir, as you can tell, I have my hands full with little Todd here, and he has a three-year-old sister to add to my full hands. She's taking a nap. I know Martin only as someone I wave to whenever I see him out or he sees me. I've been here five years; doubt we've ever talked more than two minutes at a time. I gather he was much closer to the neighbors on the other side of his house. I saw him out in his back yard with them a few times."

"Who're they?" I asked.

"The Smiths, Earl and Samantha. They moved out a month ago. Don't know where they went."

"Ms. Richardson, we don't want to take more of your time. Sorry to bother you."

She smiled. "That's okay. It was nice talking to adults, someone older than three for a change."

She may not have said that if she knew Charles better.

"Well, that was enlightening," Charles said as he slipped behind the wheel.

"Look at the bright side," I said. "Someone called you an adult."

CHAPTER FORTY-FOUR

We'd piled back in the car and were about four blocks from Center Street when Charles slammed on the brakes, uttered a profanity, and pulled off the road.

I said, "What?"

Charles pointed across the street to Virgil's apartment building, turned off the engine, and got out. Traffic was heavy so we waited for several cars to pass before crossing the street. Once we got in front of Virgil's building, I saw what'd grabbed Charles attention. Virgil's scooter was parked beside the building. A scooter with two slashed tires.

"This is beginning to piss me off," Charles said as he walked around the scooter. He pointed to a sheet of paper folded and stuck between the seat and the frame. I bent to see what was written on the paper without touching or removing it.

In block letters, it read *BUTT OUT!*

"Now Virgil won't feel left out," Charles said.

I ignored him and went to Virgil's door, knocked twice, then waited. It took a second series of knocks before Virgil opened the door, peeked out, yawned, and said, "Hey, Christopher. How're you doing?"

He had on a ratty T-shirt and black boxer shorts with pink flamingos on them. It was one of the few times I hadn't seen him in Guccis and sunglasses. He stretched his arms over his head while he waited for me to answer how I was.

He saw me glance at his shorts. "Part of my share of the divorce settlement. Want to see the fuzzy Star Wars house slippers I got?"

I bit the inside of my lip to keep from laughing then declined. I told him I was fine before suggesting he put on more clothes, then join Charles and me in the parking lot. Without asking why, he closed the door then reappeared a couple of minutes later, dressed more like I was used to seeing him.

"Suppose there's a good reason you woke me from." He hesitated, looked at the sky, then said, "my beauty sleep this sunny morning."

I motioned him to follow me. Like a good puppy, he did, then spotted his scooter.

"Holy Michelin, what in the hell happened to my tires?"

Charles pointed at the slash marks, then at the note. "Welcome to the club."

Virgil squinted to read the note before shaking his head. "To think, I was worried about the brakes needing work. Now I don't need them."

I called Cindy while Virgil slowly walked around his injured scooter.

"What now, trouble magnet?" she said with either a sneer or a muted chuckle.

I told her where I was and why. She said she was in a meeting with the mayor but would have one of her officers meet me at Virgil's. Five minutes later, Officer Spencer pulled in beside us.

He looked at the tires then at the three of us. "Gentlemen, what trouble are you creating now?"

I told him how Charles and I were driving by and saw the slashed tires. Virgil said he was sound asleep and was having a dream about being in a castle in England. Spencer bent to read the note then started taking notes. I doubted he wrote anything about Virgil's dream.

"Any idea who did it?"

Charles said, "The person who knifed a note to Chris's door then slashed three of my tires."

Spencer got an evidence bag out of his cruiser, carefully pulled up on the scooter's seat to loosen the note, then put it in the bag, before saying, "I was looking for something a bit more specific about the perp."

Virgil said, "If you mean something like his name, I would be unable to help you."

Charles shook his head in agreement.

Spencer figured he'd gotten everything useful out of us, said he'd have the note checked for prints, told us not to hold our breath there'd be any, then wished us a pleasant day.

I watched the cruiser pull into the stream of traffic, before saying, "Virgil, someone thinks you, umm, we, know something about the murders and wants us, as the note said, to butt out. Have you talked with anyone about the murders in the last day or so?"

He patted Charles on the back. "I've been taking lessons from my private detective friend here. Been asking a bunch of questions."

That's what I was afraid of. I've seen Virgil when he's been asking questions. He thinks he's being subtle, thinks no one can see through his questions to the real reason he's asking. He's about as subtle as a puppy waiting for a treat.

"Virgil, who've you been talking to?"

"You and Charles."

Charles pointed to the scooter. "I didn't slash your tires."

I sighed. "Who other than us?"

"Let's see, the other night at the party, I talked to Martin Eastman, especially since we were at his house asking about his missing boat. Nice man. Friendlier than he was when we visited his house. Then, of course I talked to Megan and Kevin since it was their party. Can you believe how much work they've had done on their house? I especially liked the kitchen countertops. Back when I was rich, I had—"

"Virgil," I interrupted. "Did you talk to them about the murders?"

"May've brought it up. They knew Thurmond, and don't forget, it was Megan's brother who was on the river near where and when I found the body."

Charles tapped his foot in the sand. "Did they say anything that seemed suspicious?"

"Like they killed the men?"

"Yes," Charles said then pushed his Tilley back on his head.

"Nope, they didn't say anything like that."

I said, "Anyone else?"

"Only Ryan, the guy I still think did it."

"Did he say anything that made you think it other than your gut feeling?"

"Not really."

We were getting nowhere fast, making about as much headway as if we were on the scooter.

I said, "Have you talked to Ben Likard in the last few days?"

"Good question. After I left the party, I walked over to the bar at St. James Gate. Ben was sipping on a Guinness. I hadn't had anything to drink since I left the party, so I plopped down on the next stool. I knew all about him losing a bunch of money to Thurmond, so I asked if he thought he'd get any of it back. I figured that'd get him talking, you know, so he'd let something slip about the deaths, that is if he was involved. I still think it was Ryan, but there's always a possibility I'm wrong."

See what I mean about Virgil being subtle?

Charles's patience ran out waiting for Virgil to continue.

"What'd he say?"

"About as much chance as a cow jumping over the moon."

Charles tilted his head. "He really say cow?"

"Nah. I've always liked the expression. Don't get to use it often. Can you imagine a cow, a real cow, jumping over the moon? Anyway, his answer was much duller. He said 'no.'"

I said, "Did he say anything that sounded suspicious?"

"Not really."

Charles said, "Talk to anyone else?"

"Not that I recall. Don't think I infuriated anyone enough to slash my tires."

A glance at his scooter would indicate otherwise.

I said, "Still think it's Ryan?"

"Absolutely."

I still didn't agree, but to be honest, I didn't have a better suspect. The three of us decided there wasn't anything we could accomplish by standing in the parking lot staring at Virgil's scooter. I told him to let me know if he needed to be taken anywhere to get new tires, that I'd take him.

On the ride home, I kept thinking Virgil had said something that triggered something in the back of my mind. I couldn't put my finger on it. Then again, my thought wasn't any more significant than Virgil's gut feeling about Ryan.

Or was it?

CHAPTER FORTY-FIVE

I had trouble sleeping knowing Virgil had said something important, but for the life of me, I couldn't recall what. As is often the case, the more I tossed and turned the less I remembered about the conversation we had standing around the scooter. I may've had trouble going to sleep, but my eyes popped open at five-thirty. I tried to go back to sleep but was as successful as I'd been figuring out what Virgil had said of significance. I got Mr. Coffee brewing then took a shower, still wondering what I thought so important before going to sleep. I still couldn't figure it out but was certain I was hungry.

The Dog opened at six-thirty and I was the first customer through the door. Zack, the manager on duty, greeted me, said it was good seeing me although earlier than usual, then told me to sit anywhere. I chose my favorite booth near the back of the restaurant. A server, who shared she was Holly, set a mug of coffee in front of me as soon as I settled. I asked her to give me a few minutes before I'd order.

What had Virgil said that was gnawing at me? I sipped coffee and started piecing together yesterday's conversation, which I hoped was clearer this morning than last night when I was vacillating between sleep and awake. I told myself I was making progress, when Cindy LaMond entered the near-empty restaurant. She looked around then headed my way.

"Morning, Chief. Care to join me?"

"At this moment I don't care about anything other than getting coffee."

She may not have cared, but she took the seat opposite me. Holly was as quick with the coffee for Cindy as she had been with me.

Cindy smiled at the server then said, "You've saved my life. If this old geezer hasn't ordered, get him French toast. I'll take a bowl of fresh fruit parfait to keep this finely tuned body running smoothly." She gave a second smile to Holly, pointed her coffee cup at me, then said, "One word out of you about my finely tuned body and I'll shackle you before hauling you off to the hoosegow."

My only comment would have been about her ordering breakfast for me. I remained silent while Holly headed to put in our orders, more accurately, Cindy's orders.

"Any more love notes?" Cindy said before taking another sip.

I shook my head.

"Any theories why you, your shadow, and Virgil have been privileged to receive such sharp attention? Theories other than you're pests."

"Not really. I doubt we know anything more about the deaths than you."

Cindy sighed, then said, "I wouldn't bet on that. Detective Adair called last night to let me know what he'd learned about Thurmond and Honeycutt." She took another sip.

"What?"

"He's learned as much about them as you've learned about minding your own business."

I motioned for her to continue.

"They're a pain in my ass most of the time, but the Sheriff's Office has excellent investigators and access to competent forensic accountants. Adair said there is no paper trail coming from either man."

"What about bank accounts?"

"That's where it gets even weirder. We know Thurmond took money, a lot of money from people who thought they were buying into companies he allegedly owned, yet they couldn't find accounts in either name or accounts with their names on them. Thurmond and Honeycutt had nothing in their residences showing a connection to anyone. It's almost like they didn't exist, which as we both know isn't true since both dead guys had been alive not that long ago."

Holly arrived with our breakfasts then asked if we needed anything else. Cindy raised her mug, and while Holly was relatively new at the Dog, she knew to get a refill.

I said, "You know Ben Likard and whomever else bought into one or more of Thurmond's companies, didn't pay cash. What about a check he paid with? What happened to it?"

"It was made out to Walter Thurmond, deposited in an account at a Connecticut bank, and before you ask, Thurmond closed the account three days later. Got the balance in a certified check, which was deposited in one of those countries surrounded by an ocean that's not the Atlantic. Then it was transferred to another offshore island we have no access to. In other words, a dead end."

"Did Adair say anything of value?"

"Yeah, he said bye. That gave me a chance to get back to cuddling up with Larry who was watching his favorite game show. Tell you what, that boy sure knows how to romance his woman." She took a large bite of her parfait. "Wow, I feel the pounds slipping off as I chew."

I smiled knowing not to say anything about her weight.

"What's Adair going to do next?"

"He didn't say he was at a loss, but I didn't get the impression he had leads. I know I don't. You sure you don't know what the three of you have stumbled across that the killer is trying to get you to leave alone?"

"Not really." I couldn't remember if I'd told her what Likard had shared about Thurmond telling him others had bought in. "Did I tell you what Likard told me about two others in this area buying into Thurmond's companies?"

She set her mug on the table hard enough that some of the coffee slushed out. "No, who?"

I told her what he'd said about one being a celebrity.

"Living here?"

I nodded.

"There're more than our quota of infamous people, but I don't know any famous ones."

"I think it's a stretch, but I asked Sean Aker about it. He thought Ryan Sparks would be a celebrity to baseball fans."

"The guy with no money, living on a sailboat, with no job. A celebrity?"

"Said it was a stretch, but he's one person who knows Charles, Virgil, and I have been looking into the deaths."

"It ain't much, but it's more than I have. I'll dig a little deeper."

Cindy got a call, whispered a profanity, then said she had to go. I told her I'd take care of her check. She said I would've even if she'd stayed, then before walking away, added, "I'll tell you one thing, Likard or anyone else who gave Thurmond or Thurmond and Honeycutt money will never see a penny of it again."

That was it. Thank you, Cindy. That's what Virgil said or close to what he'd said that'd cost me hours of sleep since last evening. Virgil told us he asked Ben Likard if he thought he'd get any of his money back. After he said it, I realized it'd reminded me of something someone had said at Megan and Kevin's party, something about getting it back. Now all I need to do is remember who said it.

Would that be as difficult as remembering what Virgil said when we were standing around his scooter?

CHAPTER FORTY-SIX

On the way home, I replayed bits of conversations from the party. I thought I'd overheard part of what Ryan and Kevin were talking about. Unless I misunderstood, Ryan asked Kevin something about getting any of it back. I got a small part of their conversation, so they could've been talking about anything, but what if it'd been about getting money back from Thurmond or Honeycutt? Ryan had told me Thurmond talked to him about buying in, but Ryan didn't have money to invest. Was there more to it? If so, Ryan could've borrowed the money from Kevin who'd inherited, as Kevin had shared, "a tidy sum" from his mother. Megan told me it was how they afforded the extensive work on their house. If Kevin loaned Ryan money, it was possible Megan didn't know about it; after all, she'd confided that Kevin handled their money. It was also possible I was putting two and two together and getting five simply because I wanted to make things fit together.

Then I remembered something else. The first time I'd

met Ryan when he and Virgil were at the Dog, I asked if he knew Thurmond. He claimed to have met him a couple of times, knew he owned businesses that manufactured equipment like wheelchairs and stairlifts. He didn't mention talking to him about buying in. But when I talked with Megan, she told me Ryan shared that Thurmond had approached him to buy into one or more of his companies. Did that mean anything, or did Ryan not think it was important enough to share with me?

Virgil told Ryan I was a private detective. He didn't say it then, but it wouldn't be a stretch to think Virgil bragged to Ryan that he, Charles, and I were detectives. Knowing Virgil believed Ryan was the killer, he could've asked enough questions to make Ryan think we were pursuing him. That would've been an excellent reason to leave notes and slashed tires.

With that said, I was no closer to proving Ryan was the killer than Virgil had been since he named him his number one suspect almost from the day he found the jon boat.

I was in front of Bert's when instead of going home, decided I'd walk to the boat ramp to see if Ryan's sailboat was nearby. I realized on the way that my plan was woefully inadequate. If the boat was there and Ryan's kayak was tied to it, was I going to yell for him, hoping he would paddle over and confess to killing the men? If the sailboat was there and the kayak was tied to the boat ramp pier, was I going to traipse all over town looking for him? Then, if the sailboat wasn't there, what? Oh well, it was a beautiful April day, the temperature was in the low seventies, so a pleasant walk would do me good, regardless of the outcome. Or so I rationalized.

Ryan's sailboat was nowhere to be seen, which meant it

was either docked at his berth at Sunset Cay Marina or he'd sailed off into the sunset to avoid being arrested for killing one or both men. What was anchored in the river near the boat launch ramp was Sean Aker's forty-five-foot Chris-Craft Constellation. I was thinking about where Ryan may've gone, when Sean yelled, "Yo, landlubber Chris!"

He was on his boat's deck and wearing cut-off jeans, a Jack Daniel's T-shirt, and appropriately, boat shoes.

"See you're goofing off work again," I said as I waved.

"I'm plotting legal strategies. My brain's in overdrive. Don't run off, I'm coming ashore."

Five minutes later, I was helping him tie his dingy to the loading ramp pier. He gracefully hopped out, pointed toward town, and said, "You had breakfast?"

I told him I had.

"Good, you can watch me eat. Got something that may grab your attention."

Zack greeted me for the second time, asked how many breakfasts I was planning to eat, then after assuring him I was only having coffee while Sean ate, we were escorted to a table in the center of the room.

Holly was quick to the table and making a comment similar to Zack's, before asking Sean what he wanted. He said, "Coffee, a lot of it, bacon and scrambled eggs, oh why not, throw in an order of pancakes."

Holly headed to put in the order. Sean looked at me. "What? It takes a lot of calories to plot legal strategies."

I told him I hadn't said anything.

"You were thinking it."

I shrugged. "Did you see Ryan Sparks' sailboat this morning?"

He shook his head. "Saw it yesterday afternoon. Does that count?"

"Yes."

"He was heading back to the Marina. Why?"

I told him I was still thinking Ryan may've had something to do with the death of the two men.

"Motive?"

I shared my convoluted thoughts about his borrowing money from his brother-in-law to buy into Thurmond's companies. Sean said it sounded far-fetched. I didn't disagree.

"Now that you mention Thurmond, that's what I wanted to tell you about."

Sean's coffee arrived. He was serious about wanting it, a lot of it. He took three sips before continuing.

"Yesterday morning I was talking to a client who's a realtor. I don't handle his closings, but he works with me on estate planning. Anyway, he was telling me he knew Thurmond. Said he knew him fairly well. Thurmond had been talking—" Holly arrived with Sean's food interrupting his story. He took a bite of bacon before continuing. "Thurmond had been talking about selling his condo. He told my client he'd come into some money and wanted to buy something on Folly. Apparently, Thurmond wasn't sure where he wanted to be on Folly although he wasn't looking for anything under a million. My client sent him a dozen or so listings." Sean took another bite then added, "That's not the point of the story. Thurmond thanked my client, told him he didn't need his services because there was a guy he knew who dabbled in real estate who'd help him. Thurmond owed the guy money and figured he could give him the money he would've had to pay the buyer's agent when he bought a house. All my client did for Thurmond was let him know about properties for sale, but regardless, that royally pissed him off since he didn't make anything unless his client bought something."

That was an interesting story, but I still didn't see how it helped me learn who killed Thurmond.

"I don't suppose you're saying your client killed Thurmond?"

"No. He was in Egypt when Thurmond was killed."

"Good alibi."

"The point is to give you one more anecdote showing Thurmond was a con man, a crook, and had enough money stashed away to buy a million-dollar-plus house over here." He looked at his watch, rolled his eyes, then said, "Marlene will be sending the cavalry for me if I don't show up in ten minutes. For some reason, she gets all antsy when a client sits staring at her while they're waiting for me."

I nodded toward his Jack Daniel's T-shirt and cut-off jeans. "You're meeting a client in that?"

He looked down like he didn't know what he was wearing. "They're paying for my outstanding University of Alabama law school education and years of incredible legal success. My sartorial elegance means squat to the client who's been sitting and staring at Marlene for the last fifteen minutes."

Sean threw a twenty-dollar bill on the table, told me to let Holly keep the change, then wished me luck doing the work of the Sheriff's Office and the Folly Beach Department of Public Safety. I thanked Sean for the coffee and information, although I wasn't certain how helpful it'd been.

For the second time this morning, I headed home. The weather had taken a turn for the worse by the time I got in the door. The early morning clear, blue sky had turned dark gray with thunder vibrating my windows. I grabbed a photo magazine I'd been meaning to look through and moved to the screened-in porch to enjoy the rain. I wondered what it would be like to be on a boat on the river or ocean in a storm. It was something I wondered but never wanted to experience.

The magazine failed to hold my attention. I kept coming back to what Sean had said. At first, I didn't see anything significant in his story about the client, but it reminded me of something Cindy had shared. Calling her would subject me to a snide remark or two, but it could possibly be worth it.

"Cindy," I said as she answered without an insult, "didn't you tell me Detective Adair found real estate fact sheets in Thurmond's condo?"

"Umm, yes. Why?"

"Did he happen to tell you where the properties were?"

"No, why?"

"Do you know what happened to them?"

"No, why? Before you answer my question with another question, what are the answers to my whys?"

"I admit I'm meddling, so you don't have to point that out, but something has bothered me since Thurmond was killed. Why was he—"

"Something's been bothering me too," She interrupted. "Who in the halibut stuck a knife in his back?"

"Ready to hear what's been bothering me?"

I heard a faint sigh then, "What?"

"What was his connection to Martin Eastman? Thurmond lived on James Island, nowhere near Eastman's house. Eastman was out of town when his boat was stolen. He claims he didn't know Thurmond. So why that boat? Surely if the killer wanted a boat there are numerous small boats he could've killed him in much closer to town. Actually, why was Thurmond even in a boat?"

"Chris, welcome to the world of catching criminals. Questions galore; answers evade. Speaking of questions, why are you asking about the real estate fact sheets?"

"When Charles and I were out near Eastman's house the other day, I noticed the house beside his was for sale. If one of the fact sheets Adair found in Thurmond's condo was for that house, it could possibly explain why he was there the day he was killed."

"I'm not going to say that's a great or even a good thought, but it's better than most I've had. If one of the fact sheets was for that house, how does it help us learn who killed him?"

"It doesn't, but isn't there a chance it could lead to something that would help you?"

"I suppose. Let me call Adair to see if the sheets were kept or are in a landfill never to be seen again."

I thanked her, leaned back in the chair, to watch the rain. Along with the rain came a nagging feeling that I knew something else. Something that I'd heard that didn't strike me as important at the time.

CHAPTER FORTY-SEVEN

It was still raining the next morning. I didn't have anywhere to go so a peaceful day in the house would be the perfect way to spend it. It would've been perfect if I didn't keep replaying conversations trying to see if there was anything I was missing regarding the deaths. Something was there, but what? Ben Likard was a strong suspect, but I was basing that on knowing he'd bought into Thurmond's con and Thurmond had refused to give him any of the alleged profits from his investment. Thurmond told Likard two others in the area had partnered with him, with one of them allegedly being a celebrity. Sean thought it could be Ryan, but what if Thurmond made up the part about one of his investors being a celebrity? If he had, that would eliminate Ryan although Ryan had talked to his brother-in-law about borrowing the money to invest. Once again, I was going in circles.

I was pleased when Cindy called to distract me.

She said, "Guess what?"

"Larry is taking you on an Alaskan cruise."

She laughed so hard she started coughing.

I said, "Guess I was wrong."

"Right and wrong."

"Meaning?"

"You're wrong about the Alaskan cruise. Right about the fact sheets. Adair told me his guys left them in Thurmond's condo in case his techs needed to go back. They didn't, but since Thurmond paid his lease through the end of the month, Adair figured everything was where they left it in the condo. Now to the part you were right about. Adair called fifteen minutes ago saying he went back to the condo. One of the fact sheets was for the house adjacent to Eastman's place. Now here's my question. So what?"

I was tempted to say, "You're the cop, figure it out." Knowledge of Cindy's moods plus my life experiences of nearly seven decades told me that wouldn't be a wise thing to say.

"I don't know."

"Then I wish you'd been right about the Alaskan cruise and wrong about the fact sheet."

If I'd chosen to respond, it would've been to dead air. She'd hung up.

Two more hours of thinking about the murders, with fifteen-minutes subtracted because I was pondering what to have for lunch, I still had the nagging feeling someone said something that meant more now than it had when I heard it.

For the second time this morning, a phone call interrupted my total lack of progress.

"Christopher, this is Virgil."

He was one of the few, very few, who referred to me as

Christopher, so he didn't have to identify himself, although it was pleasant hearing someone starting a phone conversation in a civil manner.

"Good morning, Virgil."

"I'm calling to take you up on your offer to assist me with my scooter."

"How can I help?" I glanced out at the rain hoping it didn't involve being outside.

"The day after my tires got slashed, Jamie, a guy who lives in my building, was kind enough to load my scooter in his pickup truck and haul it to the tire store. You'd be amazed how few stores carry tires that fit my primary means of transportation. Whoops, that's neither here nor there. Anyway, it's now affixed with two new tires and sitting patiently at the store awaiting my presence to pilot it home."

"And you need a ride to pick it up."

"Your deductive reasoning is above reproach. No wonder you're such a successful detective. Jamie would take me, but he must work and won't be back until late this evening, which I am sad to say, is after the store closes. Besides, since the scooter no longer has flat tires, I can ride it home, so Jamie's pickup is no longer necessary."

I would've thought Virgil asking for a ride to get his scooter would've sufficed, but I'm no Virgil.

"When do you want to go?"

"When the rain stops."

"Call when you're ready; I'll be glad to take you."

"You're a *chuckaboo*."

"Another Victorian phrase?"

"Yes, my astute friend. It means a good friend."

"Goodbye, Virgil."

"Goodbye, Christopher."

The weather might be dreadful, but Virgil has a way of putting a smile on my face.

———

It was going on three o'clock before the rain had moved on to drench other parts of South Carolina. Virgil called shortly thereafter to remind me of my offer and was waiting for me outside his building fifteen minutes after hanging up. Three thank yous later, we were pulling off the island on the way to reunite him with his scooter.

"Guess who I had a drink, or two, or three with last evening?" he said as he leaned against the door.

I was learning to detest the word guess. "Who?"

"No guesses? Hmm, anyway, the answer is." He tapped his fingers on the console like he was drumming. "Ryan Sparks."

"Oh."

"Don't you want to know what we talked about?"

"What did you talk about?"

"That's more like it. I was walking past Woody's when Ryan waved me over. He was on the porch sipping a brew. I joined him and lo and behold he offered to split a large pizza with him paying for all of it. I jumped on his kind offer since all my cash had been assigned to cover the cost of new tires. Once he added a beer to the offer, he became my new best friend, at least for the evening."

I tried again, "What did you talk about?"

"The weather, the unusually large crowds along the street, and, oh yeah, the murders."

I smiled as I said, "Did he confess to killing the guys?"

"I don't have Charles's unique skill of squeezing confessions from unsuspecting killers."

"No confession."

"Nope, but he shared something interesting. Not as interesting as his offer to buy my supper and drinks, but still interesting. It was after the third or fourth beer, he told me he'd asked his brother-in-law to lend him a hundred thousand dollars so he could become part-owner of one of Thurmond's businesses. I don't recall him saying that before. Do you?"

"It's the first I've heard about it."

"Me too. He shared it in a serendipitous moment. I asked what he planned to do with the rest of his life now that baseball was in his rearview mirror. Do sailboats have rearview mirrors? Never mind, my enquiry touched a raw nerve. He shook his head. "The poor boy began telling me how he felt his life was now adrift, directionless. I'm no expert on depression, but he gave off that vibe. Felt sorry for him, so I told him how I'd experienced something similar, although not as exciting as a possible career in professional baseball. Anyway, I told him about how I'd been wealthy, then through bad choices, bad investments, bad luck, and bad drugs, I'd lost it all."

We were less than a mile from the tire store, so I needed to move his story along. "Then he told you about borrowing money from Kevin?"

"Was still a while later. I told him how happy I was being poor but with new friends and a new attitude. Didn't cheer him much. Don't think he bought into it for another beer or so. Then it came out of the blue, his talking about borrowing money, not his deciding to try to be happy like I was."

"Did Kevin lend him the money?"

"By that time, the pizza was in our stomachs, along with a few, umm, several beers. I may not have understood everything he said a hundred percent. I suspect he wasn't expressing everything precisely either. My best recollection is he asked Kevin for the money. I'm certain he said a hundred grand, but beyond that, I'm not sure."

I repeated, "Virgil, did Kevin lend him the money?"

"Good question, Christopher."

I realized Virgil didn't have a good answer. Time for another tact. "Do you still think he's the person who killed the men?"

"That's another excellent question. I tried to find out last night without coming out and accusing him. I don't recall how I asked, he kept avoiding answering. That reinforced my thought from day one he did it."

I pulled into the tire store's lot then turned toward Virgil. "I'm going to tell Chief LaMond what you've told me. You'll probably be hearing either from her or Detective Adair from the Sheriff's Office."

"Don't know how much help I can be. Last night is still vague."

"Virgil, if he's the person who left us notes, we need to be careful. He's already killed two people, so I doubt he'd think twice about killing anyone who suspected him. Please be careful."

He assured me he would, then left to get his scooter. On the ride home, I realized I was more worried about Virgil then I let on. He said he didn't come out and directly accuse Ryan of the murders, but it's no telling what he'd said. If Virgil's interrogation techniques were taught in the police academy they'd be examples of how not to quiz someone.

I called Cindy as I pulled in my drive only to get her voice-mail. I left an abridged version of what Virgil had shared then suggested either she or Detective Adair get with Virgil to hear it firsthand.

If Kevin loaned Ryan money to buy into one of Thur-mond's companies and Ryan felt he'd been conned, it could've given him motive to kill Thurmond. It would also explain the conversation I heard between Ryan and Kevin at the party.

Could Virgil have been right all along about Ryan? It was looking more and more a possibility. If Virgil was right, it'd explain why Ryan was so down while talking to Virgil at Woody's. On the other hand, if Kevin didn't lend Virgil the money, there'd be no reason for him to have killed Thurmond, or none related to money.

The wisest thing for me to do would be to wait and hear what Cindy or Detective Adair found about Ryan. The more I thought about it, the more I worried about Virgil, especially after his conversation with Ryan. I was serious when I told Virgil that if Ryan were the killer, he wouldn't hesitate to kill again. Last night may have given him a good reason to want Virgil dead.

So, what do I do now?

CHAPTER FORTY-EIGHT

My wisest choice of action was no action. I'd wait to hear what Cindy or Detective Adair found after talking with Virgil and possibly Ryan. Not having heard anything the rest of the day and evening, I planned to call Cindy first thing in the morning, incur her wrath about pestering her, then learn what, if anything, she found. Waiting was easy to say, difficult to do. Was Virgil in danger? For that matter, were Charles and I?

Following a restless night, I was awake early and sat in the kitchen drinking way too much coffee as I waited for a decent hour to call Cindy. Before that time arrived, the phone rang with Cindy's name appearing on the screen.

"Good morning, Chief."

"Get over to the Dog and buy me breakfast, and it'll be a better morning."

"On my way."

I found her sitting at the same table she occupied the last time she let me buy her breakfast. She took a bite of toast then pointed for me to sit.

"Well?" I said.

"Hold your seahorses. Never interrupt a gal who's eating." She took another bite, a sip of coffee, then pointed her fork at me. "Okay. Here's the skinny, Detective Adair and I met with Virgil late yesterday." She shook her head. "That boy can sure be a bag of wind, charming bag, but still full of wind. Anyway, he told us the same stuff he told you, or said he did. I didn't hear anything that'd put cuffs on Ryan, but there was still enough to have a conversation with the sailor."

"Good. What did—"

"Did you forget to hold your seahorses? I'm telling the story. So, Adair, trying to show interagency cooperation, something that's in short supply you know, asked if I wanted to visit Ryan at his boat. I said sure. Well, that was easier said than done. First, his boat wasn't near the boat ramp where it's been most of the time lately, so we bopped out to Sunset Cay Marina where he has a slip." She shook her head. "It was boatless."

The hostess brought out my bagel and a refill of coffee for Cindy.

"So, where's his boat?"

"An old-timer that hangs out at the marina told us Ryan pulled out yesterday morning and headed toward the deep blue sea. Said Ryan told him it was the last time they'd see each other. Figured he was gone for good."

"What now?"

"Adair contacted the Coast Guard and put out an APB,

although I doubt the sailboat will be floating up I-26. I figure since Ryan ain't piloting a cigar boat, he can't get too far."

"Does Adair have evidence that Ryan is the killer?"

"Nothing definitive but Ryan skipping town is a strong hint."

"Have you or Adair talked to Ryan's sister?"

"First thing after leaving the marina. She acted surprised he was gone. She called his phone. No answer. I asked where he might've gone. She claimed she had no idea."

"Did you believe her?"

"She's either telling the truth or is a good actor."

"Was her husband home?"

"No. Said it was his night out with the guys, some of his coworkers. He meets them for drinks near the plant once a week."

I repeated, "What now?"

"Going to finish breakfast, enjoy a few more minutes of fresh air and sunshine, lock myself in my office so my guys can't pester me, then take a nap."

"What now about Ryan?"

"Hell if I know."

With the Chief's plan of action firmly established, I left her to finish breakfast in peace then headed to the boat ramp parking lot in the unlikely event Ryan's sailboat was anchored where he left it when visiting the restaurants, stores, and his sister's house. As I expected, the boat was nowhere to be seen. I walked across Center Street then took a seat on the picnic table in the Folly River Park to think about everything I'd learned the last twenty-four hours.

Cindy was right about it being suspicious that Ryan pulled-up anchor and headed wherever, but it didn't make him a killer. Virgil thought Ryan's brother-in-law loaned him money to invest with Thurmond, but there was nothing to prove it. If Kevin didn't lend him money, there would've been no reason for Ryan to kill Thurmond or Honeycutt. I wondered if Megan would know about the money even if she didn't know where her brother had gone.

I walked the eight blocks to Megan and Kevin's house, knocked on the door, and was prepared to ask Megan if she knew. She answered the door wearing an oversized, black T-shirt with *Talk is Cheap, Show me the Code* on the front, red shorts, and barefoot.

"Oh, hi Chris," she said then looked behind me like someone else should be with me. "Umm, come in."

I followed her to the living room. "Sorry to bother you, have a couple of minutes?"

She pointed for me to sit on the couch, then sat on the chair opposite me. "Umm, sure. You caught me on another office dress-down day." She chuckled before her smile faded then she said, "What's on your mind?"

"I was talking to Chief LaMond a little while ago. She said she talked with you last evening."

"Yes. She wanted to know if I knew where my brother was. I was as shocked as the Chief when she said his boat wasn't at the marina or by the bridge."

"I'm worried about him. I was talking to a friend who spent time with Ryan the other night. Your brother sounded down, didn't know what he was going to do next. I wondered if you knew where he might be going?"

"I'm not naive. When the head of Folly's cop squad and a Detective from the Sheriff's Office come to the door it's more than curiosity about the whereabouts of Ryan. Do they think he had something to do with the murders?"

To lie or not to lie. Maybe somewhere in between will work.

"I know they want to ask him questions about what he knew about the guy found in the jon boat near Ryan's boat."

"He's already told his story several times to everyone who'd listen, including the cops. There must be more."

She glared at me like I was holding something back or it could be my imagination since I was holding something back.

"Let me ask you something else," I said as an effort to move another direction. "Someone told me Ryan told them he'd asked Kevin if he could borrow money so he could become part-owner of one of Thurmond's companies. Do you know if that's true?"

Her hand gripped the arm of the chair, she leaned forward, then said, "That can't be true."

"Like I said, I heard it from someone. He could've misunderstood what Ryan told him."

"That must be the case. Kevin wouldn't have given away our money, couldn't have loaned any to Ryan. That's all we have, and this remodel cost a fortune. Sorry, it had to be a misunderstanding."

"You're probably right, but I wanted to ask. You're sure you don't know where Ryan would've gone?"

"I'm sure. Now if you don't mind, I need to get back to work."

Megan's smile had faded once I asked about the potential loan. I had no doubt I was being dismissed.

"I'm sorry to bother you. If you don't mind, could you let me know if you hear from Ryan?"

She sighed. "You and the police, although they weren't as polite as you when they told me to call if I heard from him."

I left on that unfriendly note. I also didn't know any more about Ryan's whereabouts or the alleged loan than I did when I arrived.

CHAPTER FORTY-NINE

That night I met Barb for supper at Chico Feo, a small, outdoor restaurant with an eclectic menu and more character than most dining venues. It was also less than a block from the house and close to Barb's Books. She wore a red blouse, navy blue shorts, and open toed sandals, attire that would've made her at home at any resort. My faded green polo shirt and tan shorts would've made me marginal anywhere but on Folly.

After ordering, I asked if she'd heard about Ryan leaving. She said Charles stopped in to see if she had any books on macramé. I asked if she was kidding. She assured me she wasn't and how disappointed he seemed when she didn't have any. He told her he'd admired a macramé wall hanging that Laurie had made. He wanted to give it a try so he could surprise her with one. I hadn't realized my friend was that bored. Barb said I needed to expand my horizons, be more tolerant of those who enjoy alternate forms of art.

I said, "Whatever."

Barb added, "Charles said you were still trying to figure out who killed the men."

"Asking questions, that's all."

"Right. He also shared you'd learned Thurmond had a fact sheet for the house beside the one where the boat was stolen. Are the police following up on that lead?"

"Yes."

"So, you can leave it up to them?"

"Yes."

"Great. Then let's enjoy the evening and not think more about it."

I agreed it was a good idea. As a result, we enjoyed mahi tacos and each other's company. Neither of us mentioned the murders, suspects, or anything else negative after that. We sat another hour listening to a local performer singing a set of original music, then I walked her to her condo.

On the way home, I couldn't imagine a better evening until I noticed a For Sale sign in a yard across from my house. Then it struck me. Something that was said when I was talking with Larry and Cindy at Rita's, the first time I'd heard anything about Ryan, and his sister and brother-in-law. Larry said Kevin worked at Boeing but wanted to get into real estate. Was I seeing everything backwards? What if instead of Kevin lending money to his brother-in-law to buy into Thurmond's scheme, he'd bought in. That could explain why Kevin appeared concerned about spending so much on the remodel. I needed to call Cindy in the morning not only to get yelled at for meddling but to share this about Kevin. After all, she was with us when Larry talked about Kevin's interest in real estate.

I opened my door and wondering about Kevin's involvement became reality.

Kevin Goodman was behind the door. He shoved me from behind catching me off balance. I tripped over the recliner but caught myself before my head slammed into the television. Kevin pushed the door closed with his foot.

My first reaction was to rush him to knock him off his feet. Seeing a knife that must've had a foot-long blade in his hand eliminated that option.

"What are you doing here?" I asked, then realized how stupid a question it was.

"Sit," he said, then pointed the knife at my recliner.

Seeing no safe alternative, I sat.

Kevin leaned against the wall opposite my chair and said, "You got yourself a mighty flimsy lock on that door. Sorry I broke it." He pointed the knife at the door. "Gonna be the death of you yet." He shook his head. "Know what a couple of people told me this week?"

More questions! "What?"

"Let's see. Said you're the nosiest person on this island. You stick your nose in things that are none of your business. You think you know more than the cops. I should've believed it when Ryan told me you were a private detective. That you, umm, never mind. Why in hell didn't you let the deaths of that damned Thurmond and his conniving partner Honeycutt go?" He pounded the heel of the knife against the wall. "Why?"

I wanted to tell him it was because one of my friends found the body, but figured the question was rhetorical. Besides, I needed all my wits to figure out how to get the knife away from him. He was taller and heavier than I am.

More importantly, the man wielding the knife was thirty years younger. The odds of my succeeding were nonexistent. The only hope I had was to keep him talking. With time, I could possibly figure something out. Lord knows I had incentive. My life depended on it.

I ignored his question. "You gave Thurmond money to become part-owner of one of his companies?"

"Why didn't you take the advice I left you?" He pointed the knife toward the back door.

He wasn't going to answer my question about giving Thurmond money, so how do I keep him talking? I shrugged. "Looks like I should've taken the hint."

He smiled, but it wasn't the kind portrait photographers seek. "Duh. Everything was fine then you came nosing around the house today. Harassing Megan, asking questions which told me you weren't giving up."

He walked behind me giving me chills thinking any second the knife blade would slit my throat. He moved to the side window and looked out. I'd been holding my breath.

"Yes, I gave him a hundred thousand dollars. Megan and I have decent incomes. With the inheritance from Mom, we could do the work we dreamed about on the house, but we had bigger dreams. Every day I build planes that'll travel the world, while Megan and I are stuck here dreaming about visiting other countries. The picture the damned con artist painted showed me how I could give Megan her dreams, our dreams." He moved back to the spot against the wall facing me.

"Did Megan know you gave him money?"

"No. That's part of the problem. She thought we had more

than we have. I took care of our finances. She didn't know how much the construction cost. Didn't know after I gave Thurmond the hundred grand we were near broke."

His knuckles turned white gripping the knife. There was no way I could wrestle it out of his hand. Keeping him talking was my only chance to survive.

"Did Ryan know you gave Thurmond money?"

"No. My idiot brother-in-law is the reason for all this."

"How?"

"Would you believe he asked if he could borrow a bundle of money to invest in companies Thurmond owned? Hell, I didn't know Thurmond existed until Ryan told me about him, even introduced us. If that hadn't happened, well...." He shook his head. "Never mind. No, he didn't know. Not at first, anyway." He moved toward the door leading to the kitchen, looked out the back door, then once again walked around the living room. "Know what else that idiot did?"

I shook my head.

"At Megan's party, he started putting things together. He figured the reason I didn't lend him the money was so I could give it to Thurmond instead. I call Ryan an idiot, but he wasn't stupid. He put two and two together, figured it out. Then of all places, in a house full of people, he starts talking about the money, wondering with Thurmond dead if I'd get it back." He moved in front of me and pointed the knife at my face. "There you were, listening to him talk about it. I hoped you didn't hear everything, but that was wishful thinking. You knew. It was only a matter of time before everything unraveled."

He was a talker. Would that give me time? He turned to

lean against the wall. I leaned forward so I could leap from the chair at him if I got a chance.

"Know what else I learned about you? You're the brains of your group of nosy nellies. That's why I'm here and not holding your buddies Charles or Virgil at knife point. Lucky you, right?" He chuckled.

"Why kill Honeycutt?"

"He didn't have to die. Thurmond told me Honeycutt was his partner in the manufacturing companies. I went to him, went hat in hand. Told him I wouldn't cause him any trouble. All I wanted was my hundred grand. He acted like he didn't know anything about it, then accused me of killing Thurmond." He smiled. "Suppose he was right. Anyway, he said all of Thurmond's records and contracts were on the laptop he stole from Thurmond's condo. The cops saw a video of Honeycutt stealing the laptop and arrested him. His bad luck, he said. His bad luck got worse. He argued with me about the money, claimed he didn't have any of it, for me to go to hell. Chris, I tell you what, it's not wise telling a man holding a knife to go to hell. Honeycutt learned that lesson. You're not going to tell me to go to hell, are you?"

I shook my head. Regardless what I said, there was no way he was going to let me live. Keeping him talking was my only hope. At some point he'd make a mistake. I was betting my life on it.

"You took the laptop from Honeycutt's house, destroyed it so the police couldn't connect your name to Thurmond, then put the destroyed computer in the trunk of his car for the police to find."

"Honeycutt already destroyed the laptop. All I did was put

it in his car. Thought them finding it hiding in there would seal the deal about Honeycutt killing his partner."

Kevin walked around the room again. I started to push out of the chair, when he pivoted, pointed the knife at my stomach, then said, "You may want to stay still. I'm getting pretty handy with one of these." He waved the knife in my face.

I sat back.

He said, "Want to know something?"

Before I responded he said, "I'm terrified of guns. Funny, isn't it?"

I saw absolutely no humor, but it answered why he'd stabbed both men. "Yes."

"All Thurmond had to do was give me my money. He'd be alive today."

"What happened?"

"You don't know this, or maybe you do, since you've been nosing around. Thurmond told me he was looking to buy a house. One of my dreams was to get into real estate where I could earn way more money. I wanted to get him somewhere private so I could talk to him. Somewhere where no one knew either of us. Somewhere where I could tell him the same thing I told Honeycutt later. I didn't want trouble, didn't want to stir up problems for him. Plain and simple, all I wanted was the money. I got fact sheets for local listings out of boxes in front of houses and said I could show him one that'd be perfect for him. It was as far away from mine as I could get on Folly, you know, in case something went wrong with our discussion." He shook his head, but his knife remained steady. "Boy, did it go bad."

"The house out East Ashley near the old Coast Guard station?"

"See why I had to stop you? Yeah, that house. I picked him up at his condo and took him out there. Then Thurmond got all pissed that I wanted the money back. He started with some damned rigmarole about how my money would grow ten times over if I left it with his companies, blah, blah, blah. I told him to con some other sucker. To give me my money. He shoved me, told me to get out of his face. That was his last mistake, a deadly one." He looked down at the knife. "Had one of these with me. Figured with Thurmond being a crook, I might need it. I would've had a gun but as you know, they scare the crap out of me." He sighed. "Anyway, after he shoved me, he turned around, started walking away like I was no more than a gnat flitting around his head. Bet the knife in the back didn't feel like a gnat."

He wouldn't hesitate to do the same to me unless I found a way to get to him. First, I had to keep him talking.

"What happened next?"

"He started running. Suppose I'd do the same if someone was stabbing me. He ran to the next yard, jumped in a little boat tied to the dock, started untying it. I couldn't have him get away. He was having trouble untying the knot. That was the last rope he'd ever try to untie. I got to him, stabbed him two more times, the last time deep. He flopped in the boat like a caught mackerel, deader than a doornail, if you don't mind me mixing my metaphors." He laughed.

I again saw no humor as I looked around to see what I could use as a weapon, that is if I got out of the chair without him getting to me first. A photo magazine on the small, round table near the chair was all that was reachable. Hardly a weapon to compete with a knife.

He saw me glance at the magazine. "Am I boring you? Don't you want to know what happened next?"

I nodded but continued leaning forward in the chair.

"I wiped my prints off the knife with an old tarp that was under the house, untied the boat with my elbow so not to leave prints for the cops, shoved the boat into the stream so it'd float wherever. Can you believe it ended up a hundred feet from poor Ryan's sailboat? Of all places, then for a friend of yours to find the body. Now here we are. Think I've said all I want to. Don't you—"

Someone knocked on the front door, then it squeaked open a few inches.

Virgil yelled, "Christopher, you here? I figured it out."

Kevin, pushed off from the wall, took two steps toward the door.

I grabbed the magazine, flung it at Kevin's head.

He ducked.

Virgil said, "What the—"

I pushed back in the chair. It smacked into Kevin, knocking him sideways.

He twisted to get his balance.

I jumped up, grabbed the top of the table and used it like a lion tamer would use a chair to shove at the lion.

Virgil jerked back to avoid Kevin and the knife.

I swung the table at Kevin. It smacked his knife hand.

He screamed, dropped the weapon, lowered his head, then butted me in the stomach.

My breath was gone. I dropped the table, doubled over, but managed to shove Kevin to the side.

Virgil must've figured out what was happening. He grabbed the table, then clobbered Kevin's head.

Kevin didn't hit the floor like a caught mackerel, but hard enough to stun him.

Virgil grabbed the knife off the floor, held it to the back of Kevin's neck, then said, "I wouldn't move if I were you."

Clint Eastwood couldn't have said it better.

I grabbed the phone, dialed 911, requested help, then fell back in the chair. I took a breath for the first time in what seemed like an eternity.

CHAPTER FIFTY

I wasn't in the mood to face anyone the next three days after my near-fatal run-in with Kevin, but Virgil insisted. Since he saved my life, how could I say no to his "after-killer-catching party" on Loggerhead's deck?

The party was scheduled to begin at seven o'clock, so I arrived at six-thirty knowing Charles would be there. I was a little surprised to see Virgil leaning against the turquoise colored classic Volkswagen bus that'd been hoisted onto the deck and converted into a bar. Charles was in animated conversation with him and didn't see me until I tapped his shoulder.

He looked at his wrist then said, "About time."

Virgil was politer with a pat on my back combined with, "Great, you made it." He may've been smiling, but it was difficult to tell through his sunglasses.

Becca, the server, handed me a glass of white wine before

I had time to move beside my two friends. She said Charles had ordered it and for her to bring it over when I arrived.

I took a sip then said, "Virgil, with everything going on the other night, I didn't ask who you were going to say the killer was."

Virgil looked down at the deck, then took a sip of beer, "Umm, same person I said it was all along. Right before I came to your house, I heard Ryan had skipped town. Flew the coop in his sailboat. That proved he was guilty." He shrugged. "So I thought."

I smiled. "You may've been wrong, but I'm thrilled you came to tell me."

Laurie was next to arrive. She spotted us, came over, and gave Charles a kiss. He was far kinder to her than he'd been with me. He thanked her for coming early, then waved Becca over to order Laurie a drink.

"Where's Barb?" Laurie asked as she looked around.

"She'll be here as soon as she closes the store," I said, not reminding anyone it was still fifteen minutes before the time we were supposed to gather.

Charles said, "Let's go to the table. Becca said they can't hold it all night."

We followed Charles to a large, round table near the elevated bandstand. Music wouldn't start for a couple of hours, so we'd be able to talk without yelling, although I came close to yelling, "Hallelujah!" when Charles said, "Supper is on me."

He'd never admit it, but that meant he was happy Virgil and I had survived the encounter with Kevin.

Barb arrived five minutes later, with, "Hi, folks. What'd I miss?"

Virgil said, "Dear Barb, it's not what you missed, we've missed you."

She rolled her eyes but still kissed the top of his head. The rest of us kept our comments in the glad you made it mode.

Charles ordered two helpings of peel and eat shrimp saying that should hold us for a few minutes. Laurie told him how sweet he was, then Virgil said, "Chris, did Megan know her husband gave Thurmond money?"

"He said she didn't. I tend to believe him, at least about that, since he handled their finances."

"Good. As the saying goes, 'Gray-mare the better horse.' Oh, for those of you who don't speak Victorian, it means praise of a wife who's more able than her husband."

Laurie summed Virgil's comment up for all of us when she said, "Oh."

For the next hour we avoided any mention of the murders and what'd happened at my house. We'd gobbled down the shrimp, quickly ordered entrees, a second drink for each of us, plenty of laughs, funny stories, and not a single Victorian phrase, more reason to celebrate.

Laurie said, "I don't want to bring anyone down, but I've been wondering what happened to Ryan Sparks. Why'd he run off if he wasn't the killer?"

I hadn't heard anything about him since the incident at the house. I was surprised to see Charles shrug. If he didn't know something, it didn't happen.

"Allow me to answer," Barb said.

She had our attention.

"Chief LaMond came in this afternoon, said it wasn't to buy anything, but to talk to another woman, someone who made sense. The Coast Guard found Ryan along with his sailboat down at Edisto Island. He was surprised anyone was looking for him. He threw his phone overboard as he left Folly."

Charles interrupted, "Why?"

"Charles, if you allow me to finish, you might hear the answer."

"Sorry, bad habit."

He could say that again.

Barb pointed at Virgil. "Actually Virgil, it's because of you. He told the police despite everything you've been through, you still had a positive attitude. Ryan wanted to emulate you, said the best way he could do that was to get away from everyone so he could think, meditate, find himself."

I said, "He didn't know anything about Kevin's arrest?"

"Cindy said he was shocked."

Virgil said, "He knew nothing about Kevin killing the two men?"

"Claimed he didn't. Cindy said they believed him."

"What about what he said at the party wondering if Kevin would get any money back now that Thurmond was dead?"

"Cindy said Ryan knew his brother-in-law invested in the company, but nothing about the murders. I suppose they'll never know what he knew or didn't know."

"What's Ryan going to do now?" Virgil asked.

"He told Cindy he was bringing his boat back here and offering to stay with his sister until she figures out what she wants to do. He said it'll give him purpose, ending him being adrift."

Becca returned and asked if any of us wanted dessert.

She heard five diners shout, "Yes!"

Charles, the man paying, added, "Gulp."

ABOUT THE AUTHOR

Bill Noel is the best-selling author of twenty-three novels in the popular Folly Beach Mystery series. The award-winning novelist is also a fine arts photographer and lives in Louisville, Kentucky, with his wife, Susan, and his off-kilter imagination.

Learn more about the series and the author by visiting www. billnoel.com.

CPSIA information can be obtained
at www.ICGtesting.com
Printed in the USA
BVHW071915130223
658422BV00012B/129

9 781958 414996